KU-151-080

Claudie Gallay

# IN THE GOLD
# OF TIME

*Translated from the French by*
*Alison Anderson*

MACLEHOSE PRESS
QUERCUS · LONDON

5310173

First published in the French language as *Dans l'or du temps*
by Éditions du Rouergue, Rodez, in 2006

First published in Great Britain in 2013 by
MacLehose Press
an imprint of Quercus
55 Baker Street
7th Floor, South Block
London W1U 8EW

Copyright © Éditions du Rouergue, 2006
English translation copyright © 2012 by Alison Anderson

The poem "How Close" from *Woven Stone* by Simon J Ortiz
reprinted by permission of the author. All rights reserved.

This book is supported by the Institut Français
as part of the Burgess programme.
www.frenchbooknews.com

INSTITUT
FRANÇAIS

The moral right of Claudie Gallay to be identified as
the author of this work has been asserted in accordance with
the Copyright, Designs and Patents Act, 1988.

Alison Anderson asserts her moral right to be
identified as the translator of the work.

All rights reserved. No part of this publication may be reproduced
or transmitted in any form or by any means, electronic or mechanical,
including photocopy, recording, or any information storage and retrieval
system, without permission in writing from the publisher.

A CIP catalogue reference for this book
is available from the British Library

ISBN (TPB) 978 0 85705 126 4
ISBN (Ebook) 978 0 85738 646 5

This book is a work of fiction. Names, characters,
businesses, organizations, places and events are either the
product of the author's imagination or are used fictitiously.
Any resemblance to actual persons, living or dead,
events or locales is entirely coincidental.

2  4  6  8  10  9  7  5  3  1

Designed and typeset in Golden Cockerel by Patty Rennie
Printed and bound in Great Britain by Clays Ltd, St Ives plc

Leabharlann
Contae na Mídhe

What is life? It is the brilliance of a firefly in the night, it is a buffalo's breath in winter.
It is the little shadow that runs through the grass and vanishes in the sunset.

INDIAN SAYINGS

It was still the calm of morning. Dustbins. The first *métro*. The concierge in the street across the way was opening his shutters. The upstairs neighbour had just come home. Anna and the girls were still asleep.

A morning like any other. I had just got up a little earlier. Because it was the start of the holidays.

I drank my coffee. Elbows on the table. On the refrigerator door were the girls' most recent drawings. Flowers on the wallpaper. Daisies with white petals, eight petals per flower. A repeating motif. To infinity.

Anna always said, there's something reassuring about the repetition of things.

We were going away. Like every summer. Our two months in Normandy. Our cases were ready in the passage, swimsuits, boots, swim rings in a box with board games, total sunscreen and rakes for collecting cockles.

What had we forgotten?

You always forget something.

After the dustmen, it was the seven o'clock bus and the woman who had the bistro downstairs taking out her chairs. She made a scraping noise with them. I had told her a dozen times, if you would lift them up, they wouldn't scrape.

She lifted them for a day or two and then the noise started again.

Anna wanted to move away. Too noisy. Too many neighbours. Too much of everything.

Or not enough. Depending.

She wanted to buy a house. In the suburbs. With a garden. She said it would be good for the girls, the air was better.

She said we could also ask to be transferred and go even further, to Dijon or Provence. Dijon I could understand. But Provence, no less. Anna was asking too much.

I did not want to leave Montreuil. I did not want to buy a house here or anywhere. I do not know what I wanted. The thought of the holidays frightened me. Like Sundays. Rainy Sundays, worse than anything. How endless the morning hours seemed. There was so much to do. I did nothing.

I made some more coffee.

Anna was in the shower. I could hear the water running.

Pruners in the street a bit further up. They were cutting the branches that touched the façades. Which meant a lot of branches. I opened the window and shouted, how will we manage without the birds if you cut all the branches!

The birds – titmice, a few robins. In winter I hung balls of fat from the bars on the balcony. I would wait by the window. It made me late for the *lycée*.

The upstairs neighbour worked a night shift. Guard at the Louvre. He did not like it when I shouted like that, just as he was dropping off.

A young woman in the building across the way. Little flowered curtains. Pink, as light as lace. She was watching the pruners. When she saw me, she gave a little wave. Her nightgown looked as if it was the same fabric as her curtain.

It was July.

It was already hot in the flat.

In the bedroom next door the twins were still sleeping.

Our house, *La Téméraire*, overlooked the sea, a few kilometres south of Dieppe. We bought it just after the girls were born. Love at first sight, said Anna.

We took out a loan for ten years.

In winter, *La Téméraire* weathers every storm. We never come in winter. Only summer. And a few weekends in the spring. We find tree trunks and lifebuoys in the garden. Sand, planks, the corpses of seagulls. It takes us days to clean it all up.

It was raining when we got there. I stopped the car as close to the door as possible. The twins took their things and went straight up to their room. They had been good the whole trip, filling up their holiday notebook. Girls' things. With boys it would have been different.

"Different how?" Anna said.

I did not feel like explaining.

We opened the shutters and began to unload.

At noon we ate sandwiches. The girls found some old *Martine* books in a box in the attic. Anna did not want them reading *Martine* so the girls read them in secret, at school or when they went to the neighbourhood library.

By afternoon it had stopped raining and Anna took the girls to the beach. I stayed out on the terrace. It was low tide. I could see the girls running. They went a long way, right down to the water's edge.

They were hungry when they got back. Anna made some crêpes. The girls went and sat outside, at the white table on the terrace.

While they were having their snack, Anna went into the bedroom and put on a new dress. Her breasts, beneath the light fabric. They were round, full. I said, you should make a nightgown with the kitchen curtains. She shrugged. After that she went to the supermarket. I looked after the girls.

The next morning, Anna stayed with the girls and I went for a drive in the 2 C.V.

It was like that all the first week, calm.

In the morning, the first one up made breakfast. Coffee. Toast with yesterday's bread.

The girls woke up at ten and then it was their turn for breakfast. Afterwards we went for a walk along the beach, then a swim, and then back home again at lunchtime.

The shutters were weather-beaten. Every year, because of the salt, they had to be repainted. Green, chromium oxide, it never changed. It's easier to touch up, said Anna.

The tyres on the 2 C.V. needed changing as well.

I went to Dieppe. The shop assistant mixed the paint there in front of me. He added the brushes. Sandpaper. It was the beginning of the holidays, I took it all without arguing.

It was the girls' birthday as well. Anna asked me to bring a kilo of strawberries for the cake.

I bought the paint, changed the tyres. I also bought a bicycle pump, but I forgot the strawberries, and yet, before I had left the house Anna had said, be sure you don't forget the strawberries, and I said, I won't.

I was nearly home by the time I realized. I had seen a green-grocer's van parked a short way behind me, by the side of the road. I reckoned that with a bit of luck he would still be there and have some strawberries. I turned around.

The van was there. I pulled over onto the lay-by. The green-grocer had already lowered half of his awning. When he saw me he stopped what he was doing. He asked me if I wanted something and I said, yes, strawberries, a kilo. He raised the awning. He put the strawberries in a bag. A brown paper bag. And as the strawberries were deep red, luscious, I asked him to add an extra handful.

I went back to the car. A muddy dirt path led away into the trees. An old woman was walking away down the path. She was carrying a basket. She took one step, then another. Her basket was full. She had to keep putting it down, changing hands.

"Would you like some help?" I said, following her down the path.

She stopped. She scrutinized me, scrutinized the 2 C.V.

I picked up the basket.

"What have you got in here that's so heavy?"

"Five kilos of pears, for jam," she said. "And the sugar."

She had a deep drawling voice.

I followed her for a hundred metres or so along the dirt path. More mud than dirt. She stopped outside a gate, an iron grille partially overgrown with ivy.

There were no other houses after that. Just the path which grew even narrower, and then the trees.

She opened the gate.

Behind it there was a garden. Flowers. And a long, low house with a thatched roof and irises growing all around. A path of white gravel.

We walked on.

There was a conservatory built on to the house, a sort of glass cathedral, and when I came closer I saw there were more flowers inside.

Behind the house a row of trees acted as a windbreaker. The cliffs were not far from there. You could hear the sea.

I remember thinking, if the girls were here, what lovely bouquets they could make.

The old lady stopped outside her door.

"You can leave the basket on the table," she said, pointing to an iron table outside the house.

She took a pear from her bag. She held it out to me. For your trouble, she said, but then added that if I took the pear she was giving me, Clémence would not have the right amount for her jam, and it would certainly cause a problem.

"Clémence is my sister. She makes jam as if we were to live another thousand years."

She waved her hand, as if to say that it was something she could not understand but that was just the way things were, and sometimes you just had to give in without trying to understand.

The pear was in the palm of her hand. She kept it there for a moment then closed her fingers round it one by one and put it back in the bag.

"Besides, jam pears are never very good. You bite into them, they're dry, a bit tasteless and they don't smell anything like Williams. But Williams are too expensive for jam, Clémence won't have them."

She held out her hand.

"My name is Alice, Alice Berthier."

She had a strong, authoritative handshake. She hesitated for a few seconds as if she still had something to say, then she turned her back on me.

"Just pull the gate shut behind you when you leave."

She headed off down what looked like a long passage and vanished inside the house.

When I got back, the girls were playing on the terrace. A game of wooden skittles I had never seen and which they had found, rummaging in the garage.

I went over to them. It was their seventh birthday.

I said, "You're seven now!" I hugged them. They laughed. A marvellous laugh, from inside, spreading across their entire faces. I told them not to move and I ran to get the camera, but by the time I got back it was too late, they had started playing again and even though they were still laughing, it was not the same laughter. I took the picture anyway.

I went to Anna in the kitchen.

Anna, her hands in soapy water.

The window overlooking the sea was open wide. A breeze brought with it the smell of salt and brown seaweed.

Anna said, "Can you make the cake?"

The recipe was on the table. The meringue cake. I knew how.

I switched on the radio.

I poured flour into a salad bowl, broke the eggs, yolks, whites, put the yolks in with the flour. The girls were shouting. I could see them through the window. They had left their skittles and were playing with the water hose. Anna went out to hang up the laundry. Reaching for the line. Her arms held high. Her dress riding up her thighs. She had got a tan.

I added the sugar, melted butter, yeast.

I spread the batter in the pan.

Then I whisked the egg whites until stiff and since we did not have a mixer I had to do it by hand. I added the sugar, a hundred grammes, and then went to look for the strawberries and could not find them.

I went to look in the car.

The girls were on the swing and Anna was pushing them. I smiled to Anna and she smiled back. There were a hundred metres between us. The red laundry basket in the grass. The scooters.

I waved, nothing, everything's fine. The strawberries were not in the car. I must have forgotten them at the old lady's. When I put the basket down on the table.

I closed the car door. I thought, it's eleven o'clock, I have time to go back, but then I looked at the dashboard and saw it was nearly noon and I had no time at all.

I went back to the kitchen.

In the place of the strawberries I put some peaches in syrup, a can Anna kept in the cupboard just in case. I covered them with the egg whites and placed the cake in the oven, forty-five minutes on the lower rack.

When Anna sliced into the cake, she could see there were no strawberries. She did not say anything. Neither did the girls.

They looked at me, all three of them.

The girls' eyes. The same as Anna's. Caramel-coloured.

After the meal the girls went up to their room. A nap, Anna's idea.

Even if they did not sleep.

I was outside on the deckchair. I could hear them. Blue sky through the lilac branches. Their voices lulled me. My daughters' laughter. I tried to guess what they were doing. What they were telling each other.

Anna wandered around the house and then came over to me. She sat down on the edge of the deckchair. She placed her hand on my ankle. Her nails were covered with a pink film. No rings, just the wedding band with our names engraved inside.

It was low tide.

Seagulls shrieking.

Anna said, do you want to go for a walk? I shook my head. The girls must have fallen asleep. I could no longer hear them.

I closed my eyes and Anna went back inside the house.

I stayed there until three. Then I drove off in the 2 C.V. I wanted to go for my strawberries. Ten minutes there and back, I thought, and then we will go to the beach.

I parked on the lay-by. The little path. The ground, too much in the shade. As if it were soaked. There must be springs not far from there, higher up.

I went up to the gate. The letter box was shaped like a bird's nest, with the two names painted on, Alice and Clémence Berthier, and I thought, I should make a letter box for *La Téméraire*.

The girls would like that.

And then I remembered that we never got any post at *La Téméraire*. We had put our subscriptions on hold, *Le Monde*, *Télérama*.

I rang the bell, and as there was no answer I rang again, leaving my finger a bit longer on the buzzer. I waited. No-one came. I went through the gate.

Alice was in the conservatory. In a rocking chair, a plaid blanket over her lap. She was reading. A cat lay on a wicker armchair next to her.

"I've come for my strawberries," I said.

She looked up and over her glasses.

"Your strawberries . . ."

"I rang the bell."

She shrugged. She pushed her blanket aside and stood up.

A door led directly from the conservatory to a pretty room that served as a sitting room. Two windows. One gave on to the garden, the other to the rear of the house.

"Look at this! She's shut the window again. Anyone would think it bothers her to let Voltaire come and go as he pleases."

She opened the window then turned to me.

"Voltaire is the cat you saw."

Two armchairs had been drawn over to the window. Hand-made cushions. Cross-stitch. Cat hair clung to the fabric.

Against the wall was a large cast iron radiator. A low table with a game of solitaire.

The cat came into the room. He looked at us, first Alice, then me, then he went to rub against Alice's legs.

"He's a good cat," she said.

The cat was purring, going from one leg to the other. His back arched.

"But you can't trust him, he's a killer. Grasshoppers, butterflies, anything that lives in the garden . . . He catches moles, too. Cats can be so terribly violent sometimes."

She sat down in one of the armchairs by the window.

"Do you like cats?"

"My strawberries," I said. "I forgot them here this morning . . ."

She took a packet of tobacco from her pocket. The packet was flattened. Amsterdamer.

She pointed to the game of solitaire.

"Would you like a game? Well, that's to say, I shall go first, then you."

She placed her tobacco on the table next to the game.

"Your strawberries . . . of course . . ." she said, moving a first peg.

When she won a peg, she removed it from the board and placed it on the rail around the edge of the game.

At one point, I recall, there were a dozen or so pegs still on the board. In bad spots. She could not win now.

She looked up at me.

"We ate them," she said.

That was all.

She had not finished the game.

Beyond the windowpane, it had begun to rain. We could hear the first drops on the roof of the conservatory.

"Bloody summer!" she said. "It's going to be a rotten one, that's a foregone conclusion."

She held out her packet of tobacco.

"Would you like one?"

I shook my head.

"You're angry about your strawberries, is that it? What can I say . . . There they were, in their bag, so tempting . . . I never thought you would come back for them. And to be honest, they weren't all that good. They looked good but they didn't taste that good, I assure you . . . We had to slice them down the middle and add sugar, and believe me, even with the sugar, they were anything but delicious. Let's go and ask Clémence to make us some tea. Will that do, some tea?"

She picked up the cat and held it against her.

"Unless you don't care for tea; she can make you something else."

She glanced at the clock.

"Clémence eavesdrops behind doors, she can't help herself. She'll be here in five minutes with the tray, believe me."

She pointed to the armchair across from her. On the other side of the little table.

I sat down.

"We've got out the extra leaves for the table. My nephews are coming. They're on holiday. They always come here on holiday. They ring us and say, we're on our way, and two days later, here they are."

She was stroking the cat with the palm of her hand. The cat was purring.

"People become such creatures of habit . . ."

She adjusted her shawl around her shoulders.

I put the pegs back in their holes.

Outside, it was still raining. A shower, thick drops splashing against the windowpanes. I thought that because of the rain, I did not have to go home just yet. I began to play. Alice was looking out at the garden. Puddles. Plants bowing to the rain.

"They tell me I ought to go and live in the south. What on earth am I supposed to do in the south?"

She turned to face the other door, the one that gave on to the corridor.

"Clémence won't come now. She can't have heard you. You'll have to come back for tea another time."

She put the cat down on the floor. She went to close the window; rain was running down the wallpaper.

"And in any case, Voltaire won't want to go out now."

She looked at the cat. And then she looked at me.

She held out her hand.

"You'll come back tomorrow. Clémence will make tea, as promised, and she will also buy a few grammes of strawberries to make up for yours, the ones we ate."

She said that with the offer of tea and a fresh bag of strawberries, well, we would be quits.

We were settling into our holidays, Anna and the girls and I. We spent our days running and playing on the beach. The water was cold but we bathed all the same. We ate mussels and shrimps, and all sorts of fish that we bought straight off the boats.

One morning we took our bikes and headed inland. The weather was fine. We had a picnic in a field, cows grazing just next to us. One of the cows had a calf. We offered it a slice of bread and butter; it was not interested.

The girls took their dolls and fastened them onto the luggage rack. At noon they served them lunch on their plastic tea set. It drove Anna crazy to see them doing that. She said she was going to burn the lot, the toy tea set, the dolls, the *Martine* books. Burn the girls as well if they went on playing that way.

Then the dolls dozed off and we had to be quiet.

People always give dolls to girls.

And if our girls had been boys?

The girls went to look at the calf.

Anna lay on her stomach on the plaid blanket; she wanted me to massage her back.

I said to her, people should do just the opposite, give dolls to boys and lorries to girls.

I began to massage her.

I told her it would be nice to have a cat.

She said, keep doing that, it feels good.

The girls came to fetch their dolls, and went off again to see the calf.

The next day when we got up it was raining. The girls went to rummage in the garage. They found some earthenware pots. They wanted to paint them. We let them. Then they wanted to varnish them. We found some varnish in an old bottle, a sort of paste that was impossible to use. I said I would go and buy some. That is why I went past Alice's place again. I stopped. It was still raining. I sat in the car for a moment, watching the windscreen wipers go back and forth.

I rang the bell and went straight in. Alice was in the sitting room. Turning the pages of a big book that was there on the table in front of her.

"I was expecting you," she said, when she saw me on the threshold.

And it must have been true, because there on the table, in addition to the book, was the tray with the cups.

The table leaves were against the wall.

"I can't stay . . ."

She looked down at my shoes, a long gaze. The tracks of water I had left on the floor.

I went to dry my feet on the mat in the entrance.

She got up.

"I'll go and fetch the tea."

I glanced at the book she was reading. A biography of the painter Roman Opałka.

"I'll explain," said Alice upon leaving the room.

I already knew. Anna had been mad about him. Before the girls were born. She had pinned reproductions of his work onto the bedroom walls. Infinite suites of numbers. Going from one to the next. From one canvas to the next. The last number on one canvas linked to the next one. And on it went, with all the numbers. His entire life devoted to painting them. One day Anna even put up a photograph of him. You don't mind? I thought it was absurd. I did not say anything. Until the girls were born, we had Opałka on the other side of the bed, gazing at us.

I pulled out a chair. The cat was sleeping on it. Curled into a ball. I took another chair.

Directly opposite, up against the wall, there was a large cupboard. With thick doors. Solid walnut. At the very top was a bouquet of dried flowers. Blue hydrangeas.

The window that gave on to the back of the house was open.

Alice came back with the tea.

It had a strange smell.

"Must you ring like that every time?" she said, setting the teapot down on the table. "It makes such a noise . . . And you rang twice, as well . . . As if once were not enough. There must be another way to let one know you've arrived."

"Another way?"

"A more silent way."

"I don't know . . ."

"You must think about it, if you plan to come again."

With the tea she had brought a plate filled with a dozen or so little dry biscuits she told me were snaps.

She pushed the plate over to me.

"Are you hungry?"

"No . . ."

"Of course you are . . . At your age, it's normal. Besides, Clémence made them herself. Everything Clémence makes is delicious, of that you can be sure."

The snaps were orange-flavoured. When I bit into them, the taste spread through my mouth. Delicious.

Not a sound. Only the ticking of the clock. The smell of cold ash. The fireplace. There was one log in the hearth. Next to it, more wood in a box.

"It's very quiet here," I said.

I said nothing more. Nor did Alice. I looked around. Paintings. Engravings. A reproduction of Braque's "*Les Oiseaux*".

Alice was looking at me. Over her glasses, while she drank her tea. Then nothing more. It was becoming awkward. Heavy.

I told her I was here on holiday. My house, *La Téméraire*, a bit further north, after Varengeville.

She knew it.

I told her I had a wife and two daughters.

"My wife's name is Anna."

She did not reply.

I took another snap. This visit was too complicated. I looked out the window. It had almost stopped raining.

I got up.

"I must go."

She did not move. I thought she had not heard me. Or had not understood.

I put my chair back, and placed my cup on the tray. I went to the door.

"What were you expecting?" she said abruptly.

I turned around. She was sitting with her hands curled around her cup, looking at me.

"Well, what were you expecting? That we'd talk for hours, as if we'd always known one another? But what would you know about getting to know people . . ."

She made a face.

"You haven't even finished your tea."

That was true. The cup was half empty. The liquid slightly green. The spoon next to the cup.

"I don't care for tea."

The book on the table. Still open.

"I don't care for Opałka, either."

"Who's asking you to care for either? Just be glad to be here. To be doing what you're doing. That would already be progress, don't you think?"

"I'm on holiday."

"And so what?"

Her voice, suddenly unpleasant. I had no desire to hear it anymore. It was just then, as I was turning away from her, that I saw the statues on the cupboard. At the very top, hidden in the shadow of the bouquet of hydrangeas. There were three of them. Their shadows against the wall.

I walked over to them.

"You have *kachinas?*"

Alice looked at me.

"You know about them?"

"Yes . . ."

She shrugged.

"I don't believe you. No-one knows about *kachinas.*"

The cupboard was too high for me to reach them.

"Native American art," I said. "An Indian tribe, the Hopis, they live in Arizona . . . *Kachinas* are thought to incarnate spirits. They give them to children, to familiarize them with the gods."

Alice got up and came over to me.

"They are not thought to incarnate, they do incarnate."

And then she turned to face me. Both arms crossed over her chest.

"How do you know about them?" she said.

"My father . . . He had an art gallery in Paris."

"Paris is a big city."

"On the rue du Bac. May I see them?"

"You may, but I've never seen Clémence do any cleaning up there, it will be dusty."

I pulled a chair over to climb on.

"Not that one, please!"

She put the chair back.

"Go and fetch the stepladder that is in the conservatory, and be careful on your way not to break any pots because then we'd never hear the end of it."

The floor was uneven. The stepladder wobbled. Precarious balance. Alice watched as I climbed.

"If you fall, I won't know what to do with you, or how to pick you up, or even who to call to notify of your fate."

The *kachinas* were there, at the very top of the cupboard, side by side in the dusty shadow of the hydrangea blossoms. Three wooden fetishes adorned with feathers and paint. One of them was made of earth, probably a Mudhead. I was not sure about the others.

"May I take them down?"

"If you like."

I handed the *kachinas* to her. One after the other. Such light wood. Hardly touching them, afraid I might rub off some of their precious colour.

"My father didn't have enough room in his shop," I said. "He piled everything up in my bedroom . . ."

I climbed down the stepladder.

I was troubled. These *kachinas* reminded me of my childhood.

"Fertility, fetishes . . . There were hooks on the wall in my room where my father hung the masks. I remember one Inuit mask,

when I woke up, it would be staring at me, it was terrifying . . .
There were *kachinas*, too . . ."

Alice came closer.

"They're impressive, aren't they?"

One of the figures had feathers on his head. A mouth in the
shape of a beak. The other one had a black face, horns on either
side. Protruding eyes.

"Superb."

"Clémence despises dust traps. If she could have reached them
she would probably have burnt them. She is quite capable of it, you
know."

She adjusted her glasses.

"These *kachinas* belonged to my father. We weren't allowed to
touch them. No-one but he could. And he used silk gloves that
were kept carefully in a cardboard box."

She went back to sit down.

"And your father, besides *kachinas*, what else did he sell?"

"African art, rare books . . . People came a long way to see him.
Do you know about the Dogon people of Mali?"

"Do you think I'm stupid?"

"I didn't say that."

"Your question implied that you did."

I was overcome with a powerful emotion. A moment of sudden
happiness. Finding them like this. Looking at them. One of the
horned *kachina*'s feet was broken. The other *kachina*, with a beak-like
mouth, had teeth like a saw. His eyes were black. Lively. He looked
alive.

"I remember a book written by an Indian from there. I can't
recall his name, just the title, *Sun Chief.*"

"Don C. Talayesva."

"Sorry?"

"The Indian who wrote the book you mentioned."

"Talayesva? Yes, that could be . . ."

Alice went to get her packet of tobacco, which had remained on the armchair, near the window.

"Not 'could be'. It was."

She rolled a cigarette.

The cat seized his chance to jump onto the table. He sniffed the cups. The biscuit crumbs.

Alice followed him with her gaze. His attentive movements, so careful not to knock anything over.

"This cat does whatever he pleases with me. Comes in. Goes out. Sits down. His Majesty. Of course it means no end of quarrelling with Clémence . . . You never answered my question, do you like cats?"

"I don't know."

"You must like them. I'm not saying that because I do, but because it's important."

She looked at me.

"Have you got a car?"

"Yes."

"Well the next time you come, we shall go and have a glass of wine at the Grand Hôtel."

"The one in Cabourg?"

"Naturally, the one in Cabourg. Where else do you expect the Grand Hôtel to be?"

She got to her feet.

"Now that you've had a good look, they must go back where they belong."

I put the *kachinas* away on top of the cupboard. The stepladder in the conservatory.

"I'll see you out."

She walked with me to the gate. And after the gate she took my arm and went a few steps further.

"We shall drink some Loupiac. If they don't serve it by the glass, we'll have a bottle, with salted peanuts and those little crackers they always serve you. We shall look at the sea. With a bit of luck, the weather will be fine. And if we are still hungry, we'll order some prawns. Or fillet of mackerel. It's excellent, fillet of mackerel, especially when it's prepared with raspberry vinegar."

She stopped there, in the middle of the path.

Held out her hand.

"You'll see, there's nothing better to do in this heat than to go to Cabourg for a drink."

I was back in the car. Hands on the wheel. I did not feel like going home. No explanation to give.

I just did not feel like it, that was all.

It happened in Paris, too. After class. I would take the *métro*. Go to Vincennes to give bread to the ducks.

Vincennes was too far away. I went to the beach. There were never any ducks on the beach. Only seagulls. The tide was coming in. I walked along the water's edge. I could hear the pebbles rattling. Like in Fécamp, along the breakwater that leads to the lighthouse. The sound muffled by the thickness of water. Thousands of pebbles.

I sat on the beach.

A couple arrived. They were walking. Arms around each other. The girl, not even twenty, wearing shorts and tennis shoes.

The boy with her body in his hands, hardly daring to touch her. They slipped behind the rocks. I followed them. They hid there, in the hollow of a cave, as if in the depths of their own prehistory.

Two lianas, I thought.

I wanted to be them.

The boy slipped his hand under her T-shirt. The girl's hips, as if they were dancing. Her naked arms. I used to reach out to Anna. In the beginning. The beginning is always so beautiful. When she desired me, she showed it, standing on the bed, her legs spread, look, I'm raining! Drops of her desire on the white sheets of the bed.

When was that, when was before?

I thought about the girls. I told myself that some day they might come here too. With boys. How would they manage? They were twins. For twins it is even more complicated.

I told myself we would have to keep them away from the rocks. Maybe sell *La Téméraire*.

I thought about all of that.

I retraced my steps. I heard someone calling and turned and saw it was the girls, they were here, on the beach.

In their swimsuits. So frail. Their legs like a grasshopper's.

My kids, I thought.

I started walking towards them. Anna had stayed behind on the terrace. The girls ran to me. I embraced them both, held them very close. Anna was watching us. I did not want her to say that I never hugged the girls, so I squeezed them even tighter.

They smelled of salt.

I remember when Anna told me she was pregnant. She said, a baby on its own doesn't grow properly, then just after that, there are two of them.

She talked about a small house, and a garden, and the dog we could get, and the girls' school, a school they could go to on foot.

It was evening. At the dinner table.

In December.

She took my hands and held them against her belly. There were strings of Christmas lights in the street. Hanging from one façade to the next. The lights twinkled, all different colours, all shining and sparkling and coming to rest against the wall of the flat.

Reflections on the ceiling.

On the tablecloth. Between us.

Anna had made meatballs. They were on my plate. I put one in my mouth and chewed. For a long time. After a while Anna said, swallow, and I swallowed.

Two more meatballs.

The lights outside. I had a headache. I would have liked to get up. Close the curtains.

I no longer knew how to eat. I was going to die. To die from not knowing any more. These things happened.

People have died for less.

Anna said, we could put the dog's kennel by the door, and hang a swing from the apple tree.

What dog was this? We did not have a dog. Or an apple tree.

I thought you were on the pill, I said.

She came and sat down again. She looked at me. It will be fine, you'll see.

I almost said, the table's too small for four.

I went out. I remember there were people in the streets. Only a few days until Christmas. I walked. Aimlessly. I thought about Anna's burning belly. Anna had lost her virginity all by herself. With a tampax. There are girls who do that. It had made me laugh.

"You don't believe me?"

I believed her. Anna never lied. Ever.

She had wanted a child. She would be having two.

My mother used to dream about Africa. A great journey. My father bought her the ticket. A return ticket. She never used the return. The last time I saw her was at the airport. She was supposed to stay for a week. She fell in love with a Bushman out there, in the great African South. She never came back. I am told I have half-brothers who run barefoot through the savannah.

I thought about all that, women, daughters, mothers. I went on walking.

Night-time. It was cold in Montreuil.

At one point I turned around. There was a dog following me.

I thought this must be the dog Anna was talking about. I did not want this dog, or a house, or what Anna had in her belly. I did not want anything. I began to walk faster. I ran.

And then I stopped running. The dog was gone.

The girls were born in July.

We still live in Montreuil.

The next day, with Anna, we made the most of the good weather, and took the girls pony riding.

The stables were out in the country. There was a beautiful view.

We booked the two-hour package.

We sat on the terraces and watched them go round and round. Their backs straight. Their riding caps on their heads. Proud daughters.

At one point Anna took my hand.

"Stop it!"

I was clicking the nails of my thumb and middle finger. She hated it. Already in the car, when I was driving.

"You don't even realize," she said.

And then, "Is something wrong?"

I do not know why I went back to see Alice. I never even asked myself the question. I took the car. Found myself outside her gate.

I went in. Without ringing.

There was a hut to the right, immediately after the gate. An assembly of boards and sheet metal partially hidden by the vegetation. I thought it was a tool shed.

Alice was inside the hut. When she saw me, she knocked on the windowpane.

"Perfect timing," she said, rubbing her hands against her trousers.

Because of the dust. A white dust, like plaster, covering everything.

She was wearing a black jumper and on her jumper was a very unusual piece of jewellery, a sort of enamel disc held around her neck by a leather braid. On her face was some of the white dust.

A table filled the entire space. On the table there were tiles. Some made of red earth. Others enamelled. There were sculptures, too, a curious menagerie made of strange heads. Misshapen. Against the wall shelves were sagging under the weight of tins filled with powdered paint. From floor to ceiling the same light film of dust. Spider's webs, as if they had been painted.

Alice pointed to the tiles on the table.

"These ones I still have to fire, and since you're here, you can help me."

She opened the kiln. It was like a cast iron beast, with a gaping mouth. She took three sculptures and slid them deep into the mouth, all the way to the back. They were little red donkeys.

She asked me to hand her the tiles in the exact order they were laid out on the table.

"These are for the kitchen," she said. "These tiles will replace the others, they're too white and too old. The mason will be coming."

When all the tiles were in the kiln, she closed the door and bolted it. Iron handles. Then she lowered the safety bar. She was like a priestess in a strange temple.

"It heats at over 900 degrees. A few degrees too hot and the colours burst."

She glanced at the dial indicating the rise in temperature.

Another glance at her watch.

"Now there's nothing left to do. Just wait."

We went out. Just outside the door. The light, dazzling.

"It's a strange little hut," I said.

"My father used it for developing his photographs."

She took a few steps along the front of the studio.

"That book you mentioned . . . *Sun Chief* . . . I think I saw it here, a long time ago. I'll have to ask Clémence to find it for us. Clémence remembers things. But there are so many books in this house, in so many boxes."

She took a few more steps.

"Clémence! Clémence! Where the devil has she got to, why isn't she answering?"

She turned to me.

"I can't see her anywhere. I expect she's gone off down that wretched path again! Oh! The gate . . . Here she comes. I tell her not to go walking in the woods, if she were to fall some day, who would find her?"

Clémence closed the gate behind her. She was smaller, frailer than her sister. Her body seemed lost in beige canvas dungarees, two big pockets on either side.

"Of course it's a lovely path, but Clémence isn't twenty anymore. When it rains in autumn it's like a torrent, barrelling down the ravines. In the summer the ravines are empty and Clémence goes walking along them. Look at her, with her basket, it's bigger than she is. She must have found mushrooms. She knows where to look. We'll have omelette for dinner tonight, that's certain."

Clémence saw us. She nodded, then went on to the door to the conservatory.

Alice followed her with her gaze.

"Clémence doesn't like it when strangers come to the house."

She glanced at her watch. The time seemed endless.

"We'll have to wait three days after the firing's done before we can open the kiln again. Three days . . . You'll be here, won't you?"

She picked up her jacket that lay on the bench.

"We said we'd go to Cabourg but it's too late . . . Although the weather is lovely. Why don't we go to Varengeville? All we need do is take your car, we can leave it in the car park in Les Moutiers and continue on foot to the church. What do you think?"

She took me by the arm. A gesture she had already made, and although it was not familiar, it was no longer strange.

"But perhaps they're expecting you, back in your house by the water?"

The park in Les Moutiers. I had been here several times with Anna. I remember the girls were still in their pram.

Then they took their first steps.

Acres of woods. When we walked past, visitors were leaving the park.

"That's Mary Mallet's château," said Alice, pointing it out.

A building in the middle of the rose garden.

"The four of us live in sixty square metres in Montreuil."

She turned to me. Her head raised. Silent for a moment.

"You have to learn to move beyond that sort of bitterness."

She leaned against the fence. She was looking at the château proudly, as if it all belonged to her, the château, the park, the flowers. The very memories of the place.

"Mary died not long ago. There are descendants, but descendants are never the same. She was a great lady. The lady of the woods. I knew her well, actually . . . When she died, they named a plant after her."

She stood there for a moment, thoughtful.

"A plant or a tree, I don't know which exactly . . . Was it when she died or shortly before? All things considered, a tree isn't enough. It would take an ocean. Can you imagine, an ocean!"

She looked at me, suddenly amused by the idea.

"Wouldn't you like to have an ocean named after you?"

I shook my head.

She shrugged. Through the fence we could see the rose garden. A few tourists were taking pictures.

"It's not Cabourg, but it's very beautiful all the same," she said.

We continued along our way.

"It really is the most beautiful garden. I'm not just saying that because it's here, but because that is the way it is. Let's come and visit it some day, shall we? But not today . . ."

She took my arm.

"Today we're going to the church. We'll have to come back one morning. In the afternoon there are often visitors and they have children with them. There's nothing more unbearable than children, don't you think?"

The path narrowed. There were dense thickets on either side. Trees, their roots laid bare. The earth was moist, loamy. In the shadier spots there was a scent of humus and moss.

Along the path on our right, protected from gazes by thick hedges, there were enclosed orchards, a manor, half-timbered houses. The gardens were on a gentle slope, down to the tall trees at the very bottom of the park. If you leaned down to look through gaps in the hedge you could see a red ball forgotten on the grass. A few statues.

Right at the end of the path was one last house, perhaps a presbytery. And then the church. Just there, on the edge of the cliff, as if on a promontory.

The church with its cemetery around it.

And then the sea.

We stopped.

Alice said, "In books they call it the sea, but I call it *the Ocean*."

The wind was blowing, ruffling the fabric of her trousers against her thighs.

Her eyes were watering. Because of the wind, she had to speak loudly. Almost shouting.

"I won't call it anything else, *the Ocean!*"

"What is the difference?"

"All you have to do is say the name, can't you hear it? In *the Ocean*, you can hear the salt, the power! You can see lighthouses . . . They're so very important, lighthouses, when there are storms . . . *The Ocean*, that's the way it is, I tell you, you cannot call it anything else."

She went over to the gate.

"Come, let's go in."

The cemetery. A few tombstones. Some of them were simple granite slabs, the oldest were topped by rusty iron crosses. On others there was a bit of earth, a few flowers, plastic wreaths. Faded petals.

Time. Frozen, settled.

Infinite.

The time of death, here.

Amidst the graves stood the church, sturdy, as if suspended. Endangered on the edge of the abyss.

Alice walked among the graves.

"One day, a very long time ago, the steeple was struck by lightning and collapsed."

She held her jacket tight against her in the wind.

"The church was not meant to be here, originally. The peasants had begun building it on the village square. But the monk, who lived here, didn't agree with that spot. So one night he went and stole the stones and carried them one by one along the path. The very path we took. Legend has it that he was helped by angels and that the angels also carried the stones."

She let her hand pass along the damp iron of one of the crosses.

"Some people say the opposite, that the church was initially built here and the inhabitants came to destroy it . . . Sometimes we think we know but we don't, really. The actual truth of things, that

35

is. You, for example: why are you here, with me, in this place, when elsewhere there is Anna? Anna and the girls . . . What is the truth? Can we explain it? No, we cannot."

I caught her eye. She was gauging me. Strange eyes.

"Don't mind me," she said, "I'm like this sometimes."

She led me to the entrance of the church.

The heavy wooden door. She lifted the latch.

"There are fine stained-glass windows. Do you know the painter Ciry? There is one of his canvases here. Perhaps it will make up for not going to Cabourg."

Immediately inside the door a flight of steps led not up but down.

Alice stopped at the bottom of the steps.

"The builder knew there would be gusting winds."

Her voice echoed. Her movements.

The light streamed through the stained glass. Burst in splashes of colour against the flagstones.

Ciry's painting was on the wall to the left of the entrance. A standing man, facing forward with his hands open, his arms slightly spread. He was wearing a white loincloth.

Alice sat on one of the pews. She had her back to the altar. Gazing at the painting.

"See how beautiful his hands are! And the light, as if it were coming from the painting itself, from his very skin . . . The loincloth, that required some daring, don't you think? Sometimes I come here just to look at this painting."

Bouquets of flowers were set out in vases at the foot of the altar. The air was damp. Cold. There was a vague scent of incense. And another less pleasant smell, that the incense did not manage to cover altogether, a smell of something rotting. Probably the flower stems, from stagnating in the water for too long.

I wondered what Anna would say if she could see me.

Alice was still gazing at the picture. Her hands crossed, one over the other. On her thighs.

"I like coming here. I like churches in general, but this one in particular. You always think you'll find a solution. In places like this ... Answers for all your questions. But that's an illusion."

She nodded to the canvas.

"Ciry lives here, in Varengeville. The house is not far from here, *La Bergerie*. It was his mother's house. We can drive by it later. I'll show you the way. Have you read his journal?"

"No."

"Then don't."

"Why not?"

She gestured limply, as if to say there was no point even talking about it.

"Just there, to the right of the altar, is a stained-glass window by Braque, *The Tree of Jesse*. Go and have a look."

"Jesse?"

"The father of David. The first of the great line of kings ... Jesus of Nazareth, you have heard of him, I suppose? Well, that was his family tree. You're in luck, the light is beautiful."

I walked up the nave. Through this church that resembled a ship. *The Tree of Jesse*. Blue tones. And among the various shades of blue, the black of the lead. The light penetrated the glass. Vibrant colours, as if they were alive.

I stood looking at it for a long time.

I came back along the floorboards. The Way of the Cross against the wall.

Alice was still in the pew.

She stood up. Walked shuffling to the foot of the steps.

"I owe you the truth about something."

The first step. She stopped.

"Those strawberries, we hadn't eaten them yet."

37

She smiled.

"But none of that matters, does it? We won't be angry over something so insignificant . . ."

We went back out.

At the entrance there were posters pinned to the wall. The timetable of services. Photographs of girls at their first communion.

"I don't know whether people really believe all this . . ."

On the square outside the church the light was dazzling. We took a few steps into the light. To feel the gentle warmth of the sun. My sandals on the gravel. My hand above my eyes.

"This sun, you know, is what I shall miss most when I die."

She pointed to one of the graves.

"That's Braque's grave."

A large stele covered with blue mosaics, a magnificent bird with its wings widespread.

"'You must also paint what is between the apple and the plate. And do you know, it seems as difficult to paint that in-between as to paint the thing itself.'"

Alice smiled.

"That's Braque, and it's so true, isn't it. Braque died the same year as André Breton . . . No, Breton didn't die in '63, he died later, in '66. I remember, Giacometti died that year, too. I always promised myself I'd go and see the Batignolles cemetery. I must remember to do that. He had an epitaph carved on his tombstone: *I am seeking the gold of time*. It's lovely, don't you think?"

"Who do you mean?"

"Breton, of course!"

She hesitated.

"That epitaph, was it on his tombstone or the announcement? I can't remember . . . It's so annoying, you know, one forgets details."

A tiny spider was clinging to the weave of her jacket. She took it in her hands.

"Did you know Breton?"

She lifted her head.

"We were on the crossing together in 1941. To New York. And then, we met again out there."

"Out there?"

"In Arizona."

She opened her hand. The spider had not moved. Alice was observing it.

"Sometimes I kill them . . . but today I don't feel like it. It's because you're here, it's your presence."

She used a twig to set the spider down in a clump of grass, a space between the two graves.

"Luck sometimes, it takes so little . . ."

She stood up.

"Do you know what they do, those monstrous trap-door spiders you find in certain countries? They inject a liquid inside their prey and the liquid transforms the flesh into a pulp that the spiders can eat."

She wiped her hands on the front of her trousers.

"That's what you've been reminding me of, since the very first day. Your first visit. You listen, you take. You give nothing . . . I don't know what you are doing here. Are you really that interested in this story? Breton, *kachinas* . . . I can see how when I talk about them your expression changes."

She looked at me. A harsh look.

She said, "I shall give you Breton if you give me Anna. Will you give me Anna?"

"I don't understand . . ."

"Anna . . . Your separation . . ."

"Who said anything about a separation?"

She let her gaze wander over the grass, the shady spot where the spider had disappeared.

"To be in a couple . . . such an impossible thing . . . a difficult, unrelenting struggle, a losing battle. One need only look at your face."

"I won't tell you anything."

"You won't have the choice."

"Stop bugging me, Alice!"

On her lips was a strange smile. Amused.

"I expected no less from you."

And after a few seconds: "So vulgar, honestly . . ."

She took my arm and we went back to walking among the graves.

"Breton was a friend of my father's. In the beginning, at any rate. It was impossible to remain friends with Breton."

The sound of the sea rose up to us. Wind in the trees.

"They met here, in Varengeville. Breton had come to the *manoir d'Ango*, to write. Then they met again in Paris and New York. It was the time of exile. The war . . . They fled. One cannot judge. Paris was occupied. I was sixteen when we left. Before we set sail, we spent some time in the South, in a villa near Aix-en-Provence, *Air-Bel* was the name of the house. All those years, the war years . . . It was a very special time. In a way we wished it had not lasted so long. And yet in a way we wished it would never end. I remember Duchamp, Peggy Guggenheim . . . They all came to the flat. All night long. I listened to them. Eventually I fell asleep. When I woke, they were still talking. But I must be mixing things up. All that, all those people and those endless discussions, it wasn't here, or in Paris, it was in New York . . . And then out there, afterwards, in the Indian territory, but neither Clémence nor my mother was there. Only my father and I."

We had walked all round the cemetery and had come back to Braque's grave. The sun on the blue stones of the mosaic.

"The journey by ship, that long crossing . . . It took weeks. We had to call at Martinique. Fort-de-France. They quarantined us. Breton was on board. With Max Ernst. And Lévi-Strauss."

Alice slid her hand deep in her pocket and brought out a piece of glass that the sea had polished.

She turned the glass in her fingers.

"I always have a few of these in my pockets . . . They become duller with time . . . Like us, you see . . ."

She placed the piece of glass on the slab.

"The first time I saw Braque was on the path we took that leads to the gardens at Les Moutiers. I was with my mother. I remember they greeted one another and then a bit further along, when he couldn't hear us anymore, my mother murmured, that's Georges Braque. I turned round to look at the man my mother had named. All I could see was his back. His silhouette, slightly hunched. The second time it was here. Behind the church. There's a bench up against the wall. And there he was, sitting on the bench."

We took the narrow passageway that led round the church to the graves on the other side. A simple mesh fence acted as protection against the void.

Trees, a gently sloping field with a few cows, and then suddenly the sheer cliff-face. The sea right at the bottom, as far as the eye could see. And more cliffs, all along the rise, further north towards Pourville and Dieppe.

The bench was there.

Alice sat down.

"At night you can see the lights of Dieppe from here, the cargo ships passing."

I sat down next to her.

"One day I shall have to take you to Honfleur," I said.

"What on earth would I do in Honfleur?"

"There's a beach there. From the beach you can see the petrol refineries and the ships coming and going, never-ending traffic, and barges too, going in and out of Le Havre."

"Le Havre? Certainly not. And besides, I don't want to cross the Seine any more. It's too far away. I'd be afraid of dying there."

"You won't die . . ."

"Of course I will."

Her face took on a sullen expression I had seen once or twice before.

"Time exists because I am going to die. I must die. Time exists because of that."

With her fingernails she scratched at the paint on the bench. Flakes of paint that she scraped away.

"And it is nonsense to tell old people they won't die, it doesn't help at all."

She turned to me.

"Some day, you too will detach yourself from things. You are young, still full of torment. A time will come when there will be no more torment."

She placed her hand on mine.

"You are at a difficult age."

"And you are not?"

"When you are this old, all you have to confront is the torment of death. As for all the rest . . ."

The sea there before us. Crushed with sunlight. The tide was at its highest. We could hear the waves crashing at the foot of the cliffs.

Alice stood up.

"Come, let's head back, it's cold in the shade. Clémence will have prepared the tea. Tomorrow you'll come again and we'll go for that drink in Cabourg. No, not tomorrow, Thursday. Thursday will be good."

"I thought you no longer wanted to cross the Seine?"

She was thoughtful.

"The Seine, yes, of course, you are right . . . Never mind, we'll go to Étretat. Or Yport. Yport is a good spot as well. They must have Loupiac there. Everyone has Loupiac! And if they don't, we shall ask them and they'll go and fetch some."

She paused, her hand on the gate of the cemetery.

"And you will tell me about Anna."

She took my arm.

"You will tell me about Anna, won't you?"

On the way home, I stopped off at the newsagent. I wanted a present for the girls. I found a cartoon book. *Gargantua*. I got them to wrap it up in golden paper.

That evening I gave it to them. It was ten o'clock, perhaps a bit later. They were in their room, where there were bunk beds, but both of them were in the lower bunk.

I showed them the cover.

"Gargantua loved Normandy," I said. "When he was tired he lay down, and because he was a giant, his head was on one side of the Seine and the rest, his body, his legs, were all on the other side."

They wanted to see the drawings.

Anna came to listen.

"His legs were so long that they made a huge bridge over the river."

The girls took the book to look at it together and go back to the first illustrations as well.

"One day, a boatman wanted to use Gargantua's body to cross the river. He climbed up on his shoe and went along his calf but since it was a very steep climb he helped himself along with his walking stick. The giant thought a mosquito was biting him. He scratched himself."

On the drawing, Gargantua's leg with the boatman clinging to it.

"And the boatman?" asked the girls.

"He dived into the Seine. A fantastic leap."

"Did he die?"

"Some say he managed to swim to the other shore."

I picked up the book. The girls were looking at me.

"And then?"

"Gargantua got old and when he was very old he fell ill and died. Since he was a giant, they couldn't bury him the way you bury other men."

"Why not?"

"I told you, he was too big."

"And then?"

"And then someone suggested cutting him up and burying the pieces right there."

They looked for a picture of Gargantua but there was not one. Just landscapes. And imagination to fill in the rest.

"His toe is here, in Varengeville," I said. "It's so fat that it's made a hill."

The girls said it was a very bad cartoon book, because of the missing drawings.

Anna and I looked at each other.

"The place is known as the Tomb of Gargantua's Little Toe," I said.

The girls wanted to go and see the place, and to take their buckets and rakes with them. We told them it was late, it was dark out. And you could not dig up the dead.

"Even dead people in bits," said Anna.

The girls asked if we were going to die too and Anna said, "Yes, of course, everyone dies."

They wanted to know what death was like and Anna said, "Death is when you're asleep, and you sleep for ever such a long time and you don't wake up."

"And everyone cries?"

"That's right, everyone cries."

The girls reread the book from the beginning. Anna found a picture of the giant in the *Illustrated Larousse*.

Afterwards it was really very late and we switched off the lights.

The next morning, in the café, Anna said, "Why do you go there?"

"It's not far," I said.

"Can I come with you?"

When I arrived, Clémence was in the conservatory. An apron tied around her waist. She was watering her flowers. In one of her pockets there was a pair of shears, two long blades sticking out.

It was hot. Humid.

It was the first time I had seen Clémence this close up. Her face. Her high cheekbones. She was slightly cross-eyed, her gaze distorted. She looked like one of those old women you see in Mongolia sitting outside their yurts.

The conservatory was overrun with plants. They were everywhere, in pots, on the ground, set on tables.

"Do you have someone to help you?" I asked.

She showed me her mouth, her closed lips, and she made the sign of the cross over her mouth, with two fingers. A shrug of her shoulders, as if to say that none of it really mattered, and then she picked up her watering can. Her back to me.

There were labels on the stems of each plant. I read the names. Some of the plants were carnivorous. If you touched them they turned black and died.

I do not know how they fed plants like that. I would have liked to ask Clémence. But she was no longer paying me any attention. With a shovel she was scraping up the soil that had fallen outside the pots.

There was a strange bird in the garden, beyond the window. In its beak it was holding a snail shell, banging it, using a rock as an anvil. On closer inspection I could see that there were other shells, all around in the grass, and I thought that in all likelihood the bird always came to that stone.

I heard someone knocking on the window. I turned around. It was Alice.

"I saw Clémence," I said, going to join her in the little living room.

"That's good."

"I spoke to her, but she didn't reply."

Alice spread her hands in a gesture of helplessness.

"Doesn't she speak?" I asked.

"No."

"Why not?"

"Do we always know why things are the way they are?"

I did not insist.

We talked about the garden. Alice told me that a man from the neighbourhood helped out with the maintenance, two hours every day, and that he was also a handyman.

"We are very fond of him. We could not live here without him."

She had found a book in her father's library, *Kachinas and Hopi Indians*. It was on the table. A big, very heavy book. Inside it were photographs of *kachinas*, and opposite each picture a detailed description. There were over a hundred of them. Reproductions in colour.

Alice got up from her armchair.

"This book is very well done," she said. "If you search carefully, you will surely find something about our *kachinas*."

I glanced up at the top of the cupboard.

"May I take them down again?"

"One must touch them as little as possible . . . But one more time, yes, that I can allow."

I put the *kachinas* on the table.

I leafed through the book.

Alice went to make some coffee.

The *kachinas* were classified according to their role among the Hopi gods. When Alice came back I had found descriptions referring to the three *kachinas* in her possession.

I read each of the descriptions, beginning with the first one, the Mudhead. And then the two others. In the same order in which they appeared in the book.

KOYEMSI KACHINA (Mudhead)
Height: 31 cm
Wood: North American poplar (cottonwood).
Natural pigmentation in black, ochre, brown, red. Feathers.
Date: late 19th century.

This figurine, representing the *Koyemsi Kachina*, is made of mud, the symbol of the earthly womb from which original man was created.

His face is round. In the place of his ears there are two balls. The head and body are painted brown (the colour of the earth).

The *Koyemsi Kachina* is a very famous clown in Hopi history. It is one of the oldest *kachinas*.

He was born of an incestuous relationship between a brother and sister, whence his provocative, obscene behaviour, which everyone tolerates however.

He can observe the world of men from the world of clouds where he lives.

When there are festivities he never appears alone, but always accompanied by eight or ten of his brothers.

This *kachina* gives presents to children (melon, sweet corn). He is the messenger of the gods but in his role as a buffoon he makes people laugh and often says the opposite of what should be said.

49

During his dances he wears a deerskin mask on his face. He represents man at the time of the Creation, before he even knew how to speak, and that is why, when this *kachina* expresses himself, it is impossible to understand his speech.

He is insolent. Spectators spray him with dirty water and urine and he takes his revenge, to everyone's delight.

GIANT KACHINA
Height: 21 cm
Poplar root.
Fine cord, raptor's feathers.
Fabric. Natural dyes, black, red, brown, blue, yellow, green, white.
Date: 1900/1910.

A very impressive figurine with a black head and two large eyes ringed with white, and long black hair (horsehair). Mouth in the shape of a beak with saw-like teeth.

Eagle's feathers attached to the head.

The shoes – boots – are white. Arms close together, right up against the body.

This *kachina* has a black beard. He is a member of the Society of Ogres. He comes out at the end of February, just after the Powamu ceremony. Before he appears he smears his chest with lime water. He then paints his hands and forearms with red blood. He comes out brandishing an axe and that is how he goes through the streets of the village.

He is always with other ogres.

During festivities he frightens the children who have behaved badly during the year.

AHOTE KACHINA
Height: 24 cm
Poplar root.
Down feathers.
Natural dyes.
Probable date: 1920/1930.

This *kachina* represents a warrior. The head is large and black with horns on either side. On his head there is a tuft of feathers and down. His eyes are round and bulging, ringed in black. The face is very expressive.

His mouth is shaped like a duck's beak.

On his left cheek is a white star.

On the right cheek is a crescent moon. His torso is painted black and yellow. His hands are white. The white kilt is held up by a traditional Hopi belt.

On his feet he is wearing blue moccasins.

In his right hand he is holding a rattle. In the left, a hunting bow.

He is an *Ahote*, a Restless One. He takes part in numerous dances. During the dance he whips intruders with yucca sticks. He stamps on the ground forcefully. His voice is deep and grave.

This *kachina* is said to come from distant planets, from the very depths of outer space. He brings prosperity to members of the clan and to the entire village. He is held to be a very beneficent *kachina*.

The *Ahote Kachina* reminds us of how short our earthly life is. How ephemeral our terrestrial existence. The spirit he embodies augurs good hunting.

The creation of this *kachina* can be attributed to the artist Quöyeteva, who was then the high priest of the Snake clan in Oraibi.

"I found that book we were talking about, *Sun Chief*. Well, Clémence found it . . . It was in the cupboard in the passage. No-one has been in that cupboard for a very long time. And there it was, in with other books."

She handed it to me.

The book was covered with a transparent sheet of paper. On the cover was the face of an Indian.

I opened it. The preface was by Claude Lévi-Strauss. I read a few sentences. Some were underlined in pencil.

*No jewellery box is too precious to house this gem of ethnographic literature.*

"Who underlined these sentences?" I said.

"I did, who else would have?"

"Your father?"

"My father died long before *Sun Chief* was translated."

There were photographs in the middle of the book. On one of them you could see a village. On another, a wooden signpost: Second *Mesa*, Shungopavy, Hopi Agency Keams Canyon . . . On other photographs, the interior of a house, a *kachina* dancer . . .

Alice sat down.

"I beg you, don't read it in my presence! Just take the book with you if you like it so much. Naturally you must give it back to me when you've read it."

I closed the book.

"That Indian, Don Talayesva, what became of him?"

"I don't know. He died. I suppose he was buried according to tradition."

"Tradition?"

"Just in the bare ground, or else in a coffin without a lid, with food and a ladder so he could climb out."

Alice took the book from my hands because I had opened it again and she could not stand watching me leaf through it.

"I saw those Indians. I went up to them. They are strange creatures. They could have built their houses in the valley, or on the riverbanks. They didn't. They chose to live on top of the cliffs."

"To be closer to their gods?"

"They think that rain can come only from the sky, nowhere else. And from their prayers, as a result."

"And when there is no rain?"

"They say that one of their number must be having bad thoughts and that they will have to send him away if they want the rain to come back. You know, they would kill you out there, for a little rain."

The book, on the table before her. Her hands folded over each other.

"I saw those cliffs turn red. I saw them turn blue and then yellow. I saw my father stride back and forth along those paths of dust, his camera in his hand, while the heat was making me sick."

"Are the cliffs like here?"

"Here and there, more or less the same, only there is no sea out there."

"What is there, out there?"

She sat with her eyes on me for a moment. And yet she was not looking at me. Something inside her, deeply buried. From far away.

"Out there the wind bites into you, and the rain, too, when it rains. And the frost. And time. I was very young. I remember. We were all absorbed in the same way."

"You say *out there* . . ."

The *kachinas*, on the table. Their recumbent shadows. She was looking at them, one after the other.

"It's a strange world . . . A world where beliefs are expressed through something altogether different. Through *kachinas*, but also drawings, sand paintings . . . They shout their beliefs through masks."

She looked up at me.

"Why are you looking at me like that?"

"I'm not looking at you . . . I'm listening."

She looked away.

Outside, through the window. The garden. The uncertain light.

"We are speaking of another world. I don't know if that is a good thing. Perhaps it would be better to keep silent."

She stayed like that for a long time. Looking outdoors. Suddenly pale. A drop of sweat on her temples.

"Would you like to rest?" I asked her.

She made a gesture. With her hand on the armrest.

"Don't be like that. Not you."

"I don't understand . . ."

"You're patronizing me."

"I don't think so."

"Yes, you are . . . You're feeling sorry for me . . . I should ask you to leave."

"Why don't you?"

She gave a nervous laugh. Almost bitter.

"I have no choice."

"One always has a choice."

"What would you know about it?"

Her voice, so deep. She ran her hand over her face, several times. Sweat on her fingers. She took a handkerchief from her pocket. She wiped her forehead. Her lips. There was a strong smell from the handkerchief. Of perfume. Lavender.

I got up.

"Where are you going?"

"To fetch Clémence."

She grabbed my wrist. Her fingers were icy, squeezing me. Like a vice.

"You are not going to fetch anyone."

"You are so pale."

"It's the coffee, it's undrinkable."

I opened one side of the window. Cool air came in from outside. She inhaled, deeply.

"The body has nothing to do with it, rest assured. Only the mind resists. Just bring me a little glass of that brandy you'll find in the bottle over there in the cupboard. Don't make any noise as you open the door."

She pointed to the garden.

"Clémence won't allow it. She swears by pills from that good old doctor . . ."

I poured her a glass.

She drank. Slowly. Her head propped against the back of the armchair.

"Let's resume our conversation, shall we? Tell me that you too would like to . . . Sometimes it all seems so disjointed to me. But in the end you will see, everything will seem clearer."

"In the end?"

"In the end, yes, you will know how to hear."

She finished her glass. Put it down on the table. Then she picked up the book. Without opening it. She held it in her hands.

"My father met him, Talayesva, the Indian who wrote *Sun Chief*. Several times. He was even a guest in his home."

She began to tell the story. It seemed to be difficult for her. Her lips still too dry. So there were times, between two sentences, when she had to run her hand over her lips, as if to renew her own saliva.

"Breton was a guest there, too. Talayesva let out a room to him in his house. There is a picture where you can see the two of them. In one of the albums. I'll show you . . ."

"And you?"

She looked up at me. Her gaze was calm.

"I went everywhere with my father."

The *kachinas*, there, next to us. Their unspeaking presence. An unfathomable world. These statues, like guardians. But what did they have to protect? The house? Or did they keep watch over something within, a mass of obscure secrets, living beliefs in the hearts of a handful of men?

That is what I said. "It's as if they're watching over something."

She said, "It was at Talayesva's house that we met the young Indian who sold us these three *kachinas*."

# THE LIFE OF DON C. TALAYESVA (1890–19 . . .),
## *Writer,*
### *Chief of the Sun Clan in Old Oraibi*

Talayesva was born in March 1890. In the dry land of Oraibi. His first name was Chuca; when he became an adult his clan family gave him his new name, Talayesva, which means *Sun Chief.*

He was almost fifty when he began to write *Sun Chief.* It was a long process. In the beginning, he did not write it down; he told his life to a sociologist who was passing through the village. The man was called Simmons. He worked at the University of Michigan. Simmons was interested in Talayesva's life and that of all the Hopi Indians. He asked questions. To get his answers, he followed Talayesva wherever he went.

He helped him watch his herd on the lands at the foot of the cliffs. It was there, in the gardens, that the beans and melons grew. It was also there that the two men met, in the shade of the spindly trees. For thirty-five cents an hour Talayesva told Simmons the story of his childhood, the rituals, the initiation.

They went along the paths, the same paths the donkeys and sheep used. They met women laden with earthenware jars, with their burdens. The women could walk for miles before finding fertile land or dead wood. Their life consisted of these long walks.

Simmons asked questions about their life.

And then he asked questions about the other life, the life of the spirits. The beliefs.

Talayesva gave no answers.

So Simmons went away. And then he came back. He often came to see Talayesva. Talayesva eventually let him a room in his house, and his sister Inez prepared his meals.

*

There was so much to tell. Too much. So, one day, Simmons brought pencils and sheets of paper and asked Talayesva to write.

Talayesva agreed, for seven cents per handwritten page. It was 1938. It would take him three years to write the book. Time did not matter. He said he would rather write than go down to keep the sheep along the *arroyos*.

In the book, this is how he described one of his meetings with Simmons:

> On 1 January, 1940 my white brother returned from the East to check on my life. I had used up almost three dozen pencils on my diary, but he wanted to know more. So I hired a man to herd my sheep and for fifteen days I did nothing but eat, sleep, and talk. When on the sixteenth he asked me for details about the ceremonies, I had to say, "What I did in the Soyal is secret. When you ask me about that, it sets the people against me."

*

Simmons had a car. With his car he would take families to visit other families in other villages. He took them to see the medicine man or to participate in festivities. Sometimes the distances were great.

You could see his car on the road and often Talayesva was there in the seat beside him.

One day Simmons asked Talayesva to introduce him to a Snake priest.

Talayesva had more and more friends among the white men. He called Simmons "my brother".

*

Hopi country. A country of *kivas* and beliefs. The feast of Wuwuchim is the first feast in the calendar of ceremonies. On that day the paths are blocked off, and visitors are told to leave. It is a night of mystery and terror, the most secret night of all. Talayesva refused to talk about it. Everything else – his life, traditions – he wrote about in his book. The legends he had heard and learned, handed down like tales, and which became the foundation of his life and of that of all the men who made up the clans.

He explained how he had had to leave his village to go to the white man's school, how he was forced to learn behaviour that alienated him from tradition. He said that one day he suffered for his modern behaviour, a very serious illness that came to him like a punishment from the gods. From that moment on he was greatly afraid, and he decided to return to honouring tradition.

He described the way of the feasts. How he, Talayesva, on the great day of Soyal, came together with all the men in the clan to repair the masks in the *kiva*.

He told the story of the great schism of 1906, when the entire village was divided in two. There were those who wanted to be friends with the white man. And then all the others.

That very evening, those who were hostile to the white man left the village. On foot. Taking the path along the ridge. Men, mules, a few carts. You could see fathers leaving daughters, and daughters following brothers, men abandoning their wives and then coming back some time later. Incapable of living apart. And yet incapable of living together.

Those who were staying behind watched them leave, from the square.

They came to a halt. Six miles further along. On land where there was nothing, and where they could build; they would call the land Hotavilla.

Talayesva was sixteen. He watched the schism tear his family apart, the way it tore every family in the village apart. He witnessed the transformation of his people. The ineluctable evolution. No doubt he sensed that contact with the white man would bring about a profound change among the Hopi nation, and his book would be a legendary testimony, lived from within.

\*

Simmons wanted to understand what the chiefs did in the *kivas*. He wanted Talayesva to describe the initiation rites. And reveal the secret of the masks. The names and words that could be uttered only in the *kivas*.

Talayesva refused to reveal them.

Simmons said that a first book had already been written by a reverend and that he, Talayesva, would only be repeating what had already been said.

So Talayesva hesitated, then spoke in turn. He told the story.

And he wrote.

One night, he recorded the chants and rituals on a dictaphone. He did it in secret, away from the village leaders.

Now he wanted a dictaphone of his own. He also wanted chairs and a cast iron stove. And running water in the sink.

One day a visitor gave Talayesva the book the reverend had written. Talayesva read it. The wisest men in the village read it in turn. They translated it for the others. It became clear to them that their secrets had been made known by the man whose name was Voth, but they reproached Talayesva for exacerbating the betrayal.

Did Talayesva sell the idols taken from the sanctuaries? Did he sell the masks that were used for the Soyal ceremony?

He was accused of opening the tombs and giving the corpses to the directors of museums, who exhibited them in their display cases.

Talayesva denied it.

And yet in the Field Museum in Chicago there were ritual statues belonging to the Soyal ceremony.

*Sun Chief* refers to this:

> *We might be better off if the Whites had never come to Oraibi, but that was impossible, for the world is full of them, while in numbers we Hopi are as nothing.*

*

The book was finished. Talayesva wrote the title on the first page, *Sun Chief*, then the date, 1941, followed by Oraibi, Hopi Reservation, Arizona, US.

Simmons took a photograph. The photograph that would be on the cover. He asked Talayesva if that was alright with him.

Talayesva stared at the giant shadow of the San Francisco mountains in the distance. These mountains, this place where one goes when one no longer belongs to the world of the living.

Simmons said he would be going back to New York, that he had friends there who would be coming to Arizona, students from Yale. He asked Talayesva if he would agree to welcome them, and Talayesva said he would be happy to receive these visits.

Talayesva stayed by himself. From afar, his red skin against the deeper red of the rocks. The cliff. A light wind lifted his hair, tossing it. You might think he was smiling, but it was the wind of sand raising the dust from the hills, the dust stirred from the peaks of the rocks, from the burning expanse of desert, a dust come from so far away, burning his eyes.

The sky of the West.

The colours – orange, red, greyish-green.

What was Talayesva thinking, now that the book was finished? Did he realize that all he had just done – all the pages he had written, going back over his life, all the long labour of remembering – all that was now disappearing from him?

Beneath a sheet metal shelter an old woman was cooking fritters in an iron pan. Next to her, ears of corn were drying in the sun, others were piled up against the wall, and still others were hanging from the beams.

The yellow gold of the ears of corn.

White flour in a dish.

And against the wall the deep orange brilliance of hot peppers.

The old woman slipped two fritters into a sheet of paper and took them to Talayesva.

She put the fritters down next to him on the stone. And returned to her shelter.

*

For a few dollars, Talayesva agreed to have his picture taken. With the money he fed his family. He bought fruit and good food.

He also bought linoleum to cover the ground in his house.

His was the first house in Oraibi that no longer had a dirt floor.

He went shopping in the big towns like Moenkopi or Winslow. He bought modern food. From his house came the smells of something other than traditional cooking. The women were envious of these new things that had come to his house. And they were envious of the fine cars that arrived and parked outside Talayesva's house.

He wrote to his white friends who had gone back to their universities. He sent them envelopes which he filled with holy flour and prayer feathers.

When they came to visit him in Hopi territory, he let out part of his house to them.

In his book he wrote:

*The chief of New Oraibi ordered me to stop taking white friends to the* kachina *dances.*

Now Talayesva was paying a young boy from the village to watch his flock. He also paid him to water his field and gather the fruit, the dried wood, and fetch the jugs of water.

The boy's name was Otto.

Otto acted as interpreter when Talayesva had visits from white men.

\*

When Talayesva was born, there were slightly more than a thousand inhabitants in the village of Oraibi. By 1959 there were only a hundred and twenty-five left.

Three thousand in all, in all the villages.

\*

Excerpt from a letter Talayesva wrote to a white friend, dated 4 November, 1941.

*Dear brother Honweseoma,*

*I would like to Reply to your kind letter thank you for the cheque with I was very happy to have it now I am broke. We havent got a cent in our wallet couldnt buy food. Thank you very much.*

*The portrait Mr Grosman made is very good. Im proud theres my portrait in the book of Yale men and soon it will be all over the world.*

*I got a lot of letters from white men who say they wanted to buy a book that was published. I think the books come from the university of Yale and theyre spread all over the United States to people Ive never met. It looks like before long Ill be a famous man. I cant really say Im pleased with the idea but the whites will call me a great man. When they write my address theyll put Chief Don C. Talayesva you recall I dont like to be called Chief or Mr Talayesva. Don is enough . . .*

*Sincerely, your brother,*

*Don C. Talayesva*

\*

Was Grosman's portrait a drawing or a painting? Was it in a museum or in a private collection? Impossible to say, or to track it down.

Perhaps it was destroyed.

Eight thousand pages were written. Where are the photographs that were taken?

Legend has it that one day Talayesva went down to pick berries along the *arroyo* and never came back.

*Sun Chief* was translated into French in 1959, as *Soleil Hopi*, by Geneviève Mayoux. The translation is careful, accurate. Lévi-Strauss helped out with the thornier passages.

André Breton had been eagerly awaiting the translation. He found the book at a bookseller's on the rue de Seine. He opened it. Began to read it on the pavement as he walked. He went into a café. And went on reading.

He recalled his voyage. Out there. Out West. The interminable distances. It was in August 1945. A trip with Elisa. And then Arizona. The high plateaux they call the *mesas*, which were the lands of the Hopi.

He read on.

Words aroused memories. Images.

He remembered Talayesva.

He brought his precious collection of *kachinas* back on that voyage.

About the book, he said that it was a revelation.

He asked others to read it. All around him. His friends. He talked about it. The enthusiasm was universal.

The book was like a vision, intimate even, as if coming from within, something he had sought so hard to find when he was there, and which had always eluded him.

With his surrealist friends Breton wrote a letter to Talayesva. The letter was dated 1 June, 1959.

*From the Surrealists to Don C. Talayesva*
*(Oraibi, Hopi Reservation, Arizona)*

*Your book,* Sun Chief, *is on sale in its French translation in all the bookshops of Paris and major cities of France. We have read it eagerly from cover to cover and we have been penetrated by your message.*

*In opposition to all the forms of oppression and alienation in modern society against which we are fighting, you represent man in all his original truth, marvellously preserved, with all his dignity as well.*

*As writers and artists, we have long held Hopi art in great esteem,* as well as that which the work of ethnologists has shown us of the spirit which informs it. One of us had the good fortune to visit Oraibi, Hotavilla, Walpi, Mishongnovi, Shungopovi, and Shipolovi, and to attend several of your ceremonies, and he has endeavoured to convey their atmosphere to us, an atmosphere we hold dear.

Thanks to you, these places, that spirit, that art have been brought infinitely closer. All mankind is called upon to draw a lesson of moral health and nobility from the story of your life.

Fervent homage to the immortal Indian genius of America; prosperity to the admirable Hopi nation with respect for and in defence of its worthy traditions; happiness, long life and glory to Don C. Talayesva.

Alice pulled back the curtain. I think that is the way she liked to see the garden. With no-one in it.

The house was silent. The clock ticking. Her breathing. She let go of the curtain.

She opened her packet of tobacco and rolled a cigarette.

I watched her. The way she moved. When she lit the cigarette. Holding it between her thumb and index finger. No-one smoked like that. But she did. She did many things the way no-one else did.

"That young Indian who kept Talayesva's flock of sheep, was he the one who sold you the *kachinas*?"

"Yes, he was."

She smoked her cigarette. The only sound the ticking of the clock. And her lips. The dry skin of her fingers rubbing against the armchair.

Ashes fell onto her jumper. She did not seem to notice.

She came to the end of her cigarette. One centimetre. Just enough for her fingers. She turned to me.

"Can you stay a while longer?"

I said yes. I could stay. In any case it was raining.

She crushed what was left of her cigarette in a saucer.

"The rain shouldn't be a reason."

She got up and went over to the door.

"This won't take long."

She disappeared down the corridor.

I waited.

She came back with a box. She set it down on the table. It was a cardboard box, like a shoe box. On the lid was a label: *Arizona, August 1945.*

She removed the lid. There were photographs inside. Black and white. All the same format, four by six. Stored in plastic sleeves. I took them out, one after the other. No portraits, only landscapes. Arid. Barren desert.

The plains of Colorado. The Rocky Mountains. Steep rockfaces. Burning stone.

Alice pointed to one of the pictures.

"These high plateaux are *mesas*."

Cliffs of stone; you imagined them windswept.

"In winter they are icy cold. Either snow-covered or waiting for rain. From year to year. One month to the next. And people live there. Their lives are hard, almost impossible. So there are those who leave, sometimes."

All those photographs, spread out on the table. There were fifty or so, maybe more. On every one of them was the same fairy-tale landscape of sculpted rocks, fashioned by time, heat, wind. The earth, which you guessed must be ochre, then red ochre. The vastness.

Alice pulled a photograph from the pile.

"This picture, this village, is Oraibi. I remember when we arrived, this was our first village. The view of the desert, from high up there, that was impressive, I tell you . . ."

She placed the photograph before me.

A few mud houses, ladders leaning against the walls, terraced roofs. A narrow street between the houses. Houses without doors.

On the square was a ladder emerging from the ground. It was the entrance to a sanctuary, the *kiva*, the sacred place where the *kachinas* gathered.

On another photograph were fields of maize, melons, beans. A dry riverbed.

The names, Walpi, Mishongnovi, Hotavilla, written on the back of each photograph.

"Was it your father who took all these pictures?"

"It was."

"All these hamlets look abandoned."

"In winter they're covered in snow. With a howling wind. In summer it's just the opposite, the heat makes them thirsty."

At the very bottom of the box were a few newspaper articles. Papers that time had faded. Damp.

Alice picked up a few photographs.

"Why do we like to talk about all this?"

She looked at the pictures.

"This feeling we get sometimes, that there's something missing . . . When we no longer have any beliefs. When we feel we're no longer capable of belonging to our own history."

There were a few pictures left on the table. There was one, just one out of all of them, that was not a landscape. It showed a group of men, twenty or more. Standing against a rock. Their shoulders covered with similar blankets.

"Who are these men?" I asked.

"Hopis, the ones who were imprisoned on Alcatraz."

Alcatraz, the prison island.

Those faces. All different and yet all bearing the same mark of solemnity.

"What had they done?"

"Nothing."

"What do you mean, nothing?"

"They refused the white man's presence – schools, church, medicine. Everything the whites wanted to impose upon them. So they were locked away."

In the photograph, standing a few metres apart from the group, was a soldier on guard.

"What became of them?"

"Some eventually cooperated. Others pretended to so that they could go home. Those who couldn't pretend spent years of their lives on Alcatraz. Or elsewhere, in other prisons."

She pointed to one of the prisoners.

"This one, the third from the left . . . He's the one who sculpted our *kachinas*."

A very young man, though his face was dark. A cross traced on his chest. The ink, somewhat faded. What remained was the imprint of the pen's nib. At the bottom of the photograph was a date, *1896 September*, followed by *Hopi Indians, prisoners of Alcatraz*.

Another photograph had been placed in the same sleeve. It showed the same group of prisoners sitting on rocks looking out to sea. It was taken from behind. You could not see their faces, only their backs. And the guard keeping watch, his rifle in his hand.

"My father bought these two photographs from a dealer in Chicago."

She held all the pictures in her hands, one on top of the other.

"If you are interested in all this, you should read Aby Warburg's book."

"Who is Aby Warburg?"

"A very learned man. He wrote *The Ritual of the Snake*. The book is essential for anyone who wants to understand."

She put the photographs back into the box.

The *kachinas* were still on the table.

"Why did he do that?" I asked.

"What do you mean?"

"The young Indian, why did he sell you the *kachinas*?"

"Poverty, you know . . . Out there, the need for money is second only to the need for rain. But you do not know what poverty is."

"I'm not well off."

Her hand. Her sudden look. Exasperated.

"Of course you are! Compared to these people . . . We all are."

"I don't like it when you are like this . . ."

"Explain yourself."

"So harsh."

She brushed my comment aside with a laugh.

"Whether you like it or not makes no difference."

She placed the lid on the box. It was time to leave. I could tell. From the silence which followed. The hostility. Palpable. Suddenly almost hateful. I picked up my jacket and went to the door.

"That man, the one who sculpted the *kachinas*, what was his name?"

"His name? I already told you. You ought to remember. But you forget everything."

She remained silent.

Then she looked up.

"Quöyeteva. James Scott Quöyeteva, that was his name."

I had promised the girls I would meet them at the beach to go for a swim, but by the time I got there it was too late. They had already gone home. They must have managed to find a break in the showers in order to go swimming because their swimsuits were on the line with the towels. Rubber rings still inflated on the table on the terrace.

Anna was in the kitchen, she had made a pastry crust and was rolling it out with the pin. I went in. She scarcely glanced at me. A vague hello.

I took a beer from the fridge. A handful of olives in a saucer. I sat down at the table.

Anna sliced pieces of Gruyère and sprinkled them over the pie crust. The girls were in the bath. The door was open. I could hear them singing, *Patty-cake, patty-cake, baker's man . . .*

The sound of water.

Of their hands.

The sound of the knife. The Gruyère smelled good. I was hungry.

I went out into the corridor to see the girls.

They had filled the bath to the very top. *Bake me a cake, as fast as you can . . .* Facing each other. Only their thin shoulders emerging from the water. When they saw me they stopped singing. The holiday sun had burnished their skin. It is strange how girls change.

It does not take much. A few days. A bit of salt and you no longer recognize them.

I said, I'll stay with you tomorrow. They looked at each other. I think they did not believe me.

I went back to Anna.

She was breaking eggs into a mixing bowl, she could do it with one hand, the egg in her palm, a sharp knock against the edge of the sink. With one hand. The other idle. Afterwards two eggshells on the table, and she did it again. I watched her. Her mouth. She was lovely.

I sat down at the table. It was hot because of the oven.

She mixed the eggs with the onions she had fried a short while before.

Salt. Pepper.

I said to her, I went for a drive. That was it, I went for a drive.

She did not believe me. She added some diced ham. Bits of olives. Her fingers were greasy. Her lips, too.

"I was there . . ." I said.

"I'm asking you nothing."

She tipped the contents of the mixing bowl into the pie crust and put the dish into the oven. Twenty-five minutes, thermostat 7.

She washed the mixing bowl and a few other things that were in the sink and which must have been left over from the girls' tea.

She dried her hands on a chequered tea towel hanging from a hook in the cupboard. She untied her apron and draped it over the back of the chair.

She told me that the girls had found a dead seagull on the beach and they had decided to open it up to see what it was like inside.

She did not want the girls to take the dead seagull up to the villa, so they went to fetch a pair of scissors.

They opened up the seagull.

They actually did.

On the beach.

Anna said she watched them as they did it. She did not think it was a good idea to stop them. But she had felt sick to her stomach, whereas the girls had not. They found it perfectly natural.

They found the nerve behind the seagull's eye.

And they found other things inside the seagull's body. And in its stomach. Worms the seagull had swallowed. One of them was still alive.

They left the body on the beach.

Back at the house they looked through books for information about the lives of seagulls. They did not find anything. They reread the story of Geppetto, the part where the old man is in the belly of the whale.

"I told them you'd take them to Dieppe tomorrow and that you'd buy them some books."

The mixing bowl was drying on the sink, with two small bowls and a knife.

The aroma of the quiche began to fill the kitchen.

Anna took my glass. She finished the beer. She drank where I had drunk. At exactly the same spot. She had flour on her forehead.

There were no more olives in the saucer. Only stones. I tossed them into the bin. The bottle. I rinsed the glass. There were ants on the windowsill. They were all headed for the same place, the stone steps, and on the second step were the remains of a biscuit that someone, the girls no doubt, had crushed.

I put my glass down in their path; they went around it. I poured out a little beer and they went around that, too.

Anna watched me.

She saw the book, *Sun Chief*.

"What are you reading?"

"Nothing . . ."

She wiped the table with a damp cloth.

"The forecast is fine for tomorrow," she said.

The cloth was one of her old T-shirts. In white cotton. A souvenir from Guadeloupe. I used to like it, back in the days when she wore it.

"I also told the girls we'd go and eat mussels somewhere tomorrow. That you would be up for it."

The following evening we went to Veules-les-Roses, we walked along the breakwater and ate mussels in a restaurant by the water. We said, for dessert we'll buy ice-cream cones. Two scoops each. We chose our flavours, just like that, as we walked along, blackcurrant-strawberry for Anna, vanilla-pistachio for me, and all chocolate for the girls.

Afterwards we went back to the beach and waited for the sun to go down. We wanted to see the green flash. There was haze. I said, we won't see it, but we waited anyway. There was no flash but the girls swore they had seen it, cross my heart and hope to die.

It was just the sun setting.

So we looked at the stars instead, and the moon and the reflection of the moon on the water. It was beautiful. The air was warm. We went to walk along the breakwater again. The girls ahead of us. I took Anna's hand. The girls wanted to take pebbles back with them and we went back to the beach to choose the nicest ones.

Anna said, "Alright then, but you're not to take them back to Paris, we'll leave them at the villa." Anna says Paris, she does not say Montreuil.

The twins promised.

We let go of each other's hand.

We took back one pebble each. After that the girls wanted

their ice cream and we bought them as promised, blackcurrant-strawberry for Anna, vanilla-pistachio for me, and all chocolate for the girls.

It was dark out.

The girls fell asleep in the car. When we got home, we looked at them. It seemed a shame to wake them up. Anna said, we could spend the night here?

She placed her hand on my face.

I opened the car door.

We took the girls in our arms, one each. They had chocolate at the corner of their lips. We put them to bed like that, without washing.

The next morning we set out the pebbles side by side on the terrace. Mine next to Anna's, and the girls' one on top of the other.

The girls wanted us to take pictures. One with just the pebbles and another with us and the pebbles. For the one with us and the pebbles Anna had to put the shutter on automatic and come back at a run.

Afterwards, since the tide was low, the girls wanted to go hunting for shells and we took our buckets. The weather was not good. But it was not raining, either. Somewhere in between. The girls put on their boots and their raincoats. Their sunhats, a bit too big. The same yellow as their raincoats.

Against the seaweed. The sand. The grey sky. All that yellow looked lovely.

I had brought the box of salt with me and I showed them how to make the razor-shells that hid in the sand come up out of their holes.

I also showed them how to find the shells. Two little holes. It was easy.

They caught a crab. Anna took a picture of the crab. She said that when we got back to the house we would draw pictures of the shells and the crab with pencils. And we would also draw the rake and the net we had used to capture them.

The twins ran along the beach to find other treasures. After that it began to rain.

We went home. We were wet. Slightly. Our hair, mainly.

Anna looked at us. She was smiling.

She said, it's a lovely summer after all.

Alice had told me it would take three days before she could open the kiln again. She had made me promise to be there, and be on time, but she did not tell me what time she meant.

Only the day.

I found her in the studio. Nervous. She hardly said hello. She was trying to clear some space on the table but when she picked something up she did not know where to put it and she turned this way and that. Her hands full. She bumped into me more than once; I must have been in her way.

Even when I hugged the wall I was still there. No doubt she was sorry she had asked me to come.

Eventually she managed to clear a corner of the table. She wiped it with a rag. A cloud of dust hovered briefly, then settled.

Alice put the rag into her pocket. She went over to the kiln. She removed the safety bolt.

"Would you like me to help you?"

"Absolutely not."

She took hold of one of the levers. She released it, then released the two others.

She turned round, halfway.

"With ceramics, you can never be sure, that's just the way it is . . ."

She opened the door.

The air in the kiln had been heated to 1,000 degrees. Then

closed in. Kept there for three whole days. It gave off a strange smell. She looked inside. She took out one tile and then another. On some of them the colours had set the way she wanted them to. On others it was slightly different. Not necessarily disappointing.

"Chance has such a lot to do with it, actually . . ."

The heat had softened some of the yellows, caused the oranges to sparkle, attenuated the greys. She lifted them to the light for a moment and then put them down on the table according to a precise diagram she had pinned to the wall directly in front of her.

"This grey-blue, have you seen?"

The three little donkeys were still at the back of the kiln.

"They are for the garden child," she said, pointing to them.

"The garden child?"

"He hangs about. We don't know who he belongs to. Clémence leaves things for him on the bench."

She placed the donkeys on the table next to the tiles.

One of them had split during the firing. She put it aside, away from the others.

"God's choice."

"You believe in God?"

"In certain passages in the Gospel, how can you not . . ."

The broken donkey, in the palm of her hand. She was looking at it.

"*In the beginning was the Word* . . . One cannot remain indifferent to a phrase like that. Naturally the rest is always open to discussion, but this *In the beginning was the Word*, that you cannot deny."

She asked me to pick up the sacks of clay along the wall that had fallen over. She said that as a rule whenever there was something heavy to be moved, she got the gardener to help her.

She shut the door of the kiln.

We went out.

The weather was beautiful.

It rained all the following night. I had left the 2 C.V. out of doors. There was a hole in the canvas cover. When I opened the door I saw that the seat on the passenger's side was soaked. I wondered how long it would take to dry.

I moved the 2 C.V. into the sun. All morning, doors wide open. The girls came to have a look. It made them laugh. Later, the sun had moved, and I had to put the 2 C.V. in another spot.

In the afternoon I went to the garage. I bought some adhesive tape to repair the canvas. The weather was fine. I drove through the countryside, windows open. Narrow roads. I met a tractor. A smell of hay. Mown flax. Now and again I put my hand on the car seat. It was not drying.

I stopped off at Alice's. Everywhere was drenched. The path. The garden. The deck chairs were filled with rain. There was laundry on the line. In the grass there were dozens of snails.

Alice was in the kitchen. On the telephone. When she saw me, she waved.

I walked in.

Something was cooking in the oven. There was a lovely smell of warm pastry. Sugar.

I looked all around me. It was an old-fashioned kitchen. The table was made of wood, a very thick surface. There was a cupboard. A stone sink. Scraps of paper pinned to the door of the cupboard, sheets from a notebook, torn along a spiral.

Alice put down the telephone.

She removed her glasses. Put them down on the table.

"That was the grocer," she said. "I call him twice a week. It's Clémence's job to make the list. The following day a young man with the sweet name of Nicolas delivers."

She folded the sheet in half then in four and slipped it under the fruit dish.

"Sometimes the grocer doesn't have the things we order, and he has to fetch them from Dieppe. Anything extra we have to agree on in advance."

"And what are these?" I asked, pointing to the sheets on the cupboard door.

"Taoist proverbs. My sister has a silent passion for such things. So we have Chinese food quite regularly. It may surprise you but that's the way it is. According to tradition, before you serve a dish you must read a short text and meditate about it. Which is why we have all those papers you see there, and which attest to our fruitful meditation."

She took down one of the papers. Handed it to me.

*To have knowledge yet believe one does not know is the height of merit.*
*To have no knowledge yet believe that one does is the illness of mankind.*

"Not bad," I said.

"On a daily basis, it is wearing, believe me."

She put the paper back in place.

"Once we have done our meditation, my sister sticks her maxims to the door and no-one is allowed to touch them."

"There's another cat in your garden," I said, looking through the window.

82

Alice came to stand next to me.

"That's Minette. She's not allowed in. She's a hunter. She kills field mice and eats them. Voltaire kills them too but he doesn't eat them."

Clémence was in the garden. She was collecting rainwater. Buckets she had placed beneath the gutters and was now carrying further along, to empty into plastic cans.

"It's for her plants in the conservatory. She thinks that rainwater is better, but with all the pollution rainwater is surely no better than anything else."

Alice went back to the table. She showed me the oven. The good smell coming from inside.

"She's made a *clafoutis*. With apricots from the garden. You might like to try some. Maybe later. It has to cook and then cool down."

A bee had come into the room. It was banging against the windowpane. Short little thrusts. Repeatedly.

"They come down this chimney. We never use it. There must be a nest, or something . . . we have to have the chimney cleaned. Although in fact they're never terribly lively by the time they come out of the flue."

Another bee came to join the first one.

"I don't understand, they always go and bash against this window even when the other one is wide open."

For a moment we watched the two bees' desperate struggle. The thud each time they hit the window.

"Why don't we go to Veules while we're waiting for the *clafoutis*?"

Her jacket was hanging from the coat rack in the hall. Her canvas hat. She took them down.

"Sea air, there's nothing better. If we leave right away we'll be there in quarter of an hour, but we shall have to hurry. Provided we are back by five. What do you say? Naturally only if you have sufficient petrol in the car."

"The passenger seat is soaked."

"What do you mean, soaked?"

"The rain during the night."

She hesitated.

"Well never mind, I shall sit in the rear. Is it soaked there too?"

I told her it was not, that it was alright in the rear.

She did pause for a moment when she saw the 2 C.V. The wide open tarpaulin. She glanced at the seat. Made a vague face and then put on her jacket. Lifted up the collar. Pulled her hat down over her brow.

"What are you waiting for, let's be off."

We left the car on the breakwater. We walked along, our eyes on the sea. The people on the beach.

"Such ugly people, don't you think?"

"No."

"That's because you don't look at them. You don't look at anything. Your gaze misses everything, that's why, you don't realize. If you really looked, it would become obvious to you how ugly things are."

She leaned against the edge of the breakwater. She took out her pouch of tobacco. I watched her. It had taken me over a year to stop. A dreadful withdrawal. And the constant fear of relapse. I no longer dared even touch a packet.

Alice looked up at me.

"Would you like one?"

I shook my head.

We went on walking. The air was mild. There were a lot of people on the beach. In bathing costumes. In the water. Others were clothed. Children wrapped up in bath towels. We stopped to look at them.

"The human body . . . The human body after the age of twenty . . . You're absolutely right, one shouldn't look at people like that. The moment you start, you can no longer stop. It becomes a reflex."

The cliff before us changed to pink. The ocean grew darker. Black in comparison.

"Have you noticed, when the sun goes down, the colours change."

"I came here the other night," I said. "With Anna. And the girls."

"And?"

"It's as if it wasn't even the same beach. Not even the same place."

A seagull passed overhead. Its shadow, for a moment, as if it had been cut out.

Alice stopped to look at a young woman on the beach. The woman was reading, protected from the wind by a blue canvas canopy.

"On the other hand, when you see them from a distance and they have their clothes on, they can be beautiful. It's the faces . . . One should never see their faces. Ever. Voices are far more important."

She took a few steps.

"You should take it up again," she added, handing me her pouch of tobacco. "That scratchy, husky voice that smokers have, as if it had been scraped raw . . . I can never get enough of it. That makes you laugh?"

"I'm not laughing."

"You're smiling, that's worse . . ."

She smoked, holding the smoke inside her. Then exhaling it. Her gaze following the light scrolling whirl.

"Tell me who Anna is."

"Anna?"

"Yes, Anna, who is she? You never talk about her."

She stopped.

She leaned against the concrete guardrail, her hands joined, one on top of the other.

"Look at those people bathing with their clothes on. That

woman in her blue dress . . . She's in the water up to mid-thigh. And she's still going in."

Alice described her in detail, as if she were fascinated.

"When she comes out of the water, her dress will cling to her stomach, and she is so fat . . . Dear Lord, how can anyone do that?"

She could not take her eyes off the woman.

"Clémence doesn't like it when I go on like this. I suppose that I've been getting nasty with age. Do you find me nasty? Why don't you answer?"

"Sometimes you are nasty with Clémence."

"Clémence is my sister so it's inevitable."

We started walking again. Taking slow steps along the breakwater. I was with her. I was listening.

"Old couples all end up living with hatred. An embryonic form of crime. In each of us. In a shared life. One day, one of the two looks at the other. How can it be any other way? It comes in waves. But you know all that, don't you?"

Alice stopped to look at me.

"Of course you do. So: Anna?"

I said, "Anna is perfection."

She smiled. And then she looked away. She gazed at the sea. The sea she called *Ocean*.

"Anna is perfection, you say . . ."

I did not feel like answering. Did not feel like going with her. Along this path where I would have to speak about Anna.

We resumed our walk along the breakwater. She seemed tense.

"Perfection does not exist. Or only in the mind or the dreams of a few ignorant fools. And you are not an ignorant fool. Although you might be a dreamer . . ."

She leaned on my arm. Her face turned towards me.

"If you had to choose between us, you would prefer Clémence, wouldn't you?"

"Choose?"

"Yes, choose. And send the other to her death. What would you do?"

"What an idiotic question."

"You're not replying."

"Things don't work that way in life."

She turned aside.

"In life things are far worse."

We had walked as far as we could. To the shadow of the cliff. It suddenly felt chilly, and Alice pulled her jacket closer.

"I am the one you would sacrifice. Obviously. Clémence inspires pity. People always think she won't manage, so they prefer her. It's her eyes, she has such a hangdog look, have you noticed? And then there's the fact that she doesn't speak."

She came closer to me.

"But I shan't hold it against you. Let me take your arm again."

She slipped her arm into mine.

"I do like to be next to you. The way it used to be. With my lovers. I did have lovers, you know . . ."

She lifted her chin to look at me.

"What would Anna say if she saw us?"

"She would say I'm mad. And that she doesn't understand."

We went back into the sunshine.

"I read a book that takes place in a concentration camp. A woman is ordered to choose between her two children. Which one she wants to keep. One feels one would die after a choice like that. But one doesn't. And what are you reading at the moment?"

"*Sun Chief.*"

"And what do you think?"

"Nothing. I'm reading, that's all."

She wanted to go back down to the beach.

I told her I had to ring Anna.

She gave a wave of her hand. I found a call box near the car park. Someone had etched *I love you Monica* on the grey surface of the dial. I thought they must mean Clinton's Monica.

I dialled Anna. I let it ring. She did not answer. She was probably not there. I imagined the telephone ringing in the empty house.

With my finger I traced the letters of Monica's name.

I wondered where Anna was.

I let it ring a bit longer then hung up.

Alice was on the beach. Sitting down. Her knees held against her. She was staring out to sea.

There was a yellow buoy on the pebbles. Dark seaweed caught in the chain.

The seagulls were shrieking.

I joined Alice.

I sat down next to her.

"Do you think Clinton ever came here on holiday?"

"Clinton? Why, has he died?"

"No, that's not it . . ."

She tossed a pebble ahead of her. To touch other pebbles. And the buoy. She wanted to reach it. She did not succeed.

"Did you know that I am not allowed in casinos?"

I said no, I didn't know.

"There are casinos all over the place here, but my favourite is the one in Cabourg. Cabourg . . . how can I explain it? Of course the view is magnificent but it's more than that. The promenade along the breakwater, the beach in the morning, at low tide. There's never a soul in the morning. Except for a few horses. The tides there are so beautiful. I may say that but in fact they're beautiful everywhere, in Fécamp and even here in Veules-les-Roses."

She turned to me.

"Shall we go somewhere for a drink?"

We found a café not far from there with a terrace in the sun. We ordered some wine. Salted peanuts.

Alice poured some salted peanuts into the palm of her hand.

"I won a great deal of money, you know."

They were roasted peanuts. She ate them, savouring them.

"I lost a great deal as well . . . That was a long time ago. Do you suppose one is banned for life? I expect I could go in again without worrying about it . . ."

She took a sip of wine.

"It's rather expensive, isn't it? Almost four euros a glass. Of course it's the best. Served in stem glasses. And with a view on the sea. A sea view always makes things more expensive. My house is worth a great deal, you know. But there are houses here that are worth far more than mine."

On the beach boys in swimsuits were opening parasols.

"They're pretty, don't you think? It's like Deauville, but in Deauville the parasols are green and yellow and red . . . They have all different colours in Deauville."

The sea was coming in. Covering the rocks, the seaweed. The yellow buoy began to float.

"It's strange, there is always wind here but today there's none."

She placed her hand on mine.

"We make a good pair, don't we?"

When we got back, it was almost five o'clock. The *clafoutis* had finished cooling on the windowsill.

I did not have time to stay.

Alice came with me as far as the gate.

"These are red Versaillaises," she said, stopping by the currant bushes. "And that other hedge you see over there is raspberries, *Rubus idaeus.* Clémence makes jam."

At the end of the garden was the man who worked as their gardener.

The cat followed us. Alice told me he had shown up in their garden a little over four years earlier. For days he had brought dead mice to the door. Clémence tossed them out but he kept at it. Then one day he brought a bird. So Alice decided to let him come in.

We had reached the car. Alice held her hand out to me.

"Will you come again tomorrow?"

Tomorrow, no, I could not.

I said, "I promised the girls."

She took a few steps along the path.

"In that case . . ."

There was laundry drying on the line. The girls' T-shirts and dresses. The bikes were there, Anna's leaning against the wall, the other two flung on the ground, their wheels in the borders.

The girls were not in the garden. They were not in the house.

I called Anna's name.

No note on the table. No note in the living room, either. I went back out on the terrace. The wind was blowing in off the sea, bringing the smell of seaweed. A rain-charged wind. I went as far as the fence and I saw the girls, all the way down on the beach. They were coming back.

My daughters. Two together. In the womb and now on this beach. Anna was with them. Anna in her flowered swimsuit. She was beautiful. She had got a suntan.

She was walking with the girls. Talking to them, first one then the other. The girls were beautiful, too. Seeing them like that, I thought, this evening I'll take them to see the fireworks on the beach at Dieppe.

I waited for them.

The sky grew dark. Almost black. The sun shining from below. A bucket had stayed behind on the beach.

Anna was holding one of the twins by the hand. They were too far away to see me.

At one point Anna looked up. I withdrew. They went into the shadow of the clouds. I walked back to the terrace.

I could not see them but I heard them. Laughing, then speaking. The twins above all. They reappeared higher up. On the path and by the fence.

The bell rang at the gate and then straight away, as soon as they came into the garden, the girls shouted with joy when they saw me.

I watched them coming. I pulled them to me and held them very close. Like that day on the beach. Closer still. They smelled of sun, salt, sweat. I could not bring myself to let them go.

I looked up at Anna. I wanted to tell her about Dieppe and the fireworks. That I would take them there. I thought, I'll give Anna flowers.

And necklaces for the girls.

I wanted all of that.

And then my gaze met Anna's.

Why was Anna so strong? How did she do it? I was on my knees. I could feel the girls' bodies against mine, their warmth.

I said, "You forgot a bucket on the beach."

"A bucket?"

Anna pointed to the two buckets near the door, next to the rake and the sand shovel.

"Everything's here," she said.

The girls let go of me and went into the house. My arms, still enclosing. Around nothing.

Anna went to give the girls their shower.

She prepared the meal.

She had developed the pictures of the pebbles. She showed them to me. The pebbles on their own and the pebbles with us.

"They're lovely, aren't they?"

I did not know whether she was referring to the girls or to the photographs.

The girls were smiling. Anna too. It was just me. I was a bit like the pebbles.

Anna placed her hand on my shoulder.

I took the photograph of the pebbles all by themselves and slipped it into my pocket.

We ate out on the terrace.

Later I went down to the beach and realized that what I had thought was a bucket was in fact a ball. Forgotten by some child. Or lost. I kicked the ball. It went and rolled into the waves. It floated on the water for a moment, a few feet from the edge, and then the current swept it away. By the time I went back up to the villa it had disappeared.

We played ludo, all four of us, outside on the terrace. At midnight we could hear the booming of the fireworks and we went to the end of the garden to see the lights in the distance over Dieppe.

On Friday, things were as usual – beach, crabs, lunch, and in the afternoon we went back to the beach. We went swimming.

The water was cold. We played in the waves with the girls for a long while. We swam. And then afterwards on the beach I gave them piggyback rides. Then back into the water when they wanted to go in.

Then I left them and went to swim on my own. Straight out to sea. I had never swum that far out. It was hard getting back in. Because of the waves. The current. I was not making headway. I could see people on the beach. I thought I would never reach them.

When I got back, the girls were wrapped up in their bathrobes. Anna had made a snack for them, bread with chocolate and a few biscuits. They were eating, their hands nearly buried in their sleeves. Their lips were blue. Their cheeks red. The bathrobes a bright white cotton.

I sat down. I took a few biscuits from the packet. Anna said, "You went very far out."

Afterwards we gathered up our things and headed back to the house.

The sea, the beach. The pale late afternoon light. Anna and the girls were walking ahead of me. I looked at them. I suppose happiness was still possible.

Anna turned around. She waited for me. She said, "Summer is lovely, after all. It's a bit like Saint-Malo in a Rohmer film."

"Rohmer's films were set in Dinard," I replied.

The girls ran ahead to the gate. They watched us coming, their heads together. Arms around each other. They looked like Siamese twins. Stuck together all along their bodies. They were laughing. What sort of images would they keep of us? What memories?

Anna took my hand.

"Maybe it was Dinard . . . We could go there?"

"To Dinard?"

"Why not?"

"It's a long way," I said.

"If we take the autoroute, it's a straight shot. We could even stay the night there."

"You want to stay the night in Dinard?"

We reached the gate. The girls had been hiding and now they hurled themselves at us. Frail little bodies, their legs like grass-hoppers.

The next day we went to Dinard. We had lunch in a restaurant by the water. We went for a walk. We ate waffles and sat on a bench overlooking the sea.

We found a hotel right on the beach. One room for the four of us. We spent the night there. In the morning we had breakfast looking out over the sea. Croissants and all the jam we wanted. The girls were happy.

We went for another walk. The weather was mild. We felt good. There were slides on the beach, and swings, and little girls in swim-suits.

The white sand, wooden changing cabins. Further along, villas with gardens. Boats and sunshine. And Saint-Malo opposite, in the distance.

Everything was there, but somehow it was not like in a Rohmer film.

We left again in the late afternoon.

It began to rain. On the motorway. The first drops as we reached Caen and then further, the full force of the storm on the Pont de Normandie. The windscreen wipers swept back and forth as best they could. I was driving. The girls were asleep. Anna, too.

The girls lying on the seat, head to foot. The way they did when they were in Anna's belly.

Anna's head to one side. At one point she opened her eyes.

"Where are we?"

"Nearly there."

"Are the girls asleep?"

"Yes."

She sat up.

"Why did you stop?"

We were on the edge of the road, in open country, somewhere between Le Havre and Dieppe.

"I don't know . . ."

A car went past, its headlamps lighting up Anna's face.

I looked at the time. It was nearly midnight.

The next day. Between two and three. A horrible time. Like dusk. Too many hours of the day still to be filled. And too many hours already gone by for us to decide to do something with the day.

I arrived too early. The house was silent. There was no-one in the studio. No-one in the conservatory. Even Voltaire had vanished.

I wandered around the garden. The redcurrants were ripe. I tasted a few, they were acid. I was tired. I had been sleeping poorly for some time now. Anna told me to take sleeping tablets.

I lay down on the bench. The sky above, between the leaves on the trees. I could see butterflies fluttering.

When I turned my head I saw that Clémence was there on the threshold to the house. She was wearing a little grey dress that reached below her knees. Her straw hat. She stood there for a moment looking at the garden and then went to tear up a few weeds growing in the gravel of the drive. She righted a pot that the wind had overturned then disappeared behind the house.

The cat emerged from a thicket. Looking hungry. He probably made the most of this hour on his own to go hunting for birds. He started up the lane. When he drew near the bench he turned his head, casting one of his habitual brief glances at me. Then he went on his way, a feather still sticking to his mouth. Haunches swaying. And on to the front of the house where, when I looked up, I saw Alice coming towards me.

She picked him up and came over to me.

"Do you know that all morning Voltaire has been waiting for you? I always know when he is waiting for someone. And I assure you, this morning he was there. Sitting on the windowsill. His paws tucked underneath him. With nothing else to do but wait for you."

She sat down next to me. The cat on her lap.

"And yet you never come in the morning."

She talked to me about the cat and then the cracked window-pane on the roof of the conservatory. Against the light we could see the dark crack in the pane.

"When it rains, water drips through. I can't find anyone to climb up on such a construction."

Alice sat up.

"Look!"

At the back of the garden. A child. A brief silhouette. The moment he saw us he ran away.

"What do you suppose that child wants?"

He had already disappeared.

"Perhaps he just likes to walk through the garden . . . perhaps he believes this garden belongs to him. It's a game for him. And besides, the raspberries are ripening, all he has to do is reach out his hand."

The cat moved from her lap to mine, then onto the bench, then he jumped down. He stretched out on the gravel. His belly in the sunshine.

"One day, Clémence found some lily of the valley that had been crushed. It drove her mad. It lasted for days. She wanted to lay fox traps. Can you imagine, fox traps! She asked the grocer where she could find them. I told her it might be the child. The child who comes to the house. She never mentioned laying traps again."

Behind us a little path meandered among the trees all the way to the cliffs. All along the path were meadows. Fields of flax. A few cows.

The blue of the sea and the acid green of the flax. The sharp cry of the gulls. She wanted to know how far I had got with reading *Sun Chief*. I told her what I had read. And that while I was reading I felt as if I was there.

She pointed to a patch of grass in front of us.

"Yesterday evening in those tufts of grass you see there, in the shade of the ferns, I saw two fireflies."

She turned to me. She held out her hand as if she wanted to touch my face.

"Your eyes . . . Your face today . . . You look ravaged."

She turned away. The cat had fallen asleep. His paws twitching lightly.

"When cats dream, their entire body goes hunting."

She turned back to me.

"I must say it is unbearable to look at you."

She did not look at me. Only the trees. The row of them which acted as a windbreak.

"I know that feeling . . . that is why I love this house so much. Because one must love, don't you think? Otherwise, I don't know . . ."

She fell silent, as if she were thinking, as if she were still not sure of the truth of what she was about to say.

"Breton was fascinated by childhood. *Perhaps it is childhood that is closest to real life.* That's what he said. Normally I detest quotations, but that one, I have to admit, deserves to be remembered. Childhood, like an impossible quest . . . That was a few years before he visited the Hopi country. I'm boring you, aren't I?"

"No."

"Tell me the truth."

"From time to time, perhaps . . ."

She burst out laughing.

"You are frank, I must say!"

It was the first time I had seen her laugh like that. I tried to laugh along with her. I could not. I had fought with Anna. It was not a violent row. Just a few words. An exchange. A sudden, unusual tension between us.

"Look! There's Clémence, at the end of the meadow, do you see her? She's holding something in her hands . . . Doesn't she look like a thief? You might think she's a hunchback, bent over like that."

Alice stood up.

"There's a spot over there that she thinks is secret. A sort of stone with a hole in it. Like an altar for offerings. She thinks I don't know about it . . ."

She took a few steps forward, her hand shading her eyes.

"Childhood is a territory, you know."

She was still thinking about the child.

"We ought to try to catch him. Steal his secret."

"What secret?"

"All children have a secret."

Little blue flowers grew in the stone wall that surrounded the house. Their strong smell of honey attracted the butterflies. The bees.

Alice picked one. She looked inside, at the pistil and stamens, almost invisible to the naked eye.

"Childhood cannot be captured. It is in the child, and it dies when the child grows up. You would have to prevent the child from growing up. Madness sometimes does that."

"Is that why you like that child?"

"I didn't say I liked him."

"But you like knowing that he comes here, to your garden."

She raised a hand. Pointed her finger.

"Do you hear the wind? It's a wind that brings rain. It smells of flax. Tomorrow it will rain, for certain."

Clémence had prepared tea for us with little orange-filled cakes that she called *madeleines de Chamonix*. They were little round cakes, with a sweet, bitter taste. Slightly doughy. You had to drink the tea piping hot. Never mind if it burned. Then sweeten it with the madeleine. And so on, back and forth, tea, then madeleine, until there was no more of one or the other.

Alice was used to this.

I was not.

She talked to me about Roman Opałka. The painter of time, as she called him. She said that one day he would die and leave behind a last canvas, and that that unfinished canvas would be more significant than any other. She would like to be able to afford that canvas.

We drank some more tea.

I ate more madeleines than I drank tea. The imbalance between the two was increasing.

I realized that this combination of madeleines and piping hot tea was part of a ritual she wanted to impose. A sort of ceremonial. A private moment where we could talk about this and that, about the trivial turmoil of life. And other moments where we said nothing.

"You must tell me things. You don't talk about yourself."

"I have nothing to say."

"Don't be ridiculous."

I put my hand in my pocket. I took out the photograph. The one of the pebbles. I laid it on the table before her, among the cups.

"I have this."

I told her about it. The days spent with Anna and the girls. Entire days. And nights.

She was looking at the photograph. She did not touch it. Merely looked at it.

"Those pebbles look alive . . ."

She pointed to each of the pebbles. One by one.

"That one is you. That one is Anna and the two over here are the girls."

She finished the tea in the bottom of her cup. She got up and walked over to the door.

"Follow me."

The door gave on to a passage. At the end of the passage was a stairway. On one of the steps there was a torch. Alice picked it up. We began to climb the steps. I could only see the steps lit by the beam from the torch. There was striped wallpaper. It was narrow. I could smell the woollen shawl Alice had over her shoulders. The stairway led to a landing with three doors. Some light filtered through a skylight. Alice went to one of the doors and pushed it open.

"I warn you, there is no electricity."

It was dark, even darker than in the passage. The shutters were closed. It smelled stuffy. She swept the beam of the torch over the room.

"I haven't come here in a long time."

The walls were covered with books. A tall stepladder for reaching the books on the top shelves. Carpets. Paintings on the walls. In the middle of the room was her father's desk. Opposite was a cupboard. Alice went over to the cupboard. She put her hand on the key.

"Everything is in here."

She turned the key.

"I don't know why I am showing you all this. I probably shouldn't . . ."

I thought she was going to add something, but she said nothing. She handed me the torch.

"You have five minutes."

She went to sit down at the desk.

I opened one of the cupboard doors. It was full of books about painting and architecture, travel books as well. Files. Boxes. Photograph albums. Everything shared the space as best it could, in wobbly piles.

Three portraits were pinned to the inside of the cupboard door. Full-face portraits.

Black and white.

"Are they Indians?" I asked.

"Hopi."

"I thought no-one was allowed to photograph them."

"My father was a photographer."

"So?"

I turned away. I could not see her. Only heard her voice. It was like being in a sanctuary.

"So nothing. He took their picture, that's all."

I opened the second side of the door. More books, old cameras.

A flat box lay along the way at the back, on top of a row of books. I opened it. Inside were two silk gloves.

I opened other boxes. Most of them contained photographs. Newspaper articles. It would take days to go through it all. I found it hard to breathe.

"This room, the shutters – couldn't we open them?"

Alice did not answer. I closed one side of the cupboard. And then there in a corner, so dark that I almost failed to see it, was a mask. It was leaning against a pile of books. Caught in the beam of light. A blue mask. Its eyes, two slits, like two living torches. For a moment, no doubt because of the shadows and the reflections of light against the coloured dyes, it was as if I had met the incandescent gaze of the man who used to wear it.

"That mask . . . Is it a Hopi mask? May I take it out?"

"You certainly may not."

I could hear the sound of the chair over the floorboards. Alice had got up.

"I didn't think you would look at everything."

She was standing right by me.

"Choose a book and let's go."

She closed the latch on the cupboard door.

"I told you five minutes."

She turned the key. The sound in the silence. I stepped back.

"Is that your father?" I asked, shining the beam on a photograph against the wall.

"Perhaps. I cannot see it from here."

"In a street . . . It looks like New York."

"That's him."

"And the others, around the table? The people in this other picture?"

"What people?"

"Sitting in armchairs. In a flat. There's a mask against the wall."

"Breton, Max Ernst . . . They're all dead, what's the point?"

"Where was it taken?"

"In New York . . . In Breton's flat."

She came to stand next to me. She looked at the photograph. There was a date. *September '41.*

She pointed to one of the faces.

"That's Duchamp."

She named each face, jumping from one to another, not follow-

106

ing a precise order, only the order imposed by memory. Or perhaps she was compelled by some other criterion, just as respectable, which may have been that of her own preference.

"That is Yves Tanguy, and Max Ernst ... Peggy Guggenheim. That man there is Fernand Léger, I don't know who that is . . . André Breton . . . Mondrian."

She named all the others.

Right up to the last one. A man seated to one side.

"And that's my father."

She took the torch from my hand.

She went to the door. She waited for me to go out then pulled the door closed behind her.

We went back down to the sitting room.

On the table everything was as we had left it, the tray, the cups, the last of the madeleines.

Alice turned to me.

"Who told you you could take that?" she asked, upon seeing the album I had in my hands.

"You said . . ."

"I know what I said! And anyway, I find your presence tiring. All these questions you ask . . ."

"I haven't been asking you a thing. You're the one who . . ."

She did not let me finish.

"When you're not asking questions, you don't say a thing, and that's worse. You say nothing to oblige me to talk . . . What do you want, exactly?"

"Nothing."

"I don't believe you. I should never have shown you all that."

She went to sit in her chair. Her back turned to me.

She was wearing the old cardigan with buttons I had always seen her wear when she was in the house and which she only took off when she went out. The buttons were little mother-of-pearl spheres, and she toyed with them, with her fingers. There were two missing. There were spots where the wool was burnt.

"And anyway, I do not know you."

Her voice, hoarse. Words in tatters, torn from her throat.

The house was silent. Clémence was not there; she had probably gone out on the path leading to the forest. The clock ticking. The sound of Alice's breathing.

The ticking like a second breath.

Voltaire was on the windowsill. He was watching the birds fly overhead. He followed them with his gaze. He knew very well that he could never catch those birds, or at least not as long as they were in flight. But he still looked at them. He was probably waiting for one of them to commit an error. For the day one of them would land there. Within reach. And then his luck would change.

Too bad for the bird.

It is always too bad for someone.

I liked the cat's calm manner.

"At home, I cannot stand the way the girls are in constant motion."

"Why are you telling me this?"

"I don't know. Perhaps you've been lying to me. All that story . . ."

"Which story?"

"About the Indians, your voyage. Maybe you never went there."

"Why would I lie to you?"

"Old people sometimes do."

"You are right, old people do lie. But they don't do it for pleasure. They want to seem interesting for a while, or their memory is no longer very sharp or they can't remember anything so they have to reinvent everything from scratch."

Maybe Anna was lying to me when she said she loved me. I did not want to think about Anna.

"Why do you leave that mask locked up in the cupboard?"

108

Alice took her tobacco pouch from her pocket.

"The Hopi old people are like those spindly trees you see along the dried banks of rivers. More alive. Not yet dead."

"You didn't answer my question."

"Masks cannot stand the daylight, you ought to know that."

She got up to fetch a box of matches from the fireplace.

"Sometimes I still dream that I am back there."

Her cigarette. Lit now. She came back to the table. She pushed the pouch of tobacco before me.

"What time is it?"

"Five o'clock."

"It's late . . ."

"Should I be going?"

"I didn't say that."

It had stopped raining. The sky was milky. It was going to rain some more, tonight and the following day.

She sat down again in the armchair.

"You really are too thin. You ought to travel, it would fill you out."

She smoked her cigarette. The whole thing. Without saying a word.

"We shall have a little wine, it will give us some vigour."

"It's five o'clock . . ."

"What difference does that make? Get up and go over to the dresser, the door on the right. You'll find two glasses and a bottle with some wine in it."

She followed me with her gaze. Every one of my gestures. I could feel her looking at me.

"You could be my son . . ." she said.

I filled the glasses and set them down on the table.

"No, that's impossible. I could never have had a son. To complete such an undertaking. Never mind everything that goes with it, watching him grow up. Accepting it. No, I never could have."

The tobacco was on the table. Between her and me. Closer to me.

"What will you say about me when I'm dead?"

"I won't say anything."

"Will you cry?"

She was swirling the wine in the bottom of her glass. It was a thick, garnet-coloured wine. A taste of raspberry.

"Of course you won't, you won't cry."

Outside it had begun to rain again. There were puddles in the drive. The earth seemed incapable of absorbing any more water. Drops on the roof of the conservatory. Streams of water down the windowpanes.

She looked at me.

"A young Indian died because he sold that mask you saw in the cupboard."

She took a sip of wine. Then another. She set her glass down.

"Delicious, isn't it?"

I drank some in turn.

That way she had of looking up at me. Of observing me. Then looking away. Her silences were worse than my own. The sentences she did not finish. Or that she gave to me unstitched.

She took the album and handed it to me.

"Open it."

It was an old album with a thick binding. Covered in red velvet. In places the velvet was so worn that you could see the cardboard. A film of gold covered the edge of each page.

Every page was protected by a sheet of transparent paper.

The first photograph.

Black and white. They were all black and white. An old Indian sitting on a rock. Wearing a canvas shirt. His hair was long, white, held in place by a dark cloth knotted around his forehead. He was staring at the camera lens.

"This is the Indian who sculpted our *kachinas*."

The man's eyes. Luminous grey.

"Eyes are the only thing," I said, "that don't age in a man."

Alice did not look at the photograph. She probably knew the album by heart.

"Often you think they are dead but in fact they are just old. That man, the Indian whose face you see there, Quöyeteva, used to speak with the spirits, and they could hear him. My father met him out there. I also met him. His teachings were among the most precious."

I turned the page. A second photograph. A village street, a goat nibbling on the lichen clinging to a rock.

"I remember how her coat smelled of dust. I gave her bread. She licked me because of the salt on my skin. The smells, back there . . . You know, people believe you don't forget smells."

I went back to the first photograph. The Indian's face. I could feel the presence of the *kachinas* on top of the cupboard. I looked up. I drew the link between the man and his astonishingly precious work. If you took away the *kachinas*, even just one of them, everything in the room would be different. I thought again of the mask.

"You should bring it down, nail it to the wall, there . . ."

Alice did not reply. I do not know if she heard me. She was looking at the picture.

"Oddly enough, it's all connected, the death of the young Indian, my father, Breton . . . And it's the story behind the mask, you see?"

I did not see.

I finished my glass.

I took the pouch of tobacco. I turned it over. In my hands. Beneath my fingers, the supple contact of the plastic. The smell. The sudden burning. The aroma of that particular tobacco.

I put the pouch back down.

"I haven't thought about all that for a very long time. On the other hand, I think not a single day goes by that I am not haunted by that story."

She pointed to the album.

"Take it, would you? Turn the next page, and the one after that, and then the one after that. That's right . . ."

She said no more.

Beneath the protective paper there was a photograph of Breton and Elisa. Standing against a mud wall. At the bottom, on the right-hand side of the photograph, was written *Walpi, August 1945*.

# ANDRÉ BRETON
## EXILE IN NEW YORK, 1941–1946

February 1941. Marseille. The ship of the *Compagnie des transports maritimes* is at its berth. The ship is the *Capitaine Paul Lemerle*.

Is it a ship? More of a tub, rotting in places. In the engine room two mechanics are trying to get the engines to hold. Perched on a ladder, a sailor is using black paint to touch up the letters on the hull.

The hold is full to the brim. Sacks of flour are arriving. It is cold. An icy wind is blowing. It howls down the narrow streets of the old quarters of Marseille. On the quay mobile guards are overseeing the loading of the calves. The animals have been herded together on the deck. Living food that the butchers can make use of throughout the trip.

Over three hundred and sixty people have piled onto the little steamer. Men, women, children, all wrapped up against the biting cold that is said to come from Siberia or elsewhere, the far north in any case. Scarves are knotted, caps pulled down tight. Over three hundred and sixty people and only two cabins, so all of them head for the hold, where bunk beds have been hastily installed by a group of carpenter sailors. Beds consisting of simple straw mattresses. That's where they will sleep. For weeks on end. On their backs. Some of them ill.

The ship still has not left.

André Breton is on deck. Leaning against the railing. With Jacqueline and their daughter Aube.

Wind whistling overhead, in the masts.

The cold in their eyes. They are weeping. There is no-one left on the quay.

Claude Lévi-Strauss is on board. With the writer Victor Serge and the painter Wifredo Lam.

The photographer Victor Berthier is there too, with his wife and his two daughters.

They are all fleeing their European homeland, for it has become truly frightening. Breton must be thinking that on the other side of the great ocean, in America, he will find a haven of peace, where words are still possible.

Hours of waiting for the ship to get under way. Impatient hours. And then at last, the engines. It is ten o'clock. The *Capitaine Lemerle* leaves the harbour. Moving slowly, as if half-heartedly.

The cold. The icy seawater. Breton strolls along the deck. Muffled up in his blue fur jacket.

The animals too are cold.

The ship follows its course along the coast of Africa. Here and there it calls at a port. Long stops where only a few privileged people are allowed to disembark. The tension rises. In Dakar the captain has to deal with an imminent riot. He threatens to send everyone ashore and interrupt the voyage if the passengers do not calm down. They kill the first calf. Free distribution of bread. Calm is restored. Finally one morning the ship heads out to sea. It is the beginning of the long crossing. Weeks long. Lévi-Strauss has managed to get a cabin, which he shares with three friends. He uses the time to write. Breton sleeps in the hold. With the others.

They left France with the February frost. Now as they enter

the tropics the heat quickly becomes unbearable. Time goes by, endlessly.

Nauseating smells. The constant pitching. Food that is impossible to eat, yet which must be swallowed. The cattle, waiting.

For washing, there are a few showers, one's body scarcely hidden by a few boards that are too thin. The wood has absorbed the smell of filth and urine. They brush their teeth with soap when there is nothing else left.

Over time, the cigarettes too begin to run out.

Breton gets up at night. He needs some fresh air. Solitude. On deck he finds Victor Berthier. The photographer is an insomniac. Together they talk about the war, then Paris. Above all about Paris. Lévi-Strauss comes to join them. It is two, three o'clock in the morning. At last a moment where life is bearable.

*

It will take three months to catch sight of land, not New York but Martinique.

Breton is on deck. That need for land. A great impatience.

The lights, the first houses. The lighthouse at Fort-de-France. This is where they will disembark. The *Capitaine Lemerle* will sail no further. They will have to wait for another ship to New York. No-one knows when it will arrive. Or even if it will arrive. It hardly matters. Breton holds his daughter close. For a start, they will be able to wash. To look human again. They leave the ship. Their meagre belongings. Their first steps. Even on land the pitching continues. They carry it with them.

Some fall to their knees. Berthier takes his first photographs.

No sooner are they on land than they are herded together. Insults fly. They are branded cowards. They are reproached for abandoning their country, for not staying behind to fight. Some are accused of being spies paid by the Nazis. People point at them. The crowd gathered there jeers at them.

The tension rises on the sunny quay at Fort-de-France. Passengers are quarantined in the camp at Lazaret. Breton is tagged a *dangerous agitator* and taken away with the others.

A few days later, released at last, he sets off to visit the island with the poet Aimé Césaire.

Days go by. Weeks.

Yet another month before another ship arrives, the *D'Aumale*, a derelict craft that is calling at Fort-de-France on its way to New York. Breton completes the voyage on this phantom ship.

*

Early July. New York. Many artists have come before them. They all live in the same neighbourhood. Painters: Fernand Léger, Chagall, Dalí, Mondrian, Beckman, Max Ernst. The sculptor Zadkine. Tanguy and André Masson and Man Ray. Art dealers too have come from Europe.

They all meet in this place that has become their country of exile and which they must use all their strength to conquer. Together.

Breton knows he must find a new path, as far as possible from the war and the impending disaster.

Their uprooting brings the men closer. New York becomes a place where strong friendships can be created.

A place for brotherhood.

Hope is restored, while elsewhere, at home in France, the war continues. The war that was only supposed to last a short time.

Together, in the cafés, they recreate the Paris of ideas.

New York replaces Paris.

1942. Peggy Guggenheim marries Max Ernst. She opens her

gallery, Art of This Century. Marcel Duchamp, Kay Sage, and the painter Matta are there. Victor Berthier takes photographs which he sells to magazines.

Breton meets Julius Carlebach, a little antique dealer on Third Avenue. Carlebach owns many *kachinas*. Duplicates, almost all of which come from the Heye Foundation, and which the curator is seeking to get rid of. Breton buys several. He also buys a Hopi mask made of folded leather, a mask he will never part with, that he will take back to Paris after the war. And hang on the wall of his studio. Until his death.

*

On the other side of the Atlantic the war is raging.

Camus immerses himself in the absurd. One after the other he publishes *The Myth of Sisyphus* and *The Outsider*.

*

Breton lives on the fifth floor of a little place on Bleecker Street. Between Jacqueline and him it is all over. They argue more and more frequently. They are drifting apart. Most of the time when he comes home Jacqueline is not there. And when she comes home, he is the one who leaves.

He suspects her of having a lover.

And they who had once sworn, had made promises to each other, now they are separating.

Breton finds a flat on 5th Street. He is forty-five years old. Lately he has been seen on his own. Taciturn. Angry, no doubt excessively so.

Has he become *the unsociable creature* he wanted to be when he was twenty? Is he once again leaving the door of his room open *in the hopes of waking up at last next to a companion he has not chosen?*

The quest for love. Unending.

*

December 1943. The wind is blowing, cold and icy, as it often does in winter in New York. Breton opens the door of Chez Larré, a restaurant across the street from his house. West 56th Street. It is noon.

He walks into the restaurant. The warmth is welcoming. He heads for the back of the room.

How many are gathered around the table today? Max Ernst and Peggy, faithful friends. Berthier is there, without Mathilde. Tanguy. There is another woman with them. A woman Breton is seeing for the first time. Whose idea was it to introduce them to each other? Breton is captivated by her guarded face. Suffering. Elisa has just lost a child. Her daughter. She almost died from the loss.

And now this encounter.

Breton looks at her.

And how does she look at him, for the first time?

He knows, immediately. She must know it, too. One love will calm another. Already in the poet's mind words are forming.

> *A mad love cannot be replaced.*
> *Cannot be erased*
> *Cannot be forgotten.*
> *A mad love never dies,*
> *Another mad love follows,*
> *That is all.*
> *And we are made of all these mad loves,*
> *Their coexistence, their strata,*
> *No matter how we search inside, all we shall ever find is mad love.*

What did they say to each other, that first day? Breton, the man who kisses women's hands. He who needs solitude so badly can no longer stand to be alone.

This is the happy period.

*

July 1945.

Breton obtains his divorce from Jacqueline and marries Elisa.

Elisa the guarded one. Intelligent.

Elisa the discreet one.

Immediately afterwards they decide to go on a trip. Lévi-Strauss is working at the French Consulate. He obtains petrol coupons for them.

Colorado, New Mexico, then Arizona. The desert, and the cliffs of beliefs.

Victor Berthier has promised to join them there, in Hopi territory. Sometime in August. With Mathilde, perhaps. If Mathilde wants to come.

Breton will write, *In the midst of much cause for despair, I had moments of brief but great joy in New York, [. . .] and I will add, under my breath, as one must, that contrary to all expectations I also encountered happiness there.*

*

August 1945.

The desert stretches for miles. Straight lines, monotonous. Here, to go from one place to the next requires an endless amount of time. They drive across a vast expanse of prairieland. When they stop, there is silence. The incessant rustling of the dust winds. Dust on metal.

*This vast Western land*, as Breton calls it. A spaciousness that makes you dizzy. At night they sleep under a tent. In sandstorms.

In the morning they head off again.

At last one evening they can see the Rockies. The great canyons. The Navajo territory, and the enclaves within that territory, at the very top of rocky cliffs: the mud villages of the Hopi Indians.

Three high sun-scorched plateaux.

*Kachina* country.

They set up their tents at the foot of the cliffs. In the morning, voices awaken them. Indians, on their way to work in the fields, offer them apricots.

Breton will say, *this fruit, a foretaste of what was coming*.

Later in his notebook he jots down a few thoughts:

[...] *landscapes made of hills, cliffs, and sand*.

\*

You have to look up. That is where they live. Near the sky and the clouds.

Oraibi. Hotavilla. These hamlets, as in the early time of the world. From a distance they look like ruins.

Ghost ships.

The earth is dry. It is not earth. It is a space where survival is harder than anywhere else.

They climb up on foot, a steep path along the cliff-face. Steps, roughly hewn into the rock. When they reach the top, the walls, the sun on the straw in the walls. Blazing. Like gold.

They walk through the village.

Women sit outside their doors. They are pounding the corn. Piles of ears of corn, set out to dry.

And the desert in the distance, all around.

Breton is fascinated. From the very first moment. These Indians.

Their gentle faces. Their pride in the midst of that gentleness.

And the poverty, the beauty, all intimately bound together.

Elisa takes a photograph of Breton sitting on a rock. He is wearing a light-coloured shirt, canvas trousers. His face is sunburnt by their travels.

It is noon. The Indians are in their houses. The children cluster on their doorsteps. On the square is a scrawny tree. It may be dead. The children are too hot. That is their daily lot. That, and hunger. Breton looks at them.

Further away, after the last house. An Indian on his knees. The skin of his back burnt by the sun. On the ground next to him are little canvas bags. In each of the bags there are coloured powders. A few pebbles. The man is drawing. Breton cannot see the drawing, only the bags full of powder and the Indian's gestures.

In the evening when Breton returns to the spot, the Indian is not there anymore. The drawing has disappeared. Swept away by the wind. Or erased by his hand.

Only the little white pebbles remain. In a pile.

*

In the evening, in the bedroom, Elisa is sleeping. Breton is writing. In his notebook.

Then he writes to Aube. A long letter. Into the envelope he slips a photograph of himself taken on the village square. Scratches a few words on the photograph itself: *For my little Aube, with all the Indian sky.* Signed, *André.*

In the bed close by, Elisa's light breathing.

He goes out into the sleeping village. The empty streets. The sudden silence, for the wind has dropped. The sky is black. Studded with thousands of stars.

Suddenly, very near, the sinister hooting of an owl.

August 1945.

Elsewhere.

The concentration camps have just been liberated.

Two bombs fall, on Hiroshima and Nagasaki.

*

The villages here; the names they have.

Shichomovi, *Hill-with-Flowers*, on the first plateau.

On the second,

Walpi,

Mishongnovi, *The-High-Place*,

Shungopovi, *The-Place-of-Tall-Grasses-Growing*,

and Shipaulovi, *The-Place-of-Many-Mosquitoes*.

And on the third,

Oraibi, *There-Where-the-Orai-Rock-Is*,

Babaki, *The-Place-of-Reeds*,

and Hotavilla, *The-Place-Where-One-Scratches-One's-Back*.

A dozen villages in all. And people. An entire nation, arriving on foot twelve thousand years ago. The women carried their children on their backs. The men walked ahead. With a few animals. They came over the Bering Strait. It was winter. The isthmus was frozen, so they crossed over the water as if it were a bridge, and when the ice melted they were on the other side. Trapped. Forced to stay there, to keep on going. To build.

Forced to migrate.

For them too, the impossible exile.

The time of the long migrations had come.

The extraordinary history of these people on the march.

What were they fleeing when they reached the Bering Strait?

Other people? What sort of hunger?

They became planters, farmers, they raised sheep. They could make corn and beans grow in soil that was like sand.

*

And those who thought they had discovered India called these men the Indians.

*

Night-time. Strangely pale. The moon glinting on the mud walls. How can anyone sleep?

Breton gets up. He leaves the house. Outside, on the square, the moon lights the entrance to the *kiva*.

The *kiva*, the sanctuary. The womb of beliefs. It is in this cavity dug into the earth that the most secret rites are held.

Breton goes closer. He can hear voices. Repeated, relentless chanting. As if each chant were bound to the next in a long prayer.

The men are preparing their ceremonies. They will dance, beat the ground, bare feet in the dust, as if the rain were to come not from the sky but from deep within the earth itself where they bury themselves to pray.

*

The heat, unbearable like this. Why did they build their houses here, at the highest point, furthest from the springs? Why here, closest to the sun?

The terraced roofs. On each roof there are iron tubs. Above, the naked sky. The tubs are empty, the iron scorching. The children's lips are dry. Their tongues hard. They suck on stones. In winter, the cold cracks their lips, transforming them into open sores.

In the seasons in between there are sandstorms. Dust in one's teeth. And in one's eyes. The children rub their eyes. They scratch their corneas. Their eyes weep, and over time they are covered with a white veil.

*

It is here in Walpi that Breton meets Victor Berthier again. They are happy to see one another. They celebrate with a meal of hot cakes at the village trading post. Alice is there.

And Mathilde?

Victor Berthier does not talk about Mathilde.

They decide to continue their journey together.

Young boys are on the lookout in the rubble at the foot of the cliffs. They are hunting for snakes. When they find one, they mark the spot by planting a stick in the ground.

Berthier manages to take a few photographs. The children, the sticks, an old woman bent under a bundle of twigs. And then he takes pictures of Breton and Elisa together. And Alice with them. And Alice with Breton, standing side by side. And then another picture, Alice all on her own on the path leading up to the village.

Some children are waiting for them. They want to sell ceremonial bows, and prayer sticks adorned with feathers. Turkey, or sparrow feathers? *Pahos* for tourists. Breton does not want any.

The children go away and then come back. With other sticks. They say that the feathers on these *paho*s are the feathers of the sacred eagle. Breton does not believe them.

Elisa laughs. She gives them sweets.

Berthier buys a *paho* anyway, to be able to go on taking photographs, it might appease them.

Breton leaves the others. He has seen a young woman sitting outside her house. By her side, a few weeks old, is a baby attached to a cradle board.

The child, practically bound.

On the path are young girls with embroidered collars. They are carrying satchels on their backs, and their hair is styled in the traditional way. When they see Breton they clap their hands on their mouths and laugh behind their fingers. On the square, goats are grazing in the dust next to a sort of pool that is used as a water reservoir. A few hens. A donkey.

Breton goes back to the others. He is content. Inside his bag is a very fine *kachina* he just bought from the young woman, after some negotiating.

*

The *kachina* is on the table, back in his room. Breton looks at it. The face, painted red. The round, protruding eyes. Two paw marks on the cheeks. And the hands, with claws. It is a Hon, a Bear *kachina*.

For Breton, identification is possible. An exchange. The sudden impression that he can engage with the invisible. He says as much:

*I want to have their power for myself.*

The *kachina* goes to join the magnificent blue Ahote he bought several days earlier in Moenkopi.

*

The hostile gazes of the men from Hotavilla. Breton has been warned. The Indians who live here do not like the white man. One must be careful. It is impossible to go near their sacred sites. A young Indian woman accompanies them everywhere. The girl is very beautiful. She wears a long skirt and a plaid shirt with a wide belt of golden metal over it. Around her neck, a chain of stones. Bronze earrings, and two heavy turquoise bands at either wrist. On her feet, leather moccasins covered with dust.

Her greeting is kindly, then suddenly her behaviour changes. She has seen the camera in Berthier's bag. She does not leave them for a moment. It is impossible for them to go anywhere near the *kivas*. Or the altars. And even other places where there seems to be nothing of interest.

*

In the evening they share a meal with a clan chief. The meal consists of pancakes and watermelon, and they eat sitting on the ground. On a red woollen mat. Geometric shapes. Breton would like to copy the patterns, but they will not allow it.

He explains that in Europe the art of the Hopi Indians is considered to be great art. That *kachinas* are on display in the finest museums.

At the end of the meal he turns to the chief and offers to buy the three *kachinas* with crenellations hanging from the wall of his house. For four dollars. The chief nods his head. It seems as if their bargain has been concluded, but then the chief says he wants to think about it, and Breton goes away.

The next day, the chief has changed his mind. He no longer wants to sell the *kachinas*, although last night he promised to. It is impossible to find out why. Breton talks with him, offers more money, then gets annoyed. Eventually he loses his temper. The sale falls through.

In his notebook, Breton will write: *Impossible to buy the three beautiful Kachina dolls with crenellations which, the night before, were almost mine.*

*

During his absence someone went into his room. They searched through his things. Nothing has been taken, neither his notebooks nor his films, but Breton is furious. He leaves the village. He knows that in a neighbouring village, Oraibi, there is an Indian who lets rooms in his house. He arranges to be taken there.

The house is Talayesva's.

Luckily, the room is free. Breton settles in until the end of his stay. With Elisa.

When the two men meet, *Sun Chief* has been finished for four years. A young Indian acts as their interpreter. His name is Otto.

\*

Otto also acts as a guide. For a few dollars he agrees to drive the car and take them on a tour of the villages.

He introduces them to Quöyeteva.

Quöyeteva is his ritual father. He is also the chief of the Snake clan.

He is the guardian of the masks. The masks are somewhere in his home. Probably upstairs. He refuses to show them. He does not even want to talk about them.

On the ground is a mat with a pitcher, two bowls, and a container. *Kachinas* are nailed to the wall. No photographs are allowed. No writing is allowed.

Quöyeteva says that nothing can withstand writing, and that to write a man's name is to take away his vital force.

\*

Shungopovi. An Indian agrees to sell Breton a very fine *kachina* with a headdress. The sale is made very discreetly, when none of the family members are present.

In one of Breton's notebooks there is a detailed description of this *kachina*:

*In the crenellated frame of a Hopi doll's head you can see the clouds on the mountain; in this little checked pattern at the centre of its forehead, an ear of corn; around the mouth is a rainbow; in the vertical stripes of the dress, the rain falling in the valley . . .*

\*

Mishongnovi. August 10. A village like an eyrie. Cliffs like fortress walls.

Impossible for Berthier to take any photographs.

A group of men is going into the *kiva*. They are wearing masks. Breton watches them closely. Every one of their gestures. As if to read them. To appropriate for himself the deep meaning of their history. He must be aware that the most important things have eluded him.

And yet.

This is so unsatisfactory, he says. To be only this.

This?

A white man.

\*

Azurite for the blue, malachite for the green, then hematite, kaolin, and obsidian. Breton is fascinated by this world of colours. It sends him back to the emotions of childhood. To his imagination.

Little is known about Breton's childhood other than the fact that it was a solitary one. Born on the evening of 19 February, 1896, in Tinchebray in the Orne. His mother, Marguerite le Gouguès, was a rigid, pious woman. Who wore a black hood. Probably too pious. So much so that she seemed absent.

A missing mother.

Nothing is known about his father other than that he was a gentle man. A worker from the outskirts of town.

Breton rarely confided in anyone. Almost never. It is known that he spent the first five years of his life away from his parents. Left in the custody of his grandfather. In Saint-Brieuc.

Five whole years.

Those years. The most alive.

The old man was taciturn, but a good storyteller. With him Breton learned to observe nature, plants, insects. Stones with strange shapes: stones of earth and clay, stones at the bottom of streams. Along the paths, those black stones with red streaks that were used to build walls, and stories. Breton would always be nostalgic for those moments spent listening to him.

Nothing is known about the grandmother.

When Breton joined his parents in Pantin, he was already five years old. Pantin. Factories. Allotments. A grey childhood in the northern suburbs of Paris. At the very beginning of the century.

He started proper school. The years of fine innocence were over. It was time for him to grow up.

Breton did not play. He was a loner. Already.

*

Every Sunday he and his parents left the small house in the suburbs. They took the train to the church at the Madeleine. The ritual was unchanging. The only source of happiness was the shop window at Bernheim's on the rue Richepance, a gallery where his mother sometimes allowed him to linger, and where he could see paintings by Bonnard, Vuillard and above all Henri Matisse.

So there was something more. An elsewhere. Another life to complement the one that was not enough for him. It was this other life that he went to look for in books. Very early on. Even though his mother had forbidden it, for she could not stand to see him spending time on an activity she considered frivolous.

Many years later he would paint this devastating portrait of her: *Authoritarian, petty, unkind, caring only for social integration and success.*

\*

Is this it, the other life he has come to find in the streets of Oraibi? His grandfather's stories – were they his first taste of the world of the imagination? Forty years later, is he still seeking a voice?

Childhood, the lost wonder.

\*

On 9 August, 1945, in the village of Walpi. Breton writes:

*This village . . . like a gigantic warship carved in the rock.*

He wanders down every path. Avid. The man is famished. There is a rebel inside him, but is he still rebelling, here, on these cliffs?

Breton, the fanatic. The violence in his words. Here more than ever, on edge.

What is he thinking when he isolates himself in this way? That he can no longer stand human company?

Poverty, deprivation. And yet beauty. The contrast is striking. He is experiencing the madness of extremes.

How often has he written, *I want to understand?*

How often has he said it, and then said it again? His hunger is insatiable.

Might it be that he is fascinated by all the beliefs this land requires of those who live here? Might it also be that he senses that no matter what he does, such knowledge will always be beyond his grasp?

*

A secret bond connects these men. And connects the men with everything that surrounds them, animals, stones, trees. Breton knows that there is a bond between this idea and his own. And it is this very powerful intuition that will compel him to say, *Here, at last, I have found proof that communion between man and nature is possible.*

*

In Hopi territory, an individual alone does not exist. Every man is part of a whole. Be it living, or inert.

There is no solitude.

*

Breton buys a postcard at the village trading post, a thick cardboard depicting the principal symbols used in painting *kachinas*. He keeps the card with him, always. Even after the journey, when he is back in Paris. But he has to confess that, however useful the card may be, it has not enabled him to unlock the mystery.

Has he already imagined how important this voyage will be?

Berthier promises to print all the photographs for him again, once he is back in New York.

*

An Indian may kill another Indian to appropriate his strength for himself. In like manner, Breton thinks he can appropriate the power of the *kachinas* for himself. He believes it is possible. Such a strong presence. Just to look at them, one is overwhelmed.

In Saint-Dizier, during the First World War, he had worked with the insane. Spent time with them. And sometimes felt so close to them.

These demented-admirable-magician-madmen wielded a brush free of all constraint, their unconscious flowing onto sheets of paper. Breton witnessed it. Drawings propelled straight from their imagination. From the unconscious to the canvas. Directly. Did this mean that he, Breton, was incapable of such a thing?

Too many constraints.

Constrained by what? The mother he does not speak of and who forced him to grow up so quickly?

It is noon in the village of Oraibi. It is as if the village were dead. On the square, the donkeys are thirsty. A woman, in the shade of an awning. On a tin roof are the charred bodies of a few flies.

Breton, his head between his hands. He observes.

\*

Breton wants to fight against force of habit. Deliver himself from the everyday. That is his obsession. Every day, life plotted out in advance. There must be something else.

*There are deep affinities between so-called "primitive" thought and surrealist thought: both aim to suppress the hegemony of consciousness, the everyday, in order to go out and conquer the revealing emotion.*

The strange world of the *kachinas* troubles him. When he approaches them, he feels as if he is touching the limits of his unconscious. A place where he can converse with that precious part of himself that is another form of himself, and which embodies the absolute purity of primitive man.

The Snake Dance is held on August 22, in Mishongnovi, and there may be another one the same day or on the following day in the village of Walpi.

Breton finds a notice in a newspaper.

*Hopi Indian Snake Dance.*
*Opens at Mishongnovi August 22;*
*And at Walpi probably on the same day.*

He cuts out the notice, slips it into his notebook.

*

Black sky. Threatening. And yet it does not rain. A few drops that evaporate before they even touch the ground. This ceremony, the dance of the Antelope.

Breton and Elisa are there, with Victor Berthier. Alice. And another woman, a friend of Breton's. The ceremonies are to be held at the end of the day but Otto advised them to be there early in the afternoon to get a good spot. A bench in the shade. They have been waiting for two hours, the sun has moved and it is very hot again. Breton is feverish. He who is usually so impatient does not mind the long wait at all.

The Indians have clustered on the terraces. A few tourists. American women. They go from door to door, looking for *kachinas.* Suddenly, without warning, a group of dancers emerges from the *kiva.* Breton takes out his notebook. Elisa tells him not to, he will draw attention to himself. He does not listen. He takes notes. He draws, a few quick lines, hardly looking at the paper. The little altar of branches, the terraces where the spectators are sitting. He draws the place where the dancers came from. Who could possibly notice him in such a crowd? On the roofs there are young people from neighbouring villages, drinking soda. A girl walks by. She is American. In her hand she is swinging a *kachina* on the end of a string.

Breton writes. Two more lines.

Suddenly a policeman is there behind him. *Give me your book!* The policeman's hand on his shoulder. Breton tries to talk his way out of it. He points to the American girl. He hands over the notebook. The policeman tears out two pages.

Elisa and Berthier are furious. They have been noticed because of him. Voices are raised. Breton has no regrets. On the contrary, he attacks. *Nothing, no-one can force me to submit to such fanaticism.*

His words are too much. Berthier is fed up. He calls Breton a sick fool and leaves.

Breton could not care less. A useless photographer! The two men look at each other. They will not meet again.

Back in his room Breton tries to remember the words he had scribbled in his notebook. From memory he draws the symbols woven on the yellow loincloth of one of the dancers.

The next day the festivities for the Snake will be held, but no-one knows whether they will be allowed to attend.

"Were you there on the day of the Snake Dance?"

Alice gave me a quick look. She was holding her glasses in one hand. Nibbling on one of the arms. An automatic reflex.

"I was there."

"And Breton too?"

"There were so many people. How could I tell who was there and who wasn't . . . Of course he was there. With Elisa."

"And your father?"

Alice hesitated before replying.

"He was elsewhere. It is always possible to be elsewhere."

The game of solitaire on the table. The sun pouring in the window, flattening the shadow of the marbles onto the board. She looked at the shadows.

"You don't want to speak about it."

She looked up at me. I felt as if I had brushed against something there, something hiding inside.

"Forgive me . . ."

"Forgive you? I'm not angry with you . . . I've been dragging you along with me. You ask questions, that's normal."

She looked away.

I looked at my watch. It was late. I did not feel like leaving.

"I was young, you know . . . That long crossing on the ship. I remember how endless it was. The smells . . . and the animals they killed, right there on deck . . . The strangest thing is that there were men and women who managed to fall in love during the journey."

Her voice held me back. Like a liana. My legs tied. I settled into my chair again.

"Your mother didn't go out there with you?"

Alice smiled.

"You say *out there?*"

"You say it, too."

"But I'm allowed to . . . No, she wasn't with us. Some people are frightened by poverty. Obscure beliefs . . . My mother liked fine dresses. I think she had a lover in New York, too."

"And Clémence?"

"Naturally, Clémence . . . But my father couldn't take both of us and I was the elder."

She had stretched her legs out on a low footstool shoved up against the radiator. On her feet, a pair of canvas mules. Her ankles were swollen. The summer heat, no doubt. Little blue veins just below the skin. Some had burst, forming tiny stars of blood.

"You should walk in the sea," I said.

Her expression. Just then. Because I had been observing her body. What a disaster, she had said one day when we were talking.

I looked away.

Her voice hardened.

"And you, at least, should practise what you preach."

She made no other comment but I saw that her fingers were trembling. The fingers of the hand that was on the armrest.

"Alice . . ."

She placed her hand once again on her thigh, with the other hand on top. She went on with her story. Something she had to tell me, suddenly urgent.

"The heat was suffocating. The air baking. You couldn't see the villages any more. There were snakes everywhere . . . Rattlesnakes, gopher snakes . . . At times you got the impression that the dancers had been bitten. You believed that they must have been. Because they danced with them. Held them in their mouths."

She settled further into her armchair. Her head supported. Her face turned to the window.

"I saw the priests go down into the rocks to capture the snakes. They did it with their bare hands. I remember the lines drawn with flour across the entrance to the sanctuaries. Those lines were like borders between the profane and the sacred. You were not allowed to cross them. The priests drew prayers in the sand. They destroyed them so that they could not be seen . . . My father managed to take a few photographs."

She pointed to the album on the table. I went to fetch it. I put it down in front of her.

She opened it. Several pages, from the middle.

"This picture . . ."

It was an altar. In a small street. On the ground was a series of little white triangles traced with flour against a blue background. Through the triangles ran long streaks of black powder: the snakes. There was another photograph on the following page.

"These frescoes are prayers. Immaterial words drawn directly from the men's collective unconscious. This dance is one of the most sacred rituals. If my father had been caught taking this photograph he would have been driven away."

She closed the album.

She opened the window. The sun came in. The scented air from outside.

"Tell me rather about your life with Anna."

My life with Anna? I did not know. As if there were nothing. Or no more words. Or I no longer had those words.

"I'm here, with you."

That is all I found to say. And I said it again, I am here, as if that were enough to explain what my life with Anna had become.

Alice nodded.

Her hand was no longer trembling.

"We will be having guests," she said. "Nephews . . ."

A chaffinch came and landed on the windowsill. Clémence left seeds for them. There were no more seeds. The chaffinch waited.

"During the holidays, we have guests, it's the custom. One must make concessions . . . That's the way it is. It would be unbearable otherwise."

The round eye of the chaffinch. Alice drew the curtain, the better to see him. The bird flew away.

"Where did you sleep when you were out there?"

"With the local people. Two mats on the floor. My father and I shared the room."

"Breton stayed with Talayesva."

"Breton always managed to have the best spot in the best place."

"You don't seem to like him very much . . ."

She did not answer.

Clémence was in the garden, raking the lane with a rake that had long, flexible tines. She worked her way up the lane until she was in front of the house.

Alice let the curtain fall back.

"She's a silent woman. She could speak if she wanted to. But she doesn't want to."

She turned to me.

"Aren't you going to ask me why?"

"Why?"

"Too late, I shan't tell you."

"The cat's not here?" I said, looking around me.

She made a face.

"I don't know why you come to see me. You don't listen to what I tell you . . . You aren't interested. You couldn't give a damn!"

"That's not true."

"Of course it is!"

She pulled up the sleeves of her jacket.

"The cat is not here. He is outside, in the garden, he kills birds and he thinks I don't know. That's what you think, too."

Her arms were thin. Her joints. Her pale skin. Almost white. She looked up.

"Do you hear, it's raining."

And so it was. The first drops on the roof of the conservatory. Alice gave a sorrowful smile.

"I must say, our conversation, today . . . We've gone off in every direction."

We listened for a moment to the calming sound of the rain. I was beginning to have a headache. A sudden sharp pain in the back of my skull.

"That day, the first time you let me into your father's study, there was a box . . ."

"There are so many boxes in that study . . ."

"That one was full of letters."

"The letters my father wrote from out there."

"Did he write to your mother?"

Alice got up. She picked up her pouch of tobacco and walked across the room to the other window, the one that gave on to the rear of the house. She looked out. No doubt she was looking for the cat. Because of the rain. And his paws when he came back. The prints he would leave all over the floor in the house.

Clémence had disappeared. Probably busy with other plants in the sheltered part of the garden.

"I was angry with my mother for not coming with us to Arizona. I was so angry I cursed her."

"That's going too far."

"No, it is not."

"All the same . . ."

"Don't start lecturing me. Not you. Please."

She came back and sat down. Her elbows on the table. Her hands joined in front of her. At right angles.

Her eyes down, then she said, "Mothers, you know . . . Mine had no lack of love or of hatred. A curious poisonous mix. It made me weak. It didn't kill me . . . But you cannot understand."

"My mother abandoned me."

"For a Bushman, I know . . ."

She pulled the album over and opened it. She stopped on the first page, the photograph of the sculptor of the *kachina*.

"I am like this old Indian, in death already."

Her heavy fingers on his face.

She looked up at me.

"That box, those letters, you want to read them . . ."

"Yes."

A vague wave of her hand.

"I won't go with you."

I went out of the room. The passage. The torch was not on the step. I always had matches in my pocket, a smoker's mania. I struck one. I had to strike another one. The flame was burning my fingertips. I was afraid of dropping the match and setting the house on fire. I thought of going back down to ask Alice where she had left the torch. I continued to climb the steps. It was when I had reached the very last steps that I felt I was not alone. I thought it must be the cat.

I struck one last match.

Clémence was by the door. Her eyes staring at me.

In her hands she held a box. She handed it to me.

Nothing else.

No other gestures.

I took the box and went back down.

I read the letters in the car. In a car park. Next to the beach.

*Oraibi, 10 August, 1945*

*My dear Mathilde,*

*We have arrived at last ... The car nearly broke down, twice. The water pump. We stopped for repairs in Illinois and then again in Kansas City. I don't know if the engine will make it through the return trip.*

*I didn't think Arizona would be like this. So vast.*

*It's late and yet it's still light out. Alice has fallen asleep. She was exhausted.*

*My kisses to you and Clémence.*


*P.S. I'm enclosing a map of the reservation so you can follow us.*


*Moenkopi, August 12*

*My dear Mathilde,*

*It is so hot. You just don't know where to go. The few animals who live here stay in the shade of the walls, never moving. The children fall asleep outside between the legs of the mules.*

*We hope we can leave our tents behind. An Indian friend has promised us a room in a real house.*

*This morning I bought Alice a tunic and some Indian jewellery. I also bought some very fine earthenware pottery.*

*My kisses to you and Clémence.*

Dear Mathilde,

A room at last. Not really a bedroom but it's better than the tent. Mats to sleep on, a table, a ladder. No windows. You go in and out through the roof.

The door doesn't lock. Just a little rope on the inside which ties to the head of a nail. To shave I use a piece of broken mirror. I have to hold it with one hand and shave with the other.

The men have slaughtered a goat. They roasted it on the village square and shared the meat with those who didn't have any. The smell of flesh was pervasive. I went and threw up. Afterwards I had to sit in the shade and the children came and laughed at me.

Alice is fine. She is stronger than I am. She didn't even look away when they killed the goat.

I bought a ceremonial bow and a prayer stick. Insignificant objects. In exchange I've been allowed to take a few pictures.

Tomorrow we'll be getting up very early. We're going to the Grand Canyon to see the coloured quarries.

My kisses to you and Clémence.

Evening of the 13th

Dear Mathilde,

If you could see the eyes of the old people here . . . Such poverty. Some of them are blind (trachoma, empty eyes). Many of them are albino, too. Sickness, infections, even the children are not spared.

When a child misbehaves, they say he is a kohopi (which means, not a Hopi). It seems it is the worst punishment imaginable.

I bought my first kachina. For two dollars. It is a Mudhead. Cheap at the price.

It is very hot. I wonder how the Indians manage to grow their corn in so much dust. It is said that the Hopi know better than anyone how to make things grow in arid soil. That's as may be, but they seem very poor nevertheless.

Alice is fine. I took two pictures of her with Indian children and several other pictures of the desert.

My kisses to you and Clémence.


P.S. A white couple has been seen on the third mesa. According to the description, it must be Breton and Elisa.


*August 15*

My dear Mathilde,

We have seen a mountain sheep. A creature with enormous horns. It's a rare breed, and we probably won't get to see another for ages.

Some young boys have captured falcons and they keep them prisoner on the terraces. These birds have something very precious to do with their ceremonies but nobody will tell me any more about it.

We met up with Breton and Elisa. With another couple from the East coast. Montreal, I think. At last we can speak French! Elisa told me we absolutely must go to Acoma. So we're going tomorrow. Breton has recommended their guide, a young Indian called Otto. The boy knows everyone. He'll be very useful.

My kisses to you and Clémence.


*Acoma, 16th*

My dear Mathilde,

The heat, unbearable. The air dries out your throat. Our guide came an hour late. We couldn't leave without him. So we had to wait for him.

*Alice thinks he's very handsome. She won't allow me to find fault with him at all. He sold me some sort of gum to suck on that is supposed to help with the sore throat I'm getting.*

*Acoma is almost abandoned. Only two clan chiefs live up there with a Hopi family. Not so long ago the village was full of people but they all went down to live in the houses of sheet metal in the valley.*

*An Acoma Indian asked for a dollar each for the visit.*

*She gave us a few apricots and that calmed me down about the dollar because I'd never tasted such delicious apricots.*

*Alice bought a piece of pottery and a shell necklace.*

*On the path we saw little grey birds, mice, and kangaroo rats.*

*As we were driving, the car was suddenly caught in a whirlwind of red sand. We had to stop and wait for it to blow over.*

*My kisses to you and Clémence.*

*P.S. Alice said the pottery is for you and the necklace for Clémence.*

*I've kept an apricot kernel in my pocket. We'll plant it when we get back to Varengeville.*

*Walpi, August 17*

*My dear Mathilde,*

*From here I can see the desert and the villages of Shipolovi and Shongopovi.*

*This morning an Indian sold me a kachina. He told me that the feathers were from a sacred eagle, but when I showed them to Breton, he had a good laugh because they weren't eagles' feathers at all but turkey feathers.*

*So I've been had.*

*With my dollars the Indian went to the trading post and bought tinned apricots. And yet they have real apricots that are delicious, but for some reason they seem to prefer the taste of the tins.*

*There are many strange things here.*

*In the envelope you will find some of the burning sand that covers everything here and sometimes gets in our eyes.*

*My kisses to you and Clémence.*

*P.S. The Snake Dance is scheduled for August 22. So we'll stay until then.*

*The 18th*

*Dear Mathilde,*

*The weather is still just as hot, despite the storm we had during the night.*

*Breton went to visit other villages in the valley. When he came back he had some kachinas. He showed three of them to me but I could see he had others, too.*

*He suggested swapping one of his kachinas for a Zuni kachina I had and which he really wanted. I agreed. So I have a very splendid warrior, an Ahote. He is for you.*

*Alice is fine. She has made friends with Otto, the guide I told you about. She is learning to speak Hopi.*

*I took a picture of the boy wearing ceremonial necklaces.*

*My kisses to you and Clémence.*

*P.S. I have collected a few more apricot kernels, just in case the first ones don't take.*

My dear Mathilde,

Terrible bellyache this morning. Most certainly due to the heat and the water we are obliged to drink.

Otto sold me a flask of chu'knga, a remedy that is supposed to cure snake bites. Elisa says it's nothing but a bit of sugared water, but even if I were bitten, I'm not sure I'd want any of it . . .

I was able to record the very peculiar noise made by the tumble-weed, those tufts of dried grass that roll along the desert.

I also managed to record some rain chants.

Alice knows how to say hakomi *(who are you?)*, halìksà'i *(listen, that is the way things are)*, and pinù'u *(I am me)*.

My kisses to you and Clémence.

*Shungopovi, August 20*

Dear Mathilde,

They are preparing for the dances. The entire village is in a fever. I wouldn't miss it for anything on earth.

This afternoon I slept. Must have been the heat. When I woke up, there were prayer sticks everywhere, outside the kiva and also along-side some of the springs.

We were given traditional food, piki and blue corn fritters.

For two dollars Otto agreed to let me visit his house. For an add-itional dollar he let me go up the indoor ladder, the one that leads to the winter floor. There I saw the most beautiful kachinas I have ever seen. Twenty or so, maybe more, and there were others on the floor. Umbilical cords hanging from a beam.

He didn't want to show me the masks, but he did show me his savings. A tin box with a few dollars inside. He says he wants to come with us to New York. He is asking me to take him with us. What am I supposed to say?

My kisses to you and Clémence.

Shungopovi, August 21

*My dear Mathilde,*

*For the Antelope Dance, there were over a thousand people. They'd come from all over, from the surrounding villages but also from Phoenix, Los Angeles, and even the East Coast. It was very impressive. So much so that you could forget the stifling heat. Breton wanted to take notes. Because of him I'm not sure whether we'll be allowed to attend the Snake Dance tomorrow.*

*I wonder to what extent all this crowd doesn't spoil the solemn nature of the ceremonies.*

*I was able to take two more photos. The Hopis think that if you take a photograph of an Indian you are stealing his soul. So I have to be very careful.*

*Otto says he can get a mask for me for next to nothing if I take him with us to New York. A mask, can you imagine? And yet I cannot accept . . .*

*My kisses to you and Clémence.*

*P.S. I have another recording, a very rare phenomenon, the rain falling and evaporating before it even touches the ground.*

I put the letters back in the box. The lid on top. I put the box under the seat on the passenger side.

It had started raining again. A fine, regular rain. I switched on the windscreen wipers. I stayed in the car for a while. I thought about the letters. I watched the rain falling.

After that I went home. The girls were waiting for me. They said, when it stops raining we'll go fishing. We got out the fishing rods, the box of sinkers, the hooks. We were missing the worms. We went into the garden. We found a dozen or so and put them in a bucket. While they waited for the sun the girls went to play skittles in the garage.

Anna saw the worms.

"Cruelty has no limits," she said.

"This isn't cruel."

"What is it then?"

"It's life. It's death."

"Is it life or is it death?"

"They go together," I replied. "You can't separate them."

She did not want to talk about it.

I put the bucket away.

As it was still raining, we could not go down to the beach. We made crêpes.

After that the girls went into the bathroom. Anna told them that they must no longer wash their faces with water. That they had to use cleansing milk and cotton. She showed them how to do it.

I watched them from the corridor. In the mirror, my daughters' faces as they learned a woman's gestures.

I went back into the sitting room. I read *Sun Chief*. On the sofa. My feet on the coffee table. I felt good.

Anna came in a short while later. She glanced at my book. The cover. The girls had rented a D.V.D., Jean-Jacques Annaud's *Two Brothers*. They began to watch it. The player was not working properly. It made a terrible noise and the image skipped. I could not read anymore. I went to watch the film with them. The girls cried at the end. I consoled them. Their warm tears.

It was still raining.

Anna said she was fed up with the rain. That we should sell *La Téméraire* and buy a flat in the south.

I did not reply. I hung around the house. The bedroom. The bed, sheets unmade.

In the bathroom, the cleansing milk on the shelf, a pink plastic bottle. With the cotton. Round precut discs. I opened the bottle. It smelled good.

"We should have had a son," I said to Anna when I went back into the sitting room.

She looked at me.

"You want a son?"

"I didn't say that."

She shrugged.

I opened the window. Little white snails had invaded the terrace. The girls came to look at them with me. They said that with all those shells, if they were empty, they could make some pretty necklaces.

We went and sat on the sofa. I told them the story of Peter Pan. After Peter Pan, there were other stories. They snuggled up against me, one on each side. I breathed in their presence. The warm scent of their hair. Their feet, in socks. The heels upside down. I decided I would not leave them anymore. To look after them. After them, and Anna.

Night fell.

That evening, in bed, Anna said, "What's wrong?"

Because I was stretched out. My eyes wide open. And I was not asleep.

The five days that followed we were constantly together. We visited the country inland, the forest of Eawy, the château at Arques-la-Bataille and the one at Miromesnil. Anna explained to the girls who Maupassant was, and she bought them a puzzle of the château.

We visited a stud farm on the road after Biville. We spent the afternoon watching horses galloping. And horses in their stalls and colts in the fields. We even went as far as Vascoeuil to see the Musée Michelet. There were statues in the garden and a dovecote. We ate in the garden, by the edge of the stream. We climbed up the tower in the château, under the eaves, the study where Michelet wrote. We bought souvenirs, bowls with cats on them. A poster of the château to hang in the girls' room. Postcards. As we had some time left, we went on to the locks at Amfreville.

We even visited Rouen. That was another day. We saw an astonishing place, a sort of cloister where they kept lepers in the Middle Ages. That day we had crêpes with cider and the girls wanted to have a taste of the cider and so we let them. It was the first time. They said it was good but they still preferred lemonade.

We bought some *sucres de pomme* and a packet of shortbread biscuits. A bottle of Calvados to take back to Paris.

On the way back we stopped at Jumièges and visited the Abbaye. Five whole days.

And for five nights Anna and I made love.

The morning after the fifth night, when we got up it was raining. We had planned to go to Étretat and hire a little boat and walk along the cliffs. Because of the rain, Anna said, "We'll go another time."

And all day long we stayed at *La Téméraire* and did nothing.

I went back to Alice's place. I wanted to return her letters to her. I recall that it was a Tuesday. The milkman had been. He always came on Tuesday. He brought two litres that he left in a special basket for that purpose that hung from the fence.

I picked up the bottles.

The garden was wet. The leaves of the angel's trumpets were hanging limply. The geranium flowers. The tulips were bent on their stalks.

Alice was in the conservatory. When she saw me she got up. The brugmansias had bloomed. It was the first flower.

She pointed to it.

"Yesterday when Clémence came to see it there was nothing, and this morning the flower is wide open."

The petals, their colour, bright blue, with splashes of mauve inside.

It was like velvet. Or something else. The inside of a woman's sex.

I remember thinking that.

Other flowers were budding. For one more day. In other pots.

"These brugmansia flowers only last a day. The flower is here now and tonight it will be dead."

I set the milk bottles down on the table. In the kitchen. The box containing the letters. Alice glanced at it quickly. She did not ask me anything.

I sat down.

She prepared the tea.

"This is Gong Fu, you're supposed to drink it slowly and not speak," she explained.

"Clémence went on purpose into the forest to fetch some spring water, from a place she knows, where the water, she says, is the purest there is. She also says you can only make Gong Fu with that water."

I did not like tea. But here I drank it. That is just the way it was. I could not possibly have done otherwise.

She smiled at me.

"All these days . . . I thought you wouldn't be coming back."

A little paper was rolled up on the tray next to the cups. It was a recent saying that Clémence had chosen.

I read it. The first time, out loud.

*Do not speak of the sea to the fish that lives at the bottom of the well, it would not understand.*

And a second time.

We drank the tea. In silence. Our gazes met. Above our cups.

Did we live in the same sea? I would have liked to ask her. I did not. No doubt I was afraid that she would reply that we lived in the same well.

A second swallow. The taste of tea. It made me shudder. The aroma on my tongue. Impregnating it. My disgust.

I put my cup down.

"I've read the letters."

"Naturally."

She was drinking. Slowly. More slowly than I was. Tiny little sips. Hardly taking her lips from the cup.

"Do you speak Hopi?" I asked.

"I did speak it. A few words. And the few words I knew, I have forgotten."

"Your father . . . with Breton?"

"They never met again."

"Even afterwards, back in Paris?"

"Even afterwards."

"And the young boy, Otto?"

"What about Otto?"

"Tell me about him."

"There is nothing to tell."

"What became of him?"

She fell silent. I thought she had not heard me. And then she said, "I don't know . . ."

She picked up her cup and turned it in her hands, round and round. From one hand to the other. She was silent. As if she could not tell her story any faster. As if a rhythm had been imposed. A sort of internal rule.

I asked her if she could show me a picture of Otto. She told me she did not have any.

"In his letters, your father says he took several photographs of him."

She gave a nervous little laugh.

She drank the last drop of tea from the very bottom of her cup and then she stood up. She went to the door.

"Come back tomorrow. Whenever you like, it doesn't matter."

I stayed alone at the table.

The cat came in. He looked at me, astonished to find me there, and then he jumped onto my lap and from my lap onto the table. His gaze. He stretched out his full length between the two cups.

A gentle purring came from him like a secret chant. I envied him for it, for his calm plenitude. How peaceful it was. This cat's tranquil happiness. I looked at him.

I kept looking at him for a long time, even when he stopped purring.

Even afterwards, when he jumped off the table and disappeared down the passage, I think I was still looking at him.

Before I left I put the cups into the sink, washed and dried them. Then left them there on the table.

I also pinned the proverb to the cupboard door, with the others.

The brugmansia flower lasted only a day.

"Like a dead body," said Alice, pointing to the limp petals. "Dark blue. Almost black."

She had made a point of showing them to me.

"Clémence hopes that each new flower will be stronger than the others. That it will last at least a second day."

She put the flower back down.

We went out to the front of the house. Little green caterpillars were nibbling at the leaves of the rose bushes. They were the exact same dark green colour as the leaves they were sitting on.

Alice shook one off its leaf and crushed it with her heel. It left an oily trace.

She crushed another. In the end there were no more caterpillars, only the greenish smudge on the gravel and the vaguely acid smell it gave off.

She took a few steps.

"See the leaves of the chestnut tree – already spotted with rust. A sign of autumn."

She picked up one of the leaves.

"Here, it's in the garden that you see the passing of time."

I had brought some brioches. Two of them, in a paper bag. When she saw them, Alice took me by the arm and led me to the entrance of the studio. She sat down on the bench, her back to the wall. She took the bag and opened it. She told me that because of that wretched brugmansia she had not had anything to eat all morning.

"When Clémence is sad she won't prepare anything. She is convinced that feelings are more important than food. With the death of that flower, that will be it for an entire day. Tonight she'll probably open one of those things you buy ready-made such as pâté in a tin or soup in a packet."

She took out the first brioche. She bit into it.

"So you can understand how very welcome your brioche is, under the circumstances."

Her trousers were stained with plaster. She had been working that morning. In the studio. She also had plaster beneath her fingernails.

"The mason came and began to remove the old tiles."

Black clouds were gathering overhead. Driven by the wind, they seemed to want to move further along. It was impossible to tell whether they were going to burst or not.

Alice started on the second brioche.

"In Hopi country, it's just the opposite, some flowers live only one night, and they die in the morning, burnt by the sun."

The cat appeared, right at the end of the little lane. A place overgrown with tall plants, and so damp that ferns grew there in abundance. He glanced over towards the conservatory and then the studio, and when he saw us on the bench he came over.

"His eyes are weeping at the moment. It must be something in the grass . . . His left eye, do you see? Like red tears. It's odd, don't you think? I wipe them but it's endless. The vet would have to come but when I called him he said he doesn't make house calls for things like that. As if Voltaire's eyes were a matter of no importance. How could I go putting him in a basket, the way everyone else does with their cats!"

159

The cat began to scratch at the ground with a careful paw, then to swipe at the red geranium flowers.

"You see how he does as he likes with me. If Clémence were to see him . . . But she's not here. And Voltaire knows it."

She turned to me.

"You don't know of a vet who would agree to make a house call?"

"No."

"It's a great pity. Have you seen his paws, how fragile they seem? But you can't go by that. Voltaire could quite easily kill a magpie. And anyway, Clémence has laid traps, they do far too much damage."

"Magpie traps?"

"She did it at the beginning of the summer. She went to the market and bought a chick. She put the chick in the cage and a first magpie came. Then Clémence kept the magpie she'd captured and used it to capture others. You see that tree over there? Well, the magpies hide in its branches. If we're not careful, they can flock together and attack Voltaire. Voltaire knows it. He is very careful. When he senses they're in the garden he doesn't go out . . . Incidentally, I wonder what Clémence did with that little chick, once she'd caught the first magpie."

The cat was looking at her. His big, trusting eyes. His grey fur against the tender green grass.

"I don't think she would have dared . . ."

And then she smiled.

"That cat is far more than a cat. He is a presence. A pure spirit."

"Like the *kachinas*?"

She hesitated.

"Yes. Like the *kachinas*. So, you have noticed, we always go back to them . . ."

"Your father loved your mother very much, didn't he?"

"Yes, of course! Why do you say such a thing?"

"The letters . . . He wrote to her every day."

"Those letters took for ever to reach her. Sometimes she got several on the same day, and some arrived long after our return."

She placed her hand on my arm.

"Shall we go to Fécamp? Fécamp is a lovely place, don't you think? We could have dinner at the Vicomté."

She crumpled the bag, now empty of its brioches. She made a ball that she rolled between her hands.

"That is the only place to eat in Fécamp. The Vicomté, and that's all there is to it."

She stood up. She went into the studio, threw the paper bag into a box and placed a wedge under the door to hold it. The sun had come back out. It was shining between the clouds.

"And with your car we could be there in no time! But we must reserve."

"What about Clémence?"

"Clémence won't come. It's her day for the hairdresser and besides, she hates eating in the evening. She always says, in the evening, some rice and some gluten dumplings!"

She bent down to stroke the cat. He lay at our feet, stretched out, his belly to the sun.

"Besides, I would like to go out with you on my own. Will you let me take your arm? The gossips will say I have a lover. You don't mind if people see you with me? I'll let you ring the restaurant, the telephone directory is in the sitting room. Reserve the round table, the one at the back, that way we can see all the other tables from there and we shan't be disturbed."

I rang the Vicomté.

I also rang Anna. I told her not to wait for me.

Alice went out just as she was, her jacket buttoned awkwardly over her plaid shirt. With part of her shirt tail hanging over her trousers. She had mud on her knee. In the car she scratched at it with her fingernail.

She did not want to wear her seat belt. She told me she could not stand it and that she would pay all the fines if we happened to be stopped.

The radio was on. She turned up the volume. She told me that she listened to the shipping forecast, on Sunday night, on France Inter. I also listened to it. I would go out and shut myself in the car.

"Even when you're in Paris?"

"Particularly when I'm in Paris."

We looked at each other. Her expression was cheerful. As for mine, I do not know. She sank deeper into her seat. Her hands flat on her thighs.

"What road are we taking?"

"The *Route nationale*, there's no other way."

"There are two roads! The one that goes along the coast and the one you're on."

I slowed down.

"You want to take the coast road?"

"Don't you?"

"It's longer."

She rolled down the window. Her elbow on the sill.

"What does it matter, we have time. Unless you want to go back. If that's the case, say so right away, and we'll make do with a few *moules* in Veules. Naturally Veules is not Fécamp . . . So, what do you want to do?"

I turned to the right down a road that ran through the fields in the direction of Quiberville, the D75, then towards Veules-les-Roses and Saint-Valéry-en-Caux. Fields of flax as far as the eye could see. Machines mowing, they looked like harvesters. Further along, on the edge of the cliff, was a herd of Norman cows and immediately beyond that, the sea.

"I was right, wasn't I? It's much lovelier to come this way."

The wind was tossing her hair. She was wearing dark glasses. A scarf tied around her neck.

"Do you know what Clémence served me for lunch today? Chrysanthemum flowers! You shouldn't laugh, it's the truth. She boiled them and then simmered them in some concoction, then she served them to me with some soy sauce and a bit of salad. I suppose the salad was fresh but still . . . Chrysanthemum flowers . . ."

"And was it good?" I asked.

"How am I supposed to answer a question like that? Chrysanthemum flowers . . . It should be obvious."

It took us over an hour to reach Fécamp. I immediately informed Alice that we would not take that road on the way back.

"And which road will we take?"

"The direct one."

She shrugged.

"In any case, you can't see anything at night."

We parked along the waterfront. It was high tide. The boats were returning to the harbour. On deck, fishermen in their yellow oilskins.

We crossed over to the far side of the quay. We looked at the boats. The cranes.

Afterwards, as we still had some time to spare, we went to the Palais Bénédictine. The shop was still open. There were paintings on the walls. We looked at them. We bought a packet of caramels for Clémence. Two umbrellas. Alice opened hers. In the boutique, and then again outside on the pavement. She said, "Now it can rain."

All the way to the restaurant with the opened umbrella. People turned to look.

When we arrived, there were already a few diners. At a table near ours was a couple with a little girl.

Alice went straight to the table we had reserved.

It was a restaurant without a printed menu. The menu was posted on the wall. Two starters and two main courses to choose from.

"Is this your treat?"

The walls were covered with wooden panels. Postcards. Posters. Alice, her face turned towards the menu.

"I'm going to try those little courgette blossoms filled with macaroons . . . Then I'll have the cod, they serve it on a bed of sauerkraut, you really must try it. And for dessert? For dessert, I really have no idea. It's always so complicated, choosing dessert . . . We'll see, afterwards."

She removed her glasses.

"And what sort of wine shall we have? What do you say to an *Entre-deux-mers*? It's very good with fish, the *Entre-deux-mers*."

She was sitting with her face cupped in her hands. She observed the couple at the next table.

"Colombe! How can you call your child Colombe, what can they be thinking, these women, when they bring their children into the world?"

We ordered. The wine was good. We spoke. About here. About Normandy. About storms.

"The only true storms are the equinoctial ones," Alice told me. "You must come back in December."

They served our starters.

"Did you tell Anna that you were coming here with me this evening?"

"Yes."

"And what did she say?"

"She said, 'If she were a younger woman, then I could fight, but in this case, no, I can't.'"

She nodded.

We spoke about out there.

"I remember . . . In the narrow streets, the mules were so thirsty they would rub their bellies against the wall. They would bang their hooves to chase away the clouds of flies stinging their eyes.

The moist eyes of mules. Old people with trachoma in their eyes."

We talked about here. And then out there, again. We always went back to it.

"The red hue of the men's skin. The women's gazes. The colour of the bows. Of the feathers. The sound of the calabashes the children played with. I remember the smells in the air, in the evening."

The cod was served with a piece of finely sliced bacon and two bunches of redcurrants.

Outside the window night was falling.

We drank some more. I drank more than she did.

Alice was laughing.

"Will you be able to drive after all this?"

All the tables were occupied. A light background noise. She stared at the people at neighbouring tables.

"Couples . . . It's strange, isn't it, everything that goes into making a couple, their existence . . . I would never have survived such a thing."

Her eyes were shining.

"You are wrong to leave Anna."

"I'm not leaving her."

"Of course you are . . . These currants on the fish are delicious, don't you think?"

She took her glass between her palms. She swirled the wine in her glass.

"You are leaving her and you do not even realize it."

She turned again to look at the couple with the child.

"I do find children hard to put up with. Is it old age? Even Clémence, there are times I cannot stand her."

She took a sip of wine.

"Do you like what you are eating?"

"Yes."

"Then why don't you say so? With you one never knows. One

does not know a thing. I can understand that Anna, at times . . ."

"What about Anna!"

"I don't know. I'm imagining. Meals, with you, day after day . . ."

She crushed a crumb beneath her nail. She was looking at me. From under her lashes.

"Have I hurt you? I did not mean to . . . I ought to ask you to forgive me. I don't know how. Would you like me to talk about out there some more?"

"No."

"What, then? We aren't going to sit here in silence? After driving all this way, that would be silly . . . Do you mind if I smoke?"

"I don't, but the others . . ."

"Who gives a damn about the others?"

She took her packet of tobacco from her pocket, rolled a cigarette, and then lit it. There was no ashtray.

"I'll talk to you about out there anyway."

The smoke, all around her. Around her face. She dropped the ash into her plate.

"What is surprising is the space, and the time it takes to go from one place to another. And after the space, the magic . . . There is magic everywhere."

She picked up her glass, handed it to me so that I would refill it.

"You are not listening."

"I am listening."

"What are you thinking about?"

"About the mask."

She put her glass down.

"I thought you were thinking about my death."

"I was thinking about that, too . . ."

"And what else?"

"That mask – did Otto sell it to you?"

"You've been snooping around houses that don't belong to you."

"I wasn't snooping. It was in the cupboard."

Alice looked at me, vaguely amused.

"You are getting angry, that's good."

She took a long pull on her cigarette and blew the smoke overhead. Into the blades of the fan.

"Is there anything else?"

"It was forbidden to sell the masks. And dangerous, too, to take them out of there."

"So?"

"So why is it in the cupboard?"

"That mask brings bad luck. And besides, the light can damage a mask. You know that."

"I also know that in Zuni country a white can be killed if he is found in possession of such a mask."

"It isn't a Zuni mask!"

She had spoken too loudly. The couple turned to look. Other couples, too, at neighbouring tables.

She picked up her fork.

"You are wrong to insist."

She stabbed the head of a mushroom which she then circled around her plate for a moment.

"As for the mask, my father bought it. Sometimes poverty is so great that some people will agree to part with what they have. No doubt they have no other options."

She looked up.

"You look at things the way whites do. You see only the surface."

The *patron* came over to us. He picked up the plates, suggested some desserts.

"*Fondant à la poire, crème brûlée*, chocolate profiteroles ..."

Alice could not decide.

"Choose for me."

It was impossible.

"So choose for yourself and I will have the same thing."

I asked for some *fromage blanc*.

Alice made a face.

"*Fromage blanc*, no, that won't do. Well, you have your *fromage blanc*, and I'll have a *crème brûlée*. And after all that we'll have coffee."

She folded her napkin in two, then in four, to make a square that she put on the table.

With her hand she smoothed the square of cloth. Then the tablecloth. The edge. She arranged the fold on the side.

"That mask you refer to was wrapped in a piece of cloth. With string around it. My father hid it at the bottom of a bag. The bag was on the back seat of the car. We were checked just before we left the territory. They opened the boot. They didn't look to see what was in the bag."

The *crème brûlée* was served in a glass bowl with a mint leaf. A dry biscuit. A few strawberries. With the end of her spoon, she cracked the fine caramel crust covering the *crème*.

"Emotion. That is what my father was looking for. Breton, too. All of them. They all had the same thing in mind. And belonged to the same movement."

She took the biscuit between her fingers.

"The world of *kachinas* is a world of violence. Of emotions . . ."

"You didn't answer my question."

"What do you want to know?"

"Was it Otto who sold you the mask?"

She put the biscuit back on her plate.

"Yes."

"And did you take him to New York?"

She looked out of the window at the pavement, the street.

"Look, it's raining. We'll be able to open our umbrellas when we leave."

The next day, Anna and I quarrelled.

"What do you want?" she said. Because I had got back very late.

She told me she had gone over to Alice's place, had waited about. She told me she did not understand.

"You have a job, two daughters . . ."

"It's not that simple," I said.

She went out, slamming the door.

The girls cried.

I held them close. I told them, "It's nothing," but I could see perfectly well that they did not believe me.

I let a few days go by.

On Wednesday there was wind. Enormous waves. The girls were in their room. They were drawing. Anna was doing crosswords in one of the big armchairs in the sitting room. I asked her if there was anything she needed. She shook her head.

I went back to Alice's place.

The mason had removed all the tiles. He was installing new ones, enamel. There were newspapers on the floor to protect it. There was a smell of plaster. Glue.

The mason had blue eyes. Alice told me she was paying him on the black. We looked at each other. It made us laugh. We were happy to see each other.

She took two bowls from the lowest compartment in the fridge. Plums.

"You prepare them the day before. Twenty-four hours in a mixture of wine and sugar, and Clémence adds cognac."

We sat at the table in the kitchen because Alice did not want to leave the mason.

"You've got a nasty look on your face today," she said.

Anna had told me the same thing.

I tasted a plum. There was something else in the juice besides the cognac. I could not tell what it was. A liqueur, some sort of plant. With cinnamon.

It was strong. It was good.

I thought it might be Bénédictine.

Even the stones, when you sucked them, had that taste.

Alice would not take her eyes off the mason. The tiles were all different. There was a plan. Even with the plan, she insisted on checking the mason's work.

"It's stopped," I said, comparing the time on the clock with my watch.

"Even when it's stopped, a clock gives the correct time twice a day. All you need to do is wait."

She stared at me, vaguely amused, the way she had the first day when I had helped her carry her basket of pears.

"Nothing new?"

"Nothing."

I finished my plums. And then I finished hers because she did not want any more.

The mason put away his tools. He said he had finished for the day. He would come back the next day.

We stayed, the two of us. Looking at the tiles. Ten of them had already been set. Alice got up and wiped them with a rag to remove the dust.

"Can you hear the gate? That's Clémence coming back . . . In a moment, you'll see, she'll stop next to that dreadful plant she is trying to save, God knows why, the one with the berries. I won't look. You look, then tell me."

"What do you want me to tell you?"

"Whether she is looking at her plant with the berries."

"She is looking at it."

"I do not understand! If you touch that plant it gives you spots. And now what is she doing?"

"She's removing her shoes."

"She's going to take off her jacket, too, and she'll hang it on the coat rack, on the third hook even though the others are empty, but it's always like that, the third one, the yellow one. Lean forward and tell me . . . Is it the yellow one?"

"It is."

She snapped her fingers.

"Dear Lord, to be that predictable!"

She came over and sat down again. She was looking at me. Her head propped on her hands. She was wearing a plaid shirt. A man's shirt, made of thick cotton. The sleeves were too long.

"Is there something wrong?" she said.

I said no, everything was fine . . .

"There is something wrong, I can tell! It's Anna, isn't it?"

"Yesterday, in the street in Dieppe, I followed her. She didn't see me."

"What do you mean, followed?"

"As if I didn't know her."

"Why did you do that?"

"I don't know."

She was fiddling with the plum stones. With the end of her spoon, in the bottom of the bowl. She was arranging them in rows. And then in the shape of a star.

"What else?"

"This morning, in the bed, she was sleeping."

"So?"

"So nothing. I looked at her."

"When you live with someone, things like that, you know . . ."

"What things?"

"Such things . . . It's pointless trying to fight them."

I looked away.

Alice smiled.

"My gaze is bothering you . . . I am so old, you know, I can hear everything."

She glanced at her watch.

"Aren't you going back?"

"No . . ."

"In that case, I want you to listen to something."

We went into the sitting room.

She opened a drawer and took out a case which contained a recorded tape. She slotted it into the player.

There was a scratchy sound as it began to play. A sort of rustling then, in the background, a hubbub of cars, horns, an ambulance moving away in the distance, voices, footsteps, doors creaking, more voices . . .

She paused the tape.

"What did you hear?"

"A city."

"It's New York," she said.

"It could be New York or anywhere . . ."

"It's New York. Now, listen carefully. In all likelihood you won't have any other opportunities to hear this."

The tape continued to unwind.

Men's voices. Chanting, voices rising, a pounding rhythm, very deep, and in the background what seemed to be the sound of rattles but which may also have been a melody on a flute.

She paused the tape.

"These men are singing to give strength to their masks. They are singing so that the cloud-men will hear their prayers and cause the rain to fall."

"The cloud-men?"

"The ancestors . . ."

Another sound followed. This one was barely audible.

Alice gave me a questioning look.

The tape continued. A few more rotations. Then it stopped, with a sharp click.

She rewound it.

"You're not paying attention. Even the obvious – you don't see it."

I listened for a second time. In vain.

"The sound you have just heard is a dust storm, driving bushes along the ground . . . you know, those clumps of dried grass that roll along and terrify the horses . . . I've forgotten what they're called . . . Probably the horses think they are animals, some sort of mad dog like the ones that run through the desert sometimes, alone or in packs."

She pressed the play button again.

I listened to what followed. And it sounded like nothing but silence. But it wasn't; a scarcely perceptible whispering. Nothing else. The tape stopped.

"Did you hear?"

"What was there to hear?"

Alice looked at me. She was holding her glasses in her hand. One of the arms wedged between her teeth.

"It is nothing I can tell you. You alone . . ."

She removed the tape from the player and put it back in its case.

"We'll listen again some other time."

She came back over to me.

Her back in the mirror. Reflections from the lamp on the ceiling.

"You don't speak . . . How am I supposed to put up with you?"

"I can leave if you'd like."

"That's it, leave . . ."

The tension between us. Abrupt. I stood up.

Alice did not move. She was staring at a place on the floor somewhere between us.

"But you will come again, won't you?"

Her voice, even lower than usual.

"We have more to talk about . . . Not everything has been said."

She smiled briefly.

"I won't have the strength to start again. With someone else. Neither the strength, nor the time . . ."

She caught up with me when I was already in the passage. My hand on the latch.

"I remember now, those dried bushes that roll along, driven by the wind, that terrify the horses . . . Tumbleweeds."

The next day, Anna took the children to the cinema. I cannot recall what film they saw. Although they did tell me before they left.

The 2 C.V. was at the garage. A spot of oil, the day before, beneath the motor. A part that needed changing.

I went to Alice's on foot. It began to rain when I was halfway there. Mud. Puddles. Impossible to cut through the fields. When I got there, the gate was locked, I had to ring and wait for Clémence to come and open.

One umbrella for the two of us.

She left me in the entrance. My feet on the doormat. My shoes covered with mud. I had to remove them. There was a fire in the hearth. I stood in front of it. My trousers, my sweater. The wool, steaming.

When she saw me, Alice let out a long sigh.

"You can't stay like that," she said. "There is a wardrobe full of clothing at the end of the passage. Just go and rummage around in there."

I left my sweater by the fire. I went out into the passage. The cupboard, right at the end. In the wall. Closed with a bolt. I pulled it open. Inside, there were blankets. Clothes, trousers, shirts, sweaters, everything you could possibly want, and for virtually every size.

There was a smell of wool. I took a pair of beige corduroys, a cotton sweatshirt, and a pair of socks. I could hear the mothballs rolling about when I pulled out the clothes. I did not want to get changed out in the passage. There were two doors. I opened the first one. It was a small storeroom. I slipped inside. The trousers were too big. I found a plastic bag and rolled the rest of my wet clothes up inside it.

I went back out.

I opened the other door. I do not know why. Curiosity, I suppose.

There was an odd smell in the room. I hunted for the light switch. With the palm of my hand. On the right. Along the wall. A sudden violent burst of light.

The room was big, the walls wood-panelled. A crystal chandelier hanging from the ceiling. That was the source of the light. Beneath the chandelier, a huge table. On the table, a tablecloth and place settings. Twenty or more, and then candlesticks.

I went closer. There was bread in baskets, dry, grey slices. I touched them; they were like stone.

A carafe. Empty. Traces of sediment inside.

Some of the chairs were set normally at each place and others were in disorder, which suggested that there had been people here who had left the room suddenly.

A shawl over the back of a chair. A jacket. A teddy bear.

As I turned away, I saw there was a Christmas tree at the end of the room. Garlands. A few baubles.

The needles had fallen from the tree, and what was left, a few dried branches, made me think of a crucifix.

At the foot of the fir tree, still in the place where someone had once put them, were presents that were no longer presents but boxes covered in golden paper. Ribbons that had been nibbled away.

A child's coloured drawing.

Alice had pulled a chair up to the fire. A log had been placed on the andirons. She watched as it burned.

She did not move.

She did not turn around.

She just leaned forward. She took the poker and scraped at the embers to lift them and get the flames going again.

"It was Christmas 1946."

That is what she said.

She put the poker down.

She pointed to the chair next to hers.

I did not feel like sitting down. I wanted to hear her. Hear what she had to say to me.

Without being close to her.

She smiled. She looked at the fire. Living flames, throwing their red light onto the floor around her.

"It was December. There was snow. My father wanted to take pictures of the falling snow. He went to Étretat. Snow, water . . . He went down to the foot of the cliffs. He went a long way out. The tide came in. Equinoctial tides, they're the worst . . . We found his body three days later. My mother was here, with the guests. In that room with the Christmas tree. It was Christmas Eve, you see . . . She was waiting for him. The police said it was an unfortunate accident.

My mother closed the door. She did not want anyone to touch the room. Ever."

Alice sat for a long while without saying a thing, then turned to me.

"That's enough for today. You have to get back to Anna."

"Anna . . ."

"Anna. And the girls. You must go and be with them. Make the most of this break in the rain to get home again."

My sweater had not dried.

"You can pick it up later."

"I'll come back tomorrow."

"Not tomorrow. Let a few days go by."

It was not so much the thought of seeing Anna and the girls. But the desire to be alone. I took the car and went to the beach. The tide was still far out. There was some wind and children were searching in the rocks for crabs.

I walked along the foot of the cliffs. Places where there were fallen rocks. Alice's father had died in a place like that. A dream décor. For a death. A photograph. One photograph too many, I suppose. And the others, at home, waiting to celebrate Christmas.

Alice had told me that an Indian could kill another Indian to appropriate his strength. Similarly, the sea could kill a man.

I went back to the port. I found a table out of doors. I ordered a glass of sugared water, but the waiter told me he could not serve a glass of water like that.

He told me to order something else, a coffee for example, and then I could have my glass of water with it. I had already drunk too much coffee, that morning, the night before too, with Anna.

"You don't have to drink it," he said, "but if you order a coffee, I'll give you your glass of water."

That's what he did. He brought a coffee in a cup on a tray, and next to the cup there was also a glass of water and some sugar. The sugar was in lumps, paper folded round it. He told me that it was not his job description to put sugar in his customers' coffee.

I pointed out that it was not coffee but water and he said it was all the same to him and he did not want to discuss it.

I stirred the water with a spoon.

A dog came up to me, determined to stay.

A little black beast, an affectionate sort of cocker spaniel with soft moist eyes. I gave him the biscuit wrapped in cellophane that came with the coffee.

There was no-one left on the beach.

I thought, I'm going to leave Anna, and then I said to myself, what will I do if I no longer have Anna?

Anna and the girls.

I said, when the shade reaches me, I'll leave. The shade came. I waited for it to cover the entire terrace, as far as the slide.

The dog had vanished.

The waiter took my cup away. He gave me an odd look. I suppose I had sat there too long, for just a coffee.

When I got home, Anna was on the terrace in the rocking chair. She was wearing the plaid T-shirt I had given her for her birthday, and flip-flops with flowers on them. The low-angled evening sunlight. A blanket on her legs. She was reading.

The girls were not there. At least not in the garden. Perhaps they were in their room.

Anna did not move.

She just said, "Who is that woman you're seeing?"

"That woman . . ."

"I don't want to know her name. Just what it is that she gives you that I don't give you."

She waited.

I think she closed her eyes. Her finger stuck between two pages. I suppose she wanted to go on reading once I had given her an answer. But what answer could I give?

Alice's story haunted me. I looked at Anna. I was thinking about elsewhere. Alice's words. Her voice. Even at times when I played with the girls. It was nothing to do with her. Or against her. It was me, only me.

I had no answer for her.

Not even a rough idea.

"I need to go there . . ."

Anna let go of her book. She stood up and went into the house. I stayed behind. Unmoving. Staring at Anna's flowered flip-flops. And then at the closed book. The lost page.

I let several days go by before I went back. Trying to resume a normal life with Anna.

I went back to Alice's one day the following week. She was in the studio cleaning a sculpture, a sort of misshapen head on which you could see the face and profile all at once.

She told me she had sculpted the face a long time ago and from time to time she felt the need to come and look at it.

She told me this right away, the moment I came in.

"Duality, good and evil, black and white . . . all the contraries one can oppose are brought together in this face."

She was wearing fur-lined boots. Because of the dirt floor. Always so damp.

With her fingertip she drew a circle in the dust and then another circle inside the one she had already drawn.

"They do this with coloured powders. Make drawings that the wind erases."

There was a little aeroplane on the shelf behind her. A construction of wood and twine. When she saw I was looking at it, she explained it.

"Max Ernst made it. And he gave it to me."

Cardboard propellers. The blades edged in red. A piece of cloth for a flag.

"The plane was in my room in New York for a long time and then when we moved I put it in one of the cardboard boxes, and the box got lost. I found it again years later."

The name, Ernst, in black paint on one of the wings.

"They got together frequently at the flat. My mother didn't like it. She would stay in her room. Breton was still with Jacqueline."

A box. Pieces of shattered earthenware. I rummaged through it.

Alice continued to busy herself with the sculpture. With a little brush she removed the dust in the recesses.

"Ernst and Breton had a falling out. Because of Cézanne, or Giacometti, I can't remember which . . . In any event Breton got angry with everyone."

A drawer. I opened it. It was full. Shells, pieces of string, a few blue stones. An empty domino box. A doll. And in the middle of all that bric-a-brac, in the dust, I found a small photograph. It was Alice. Very young. Not even twenty. She was standing against a wall in a room. Wearing a heavy cotton dress. The wall was made of earth. The same colour as the dress. You could make out a ladder in the background. And a necklace she was holding in her hand. Hanging from her fingers. As if forgotten. An entire section of the picture was blurred because of the light falling from the roof behind her. In contrast, her face was very sharp. Very lovely. Those eyes, and that strange pallor.

I turned around.

I looked at her as she leaned over her sculpture. Indifferent. Isolated.

So much time separated these two pictures. From the very lovely woman she had been, to the old woman.

Are we so different at the end of our life from what we were in the early days? When we were really only beginning to live?

I put the picture in my pocket and closed the drawer. I went back over to her.

We set off on a short walk around the garden.

"This boxwood, when we planted it, was quite small, a few inches. We never trimmed it and now look, it's out of all proportion. That is why there are so many birds, they use it as a refuge."

"In his letters your father says he brought back apricot stones."

"He planted one. Over there. At the far end of the meadow. You can see the branches from here."

We continued along the lane.

"Sometimes the neighbour lets his sheep out, all he has to do is open that gate hanging from a post. From the other side the sheep nibble at the bark of the fruit trees and you have to be constantly out of doors keeping an eye on them."

She pointed to the apricot tree.

"Go and have a look. I'll wait for you here."

I went deeper into that part of the garden which became a meadow once you passed the boxwood hedge. Grasses, ever higher. A peony growing among the brambles. An earthenware jar. A chair lying on its side. The apricot tree was right at the end of this wildest part. A place of loamy earth, rich with smells, almost cloying. I reached the tree. A few apricots were hanging from its branches. I took one. The inside was juicy. Honey-coloured. In my mouth I had the sudden impression I was swallowing the sun.

I put the stone in my pocket.

"The apricots have worms," I said when I went back to Alice.

"They ought to be treated. We haven't done it."

"That's a pity."

"What is a pity? Not to poison the earth? Whereas all you need to do is scratch a bit with the tip of a knife . . . You don't believe me when I tell you it is an apricot tree from out there, and yet you kept the stone. I saw you. Where are you going to plant it?"

"I don't know. At *La Téméraire* . . ."

"It's too close to the sea, it won't grow."

We went back to the house.

"There are places like this garden which require our presence.

Wherever we are. So needy. Even when I am no longer here, you will have to come back. The little gate is never locked. I will write it on a piece of paper for you to keep, if by any chance Clémence tries to forbid you from coming in."

She made a strange face.

"Clémence will forbid everything when I am no longer here."

She stopped. Raised her finger.

"Do you hear the magpies? It's the cat. He's behind there. He must have climbed up the magnolia tree and now he's hunting."

A hammering sound was coming from the kitchen. Clémence had got it into her head that she wanted to change one of the shelves. The shelf was painted white. She wanted to instal one in wood.

"I'm going to ring my notary. To add it to my will."

"It?"

"The fact that they must bury me in the garden and nowhere else, especially not in Paris or one of those wretched places surrounded by concrete. And if they don't, it's too bad for them, all my money will go to protect the seals."

"You're fond of seals?"

"Not particularly, but it's either the seals or the Little Sisters of the Poor . . . I have my preferences. Some people are going to be bloody annoyed, I tell you!"

She turned to me.

"Don't you think I'm right?"

"To want to help the seals?"

"To make it an unconditional clause."

"I don't know."

"Of course you know, you're just not telling me. That's the way you are, you don't take sides, I must get used to it."

I pointed to the window that gave on to the kitchen.

"Perhaps I should go and help Clémence," I said.

"If it amuses you . . ."

Clémence was standing below the shelf. A screw was stuck, buried in thick layers of paint. No doubt it had been there for years.

It took me a long time to scrape off the paint. Then I had to loosen the screw from the wood.

"Now all you have to do is buy another board," I said, handing her the screw.

She smelled of violets.

I showed her the apricot stone I had in my pocket. She looked at it and nodded. She had a tiny little mouth. Her lips hardly visible. Alice came to see what we were doing. She said something to Clémence and Clémence replied, a few gestures.

It was a strange sort of conversation.

Alice turned to me.

"She says that when I die she will kill the cat."

She shrugged.

"Of course she won't do it. Deep down she is too fond of the cat. She cannot do without him. And besides, who knows, perhaps she will die before me."

She took my arm.

"Do you know what we should do? We should go to the beach, and hire one of those cabins with two deckchairs, and we shall spend the rest of the afternoon looking at the sea."

She glanced at her watch.

"Afterwards, if there's still some time, we shall go to Dieppe. I know a place, an Irish pub. We'll have a few whiskies. Dieppe isn't very far . . . I'll pay for your petrol if you like."

"That won't be necessary."

She looked at me, amused.

"The whisky, then! That's it, the whisky is on me."

We took the car, went to the beach and hired a cabin with two loungers.

The air was mild, almost hot. The sea was beginning to cover over the first rocks by the breakwater.

There were children playing on the beach. In the distance, the red and white spots of a few sailing boats.

Waves, sunlight. I closed my eyes. Luminous bursts of red and yellow. Through my eyelids I could feel the heat. I could hear children laughing, and the sound of the sea.

A woman's warm laughter. There was desire in her laughter. She must have had a man there, by her side.

"I'm going to leave Anna," I said.

That was it. Those words, exactly, in that order.

Alice did not move. I thought she had not heard me. Some children went by, running. They reached the water's edge. Then the water. Their thin legs, splashing about. Their shouts absorbed by the sound of the sea. But you could still see their sweeping movements. As if in a silent film. And their eyes were wide open, because this was the place where the waves lifted them up and rolled them over to land them with their noses in the sand.

"I'm going to leave Anna."

The children went on shouting. They spat out what they had swallowed. Water, salt, sand. Their lives of pure childhood, drenched in sunlight. Like them, I would have liked to spit things out. To be capable of it.

Alice placed her hand on mine.

"Those children playing in the waves, don't their parents know that this is the most dangerous part of the beach? Or do they want them to die?"

"You're not listening . . ."

The littlest ones could no longer stand being rolled around like that. They came back out. Exhausted.

"I am listening to you. You said, I'm going to leave Anna. And you said it twice."

The pub, a long room with a low ceiling and wooden beams.

On the tables there were books you could take away with you, and you could leave others in their place.

We chose a table at the back, near the pool table.

"A glass of whisky, will that do?"

A record was playing, Billie Holiday, I remember because Alice asked me what the music was, and as I did not know, she asked the waiter and the waiter said, "It's Billie Holiday."

We talked about the girls. She wanted to know whether I was a good father. I did not know. I told her that the girls loved me but that did not mean anything.

She looked up at me.

"Sometimes daughters can kill their fathers."

She put her glass back down.

She hunted for something in her pockets, first in her jacket then her trousers.

She had forgotten her tobacco.

I went up to the bar. On the beam, *Vox populi, vox Dei*. Carved into the wood. A large mirror. The entire room was reflected, the tables, the podium, the posters. Alice had pulled her scarf to her face and was breathing in its odour. Silent fan blades stirred the air. The walls were dark brown from the nicotine. The ceiling, too, in places, almost black. I came back over to Alice. I put the packet down in front of her.

She waited for me to sit down. She took out her matchbox and her rolling paper, fine sheets, you could see through them. She laid everything out on the table.

"I killed my father, you know . . ."

She said it calmly, as she lifted the little plastic disc that served to seal the packet of tobacco. She looked up. A faint smile. As if she wanted to diminish the impact of what she had just said. Diminish it, or mock it.

"I killed my father . . . Of course no-one wants to hear a thing like that."

She opened the packet. The aroma.

"You don't believe me, do you? You never believe me when I tell you the most serious things."

She placed a pinch of tobacco on a piece of rolling paper. Her fingers were trembling. Shreds of tobacco fell on the table.

"Would you like me to help you?"

Her gaze. Harsh, without warning.

"You and I . . . this is becoming . . . impossible."

She said nothing else. She rolled her cigarette. It took her some time.

And then she reached her hand across the table. Palm up.

"Give back the photograph you took, for a start."

"What photograph?"

"The one of me. Don't act all innocent."

I took the picture from my pocket. I put it on the table. Alice's face, in that room with its dark walls.

"What were you going to do with it?" she asked.

"I don't know. It was in the dust."

"So?"

"So, nothing . . ."

She looked at the picture. For a long while. Her hand only a few inches away. Curled on itself.

She looked away.

"You are right, it may as well stay with you."

I was thinking about what she had told me about her father. I did not know why she had said that. I did not dare ask any more questions.

She asked me if I could find the Billie Holiday record for her and I said yes, that should be possible, I just had to go back into Dieppe one day when the shops were open.

She began talking about Breton again. About the *kachinas*. She told me that the man who had sculpted the *kachinas* was a high priest. She had met him. A first time, at his home. With Breton and Elisa. And the second time when he was dancing with the snakes.

"That second time I saw him just as I can see you. That close. I could have touched his face . . ."

For a moment I thought she had gone mad. Always talking about that time. Dwelling on it.

She told me that Otto was the spiritual son of that great priest.

"When Otto was born, Quöyeteva was over fifty years old. His children were already grown. He wanted Otto to be the chosen child. The one who would receive his teachings . . . We all dream of such a thing, a child who will be the sum of all our successes and who at the same time will make up for all our failings."

# LIFE OF QUÖYETEVA
## PRIEST OF THE SNAKE (1875–1946)
## AND OF OTTO (1925–1945)

Quöyeteva was twenty when the government authorities came up the road leading to the village of Oraibi. They were coming to arrest him. Not just him, but several other Indians as well, twenty or so in all. The names of some were Polingyawma, Heevi'ima, Yukiwma, Qütsventiwa. There were high priests and clan chiefs among them.

They had all refused to send their children to the white man's school. They had refused to obey the missionaries who were preaching the word of Jesus Christ.

Alcatraz, the prison island, a prison without bars. A scrap of land thrashed by the wind.

Alcatraz, like the ends of the earth, hell.

Quöyeteva spent long hours sitting on the rocks. Weeks went by, months.

Some of his friends agreed to cooperate and were sent home. He remained unsubdued.

*

The government authorities came to fetch Quöyeteva. They took him to San Francisco, they made him visit the white man's institutions. A school. A hospital.

They told him that it was not *kachinas* that would cure epidemics. They showed him pills, and needles that entered the skin. Drops to heal eyes. Drops as transparent as water. They told him that this was what brought cures.

They also explained that clouds were not the souls of the dead, but the result of water that has evaporated.

Quöyeteva did not listen.

He did not allow the white man's words to enter him.

\*

A summer and yet another autumn.

One night snow fell, covering the island.

And one day, they set him free.

\*

It was at the beginning of winter. The stars, the Great Bear, the time of the first festivities, Solstice and the Feast of Soyal.

Quöyeteva went home. On a train with a steam engine, from San Francisco to the station at Holbrook. He walked the rest of the way. Over one hundred and fifty kilometres across the desert.

\*

He spent the first night alone, in the *kiva*. He did not sleep.

The waves off Alcatraz were still pounding in his blood.

On his thigh was a wound covered with a poultice made of earth. He scratched at it with his fingers, spread a new layer of green ointment he took from a case tied to his belt.

How long did he stay there?

He knew that the children of his village had been taken by force to the white man's school. That they had cut their hair and changed their names.

He knew that the white man had supplied modern wooden planks and stones to repair the houses. That they had provided tools. Clothing. Which some of the Indians had agreed to wear.

He knew that the white man had given presents to the children.

He also knew that his mother had died, taken by the great epidemic. Smallpox. She along with so many others. Hundreds at a time. From Walpi to Shongopovi and Moenkopi.

Dead bodies everywhere. In the streets. Corpses burnt. Thrown from the tops of cliffs.

And he, Quöyeteva, was not there to put his mother in the earth.

*

The last days of December. The shortest days. The coldest nights. The moon is full.

The first *kachina* comes from the heights of the cliffs. He is clothed in a long white robe. His head is covered with a turquoise-coloured helmet. He advances, his body leaning on a stick. He is the Soyal *kachina*, who announces the beginning of ceremonies. The children are laughing. The women come out. The entire village gathers on the square. They all watch him coming.

All alone, in that lunar place.

With him the crops will grow again, seeds will sprout.

He walks around the houses, carrying his blessing. And then he continues on his way to the other villages, Shipolovi, Min-shongnovi, Walpi . . . The children climb onto the roofs to see him again.

197

The men stand in a cluster.

The time has come to wear the masks.

*

September. Quöyeteva married Bessie, a daughter of the Bear Clan.

Time went by.

Bessie gave him sons.

On the day he turned six, Quöyeteva's firstborn son was abducted by the white man, taken away with other children to a boarding school in Keams Canyon.

Quöyeteva was afraid that they would take his other children.

Bessie said he was a good husband but that he had a bad reputation. She knew he took part in commando operations and that he was repossessing by force the masks the white men had bought. She told him he would get into trouble with the American government.

She was afraid.

One day, she would put all his belongings outside and tell him to leave.

*

Otto was born in Oraibi in the month of February of the year 1925. He was not Quöyeteva's true son. He was his ritual son.

It was for the feast of Powamu. That night it had snowed and the wind was driving icy drifts against the walls. His mother had waited for hours, squatting. Otto did not want to be born, so one of the clanswomen, who was also a mother, came and wrapped her powerful arms around the mother's belly and squeezed very hard. She did this several times. Otto eventually came out but he did not want to breathe.

Quöyeteva slipped a finger into his mouth. To force him. Otto

198

was still not breathing so Quöyeteva slapped him and took him by one foot and flung him outside into the snow. The elders told the story that Otto's cry could be heard very far away, on the far side of the Grand Canyon. That it could be heard as far as the mountains of the Elders. And when the dead ancestors returned, they said that they had heard the cry.

Otto's first name was *He-who-cries-with-the-snowflakes*.

*

Night is falling. The plain is turning the colour of rust. A tree in the distance, like a skeleton.

The desert, silent.

Grey glints of light on the hills. Prussian black, sienna umber. The road is scarcely visible, a mere track, slightly darker against the burning expanse of the plain on either side. This is the road for Moenkopi and Flagstaff and, further still, Phoenix and the rest of the world. A dusty track. Rare bushes. A few dead horses.

For days the wind has been blowing. Skimming the ground. In the narrow streets the dogs are going mad.

Quöyeteva makes his way along the cliff. Makes his way even where it is no longer possible to go. He buried a poplar root there. Over a year ago.

The root, in his fingers. Dry. It has taken strength from the earth. Its odour.

It weighs nothing in his hand.

With the root he will make a *kachina*.

*

In the *kiva*. Quöyeteva cleans the root. He smoothes it with a rag and with his hand. When the root is ready he takes his knife and

199

attacks the wood. Creates the shape, the head, the body. The *kachina*'s arms, in front of its body. Its legs. He is not inventing. He is reproducing what his ancestors did, the same gestures. He is transmitting. With his blade. Patiently. One by one he removes wood shavings. He does it by following a model he has kept within. The one his forefathers taught him. The shapes, repeated and unchanging.

To make visible that which is not.

And when the shape has been given, he mixes gypsum with a shining powder, galena. He spreads a first coat. A luminous white.

When his real father died, Quöyeteva placed a ladder on his tomb so that he could come out and reach the other worlds. Is it true that the dead can hear the prayers the *kachinas* have brought them?

Quöyeteva paints. The body and the face. The black face, two horns, black and white. Striped. Protruding eyes. Yellow for the torso. Pigments he obtained from far away, from the quarries of the Little Colorado.

He is expressing the Hopi beliefs. In this he is like every other artist on earth who labours for his gods. He belongs to the pantheon of the great anonymous artists, the painters of temples and churches, sculptors of black virgins in Vézelay or elsewhere, the sculptors of original sin in the choir of Notre-Dame-du-Port in Clermont-Ferrand.

All elevated by the same force.

They convey emotion.

Voices raised in song tell of mankind's faith. *Kachinas* have the same power of speech.

All it takes is one mistake in one of the motifs for the *kachina* to lose that power.

Quöyeteva knows this.

He works attentively.

On the face are sacred motifs. With the tip of the brush. Star, then moon. A fine, regular line. A white line on a black background. A goldsmith's labour. The eyes. The symbols, precise and immutable. One more stroke. He puts the brush down.

When the paint has dried, he slips a little rattle into the *kachina*'s right hand. In the other hand, a hunting bow, the wood painted the same black as that of the torso.

He steps back.

The *kachina* is ready.

It is a warrior. An Ahote. A Restless One.

He keeps it for two days in the *kiva*, and on the morning of the third day he gives it to Otto.

And Otto takes it.

He plays with it.

With it he learns the pantheon of his ancestors.

\*

Otto was seven when Quöyeteva initiated him into the rituals for the first time. That day he took him by the hand and led him away from his mother. He took him to an aunt who washed his hair with the sap of the soaptree yucca. She covered his face with flour. Then she led him into the *kiva* where the *kachina* dancers were waiting. A dozen of them, standing against the wall. They were wearing masks. Otto saw them. He heard them. Their breathing. He had never seen them so close before. The deep song they uttered. He knew that the *kachinas* came from far away, from the hills of San Francisco, he knew that some of them came from the stars and the worlds beyond the stars.

Worlds that were invisible to human eyes.

His heart began to pound. Opposite him, so close that if he

reached out he could touch him, was *Ang-ak-China*, the *kachina* with the Long Hair. His eyes like two slits. Otto stared at him. And suddenly he turned away because the *Ang-ak-China* had just lifted his hands to his mask. He raised the mask. Otto knew it was forbidden to see the face of a *kachina*. He closed his eyes. When he opened them again he saw the blue mask of the *Ang-ak-China*. But the mask was no longer covering a face. A hand held it.

So Otto looked up. Slowly. From the hand holding the mask along the arm. Up to the face. And what he saw then was petrifying. No longer were there any spirits before him, only the men from the village. Uncles, neighbours, brothers. He recognized all of them.

And in the man holding the blue mask he recognized his father, his ritual father,

and he understood

and he had to keep himself from crying.

*Many years ago*, said the high priest then, *a child was whipped to death for revealing the secret.*

\*

Otto used to like the *kachinas*. He used to like waiting for them when they came again with the winter, and learning to know them and recognize them. He used to like being afraid of them.

Now there were days when he was angry with those who had lied to him.

Otto learned the stars, the movements of the sun. He learned to read the secret traces on the rocks. The quarters of the moon that heralded the solstice.

Otto learned the names of all the feast days honouring the world: Soyal, Powamu, Wuwuchim . . .

Quöyeteva said to him, you will be a great chief.

Later, you will have to sing. You will also learn that.

And then to dance.

To dance with snakes.

And you will learn to paint the *kachinas* that will be used for teaching.

Later you will be the guardian of the masks.

Otto listened, but he sat through his entire teaching without saying a thing.

Until the day Quöyeteva let him wear his first mask. It was the blue mask.

The supple leather beneath his fingers.

Otto learned the history of all the Hopi myths and legends, the migration of the clans, the founding of Oraibi and the secret of the sacred tablets.

*In the beginning, the water covered almost the entire flat world under our earth. For a while, life was good. It rained all the time, the plants grew, and there were flowers everywhere. And then one fine day things changed.*

He learned the secrets of the four worlds and how to use the powdered paints to pray to the gods.

*Everything was carved symbolically on the four sacred tablets that Màsaw gave to them.*

He listened. He was a silent child.

*When the people of Shongopavi lived at the foot of the* mesa, *and the Twins of the War lived to the north of Oraibi, they noticed that many of the Hopi went to the west, to the Blue Canyon.*

And when Otto had heard all the legends, Quöyeteva took him into the *kiva* of the snakes.

He said a pure heart need have no fear of the poison.

Thus Otto entered into the world of the spirits.

He became *He-who-has-kept-the-silence*.

*

Otto was nine years old when he touched a snake for the first time.

At the age of ten he washed the snakes. According to the ritual, with water mixed with sand.

He fed them.

At fifteen, he took care of them.

And one day he was bitten. Fever, for days. So great that he did not know whether he was alive or dead. There were faces at his bedside whose names he no longer knew. Nor their shapes.

He no longer knew that they were faces.

And then one morning Otto was back on his feet. He walked to the door. He opened his eyes wide. He was alive.

*

Quöyeteva taught Otto the truths of the Hopi world and the four worlds from before. He showed him the paths that led to the salt reserves in the Grand Canyon. He also showed him the paths that led to the lands of colour.

Smells. Earth. Light.

Shadow.

Together, everywhere. The priest-man and the child.

A stubborn child. Tenacious.

But the child was looking elsewhere, to the east, to the land that touched the horizon, and which beckoned to him.

And one evening, for the first time, the chosen child drew a path. And on the path he drew a train.

A train that was leaving.

\*

The snake was a pledge. Without the snake the rain did not fall. The corn died.

The snake housed the soul of the witches. To kill a snake was to set that soul free.

One day when he was by the *arroyos*, Otto killed a snake. To punish him, Quöyeteva tied a rope to his ankle and dragged him to the village. He made him spend the night out of doors. He wanted the coyotes to eat him, but the night passed and the coyotes did not come.

Otto stayed all night trembling against the wall. The next morning the inhabitants laughed at his fear.

After that Otto would do other foolish things but never again would he kill a snake.

\*

The rose bushes on the cliffs had bloomed. Quöyeteva was picking the leaves to make remedies. And then the flowers withered. Snow fell.

Winter already. A few more months and new buds would form.

Thus, the work of time.

Otto grew up.

His grandfather died. As did a clan uncle.

Otto looked up to the sky. He was not sad. Quöyeteva said that men died but they came back in the shape of clouds. He said that the living and the dead make a unity of a single substance.

*

Otto grew some more. He became big and strong. He did not want to learn to dance with the snakes.

*

There were more and more white men in the villages. Quöyeteva said that they must no longer obey them. He also said they had to set fire to the missionaries' barn.

The white men replied that men are sheep and that God is the shepherd of them all. They wanted to replace the Hopi gods with their god.

Quöyeteva burst out laughing. He knew what shepherds do to sheep.

*

Otto was sixteen when for the first time he agreed to let a white man take his photograph. He did it for one dollar.

Behind Quöyeteva's back.

With the money he bought a postcard: a train. For months he kept the postcard. Under his shirt. The paper got bent, absorbed his sweat, the colours stuck to his skin.

One day there was nothing left of the train but shreds.

*

Quöyeteva did not know whether his tribe was fated to open up to the outside world. He knew that closed worlds can suffocate. He was afraid that his people would die without having found their place.

He said they must refuse presents. Even if the presents were tempting.

He knew Talayesva. The two men often met and they quarrelled. They ended up not speaking.

Quöyeteva said that the writer would agree to do anything for money. He even let the white man sleep in his house.

He saw Otto go several times into his house. Otto was learning to speak like the white man. He knew their language.

When they asked him to, he acted as an interpreter.

This made Quöyeteva furious. But in the village of Oraibi the Hopi had agreed to treat the white man as their friend.

If he continued to rebel, he would end up back on Alcatraz. Or in another prison that he would never leave.

*

The seasons passed. Quöyeteva had a herd, twenty or more sheep. He was growing peas, tomatoes, and sweet potato plants. The sun dried them.

The soil, almost dust.

He hung eagle's feathers from the beams outside his house. They swayed in the wind. And the wind carried his prayers to the gods.

One night Otto took the feathers down and sold them to the white men.

*

Bessie gave Quöyeteva another child. A daughter. The day she was born Quöyeteva was in Phoenix with other Indians. They wanted to repossess a ceremonial mask. A very fine *Sipikine* which a white man had bought and which was to be sold at auction.

This was not the first time they had done this.

The newspapers accused the Hopi of repossessing what had been legally sold by their chiefs.

Police guards came to Hotavilla. They found Quöyeteva sitting outside his door.

Quöyeteva said all he was doing was staying there to look after his family.

And he showed them the cradle where his infant child of a few days lay.

*

Otto forgot about tradition. Already, he no longer drew the way the ancestors had. He no longer spoke like them.

He said that in San Francisco men captured electricity and made it run through wires, and that this brought light to the interiors of their homes. He said that the water there flowed along pipes and came out into basins, all you had to do was turn a tap. As much water as you wanted.

He said that there was no longer any need to wait for rain.

That there was no longer any need to pray.

He said, too, that snakes could be killed.

*

In France there had been the Great War. The one they call the First World War.

Breton was studying medicine, then. He was mobilized. He worked as a doctor in a psychiatric centre. He studied Freud.

*

Quöyeteva fed the masks, coated them with honey and grease, and he made offerings to them, of tobacco and flour.

The masks. All the masks.

Among them was the blue mask.

Quöyeteva slipped it onto his face. He kept it there for a short while.

His sweat soaked the leather.

And later, when Otto danced, it would be Otto's sweat.

*

Years went by, where we know nothing of Quöyeteva's life.

*

Quöyeteva said that only those who have bad thoughts can be bitten by snakes. His thoughts were pure. He was not afraid.

Otto refused to wear the masks. He wanted to go to Phoenix, or New York. To university.

When he said this, Quöyeteva did not listen.

*

The daughter Quöyeteva had with Bessie lived in Oraibi. She pinned her hair up with flowers. She was looking for a husband.

His eldest son had gone to live with his wife in Moenkopi. His other son was in Winslow, where he opened a shop selling local handicrafts. He made *kachinas* for tourists. He used acrylic and chicken feathers and sold them as local art.

*

Quöyeteva knew that if he sold *kachinas* he could buy fruit and bread and tobacco, too. He was afraid that when night came white men would steal the prayer sticks that were planted outside his house. One evening he posted Otto there as a watchman. In the morning two of the *pahos* had disappeared. Otto said he had fallen asleep and that the white men seized the opportunity to steal the *pahos*.

But in the afternoon of the same day Quöyeteva saw Otto leave Lorenzo's trading post with modern food, and he understood that Otto had lied, and that he had sold the *pahos*.

\*

Quöyeteva said the door must be left open. The door of intuition. So that everything might move through there. Going in, going out. It was in this way that the relationship between all things could be created.

Quöyeteva was afraid of dying before finding shelter for his family. Shelter, that secret place where the chosen would go when the world was destroyed.

And the others, those who were not chosen?

Otto said that the white man was going to destroy the world, but that there would be no other worlds after this one. This world, which was about to be destroyed, would be the last.

\*

There was what Quöyeteva said.

And there was what Otto said.

\*

The masks were the infinite patience of the people of the *mesas*. Their poetry.

But one day a man looked at a mask and as he looked at it he saw something else.

That something else was Beauty.

And the importance of that beauty overwhelmed him, like the truth. Before knowledge itself. Before it could even be named.

Before anything else.

And his way of looking at the world changed.

The sacred thing became a work of art.

*

August 1945. Otto met Victor Berthier. He agreed to have his picture taken. For one dollar. With his ceremonial necklaces.

For another dollar, he showed him the *kachinas* in the winter room.

*

The masks contain the spirit of the Hopi people. To steal a mask is to touch that most precious part.

Otto knew this. And even so, one morning, he went up to the winter room and stole a mask.

The blue mask, the *Ang-ak-China*.

A child said he saw Otto running away with the mask. And then selling it to a white man.

Quöyeteva replied that it could not have been Otto. The child must be mistaken. Or else he had lied.

They caught up with Otto along the great road. With money in his pocket. He did not defend himself.

Quöyeteva could no longer look at his face. Or meet his gaze. Otto, that son who had been so precious to him.

He looked away.

He took the banknotes and burned them.

\*

The white man is evil. He causes envy to be born in the eyes of the younger Indians. That is all Quöyeteva can say. Envy, the word murmured.

He puts on his ceremonial loincloth. He smears the powdered paints over his body. The other dancers are waiting. Down in the *kiva* the snakes raise their heads. Their mouths open, hissing.

It is hot. The heat of dust made almost electric with the men's tension. The dancers. Over fifty of them. Their faces covered with black grease.

Quöyeteva goes out first. In his hand is a snake, an enormous rattler. One of the finest. This sudden passage from shadow to light.

When the crowd sees the snake they fall silent.

Quöyeteva looks all around him. The silent crowd. This is one of the most solemn moments. A dance offered to the gods. He holds the snake above him, at arm's length. The sun is leaden.

A hoarse murmur leaves his throat and the other dancers'. The chants. Suddenly the silence is broken. Abruptly. Violently. The din of the rattles and the dancers surging forward. As if they have come from the earth.

A thousand people hurry to the roofs and terraces.

And in each dancer's hand is a snake.

Quöyeteva brandishes his. He looks at it. With the sun behind him, dazzling in a sky that is almost too blue.

For a brief while, the encounter between the dancer and the snake. The great priest and the intercessor. And it is that very thing, that expectant tension, which makes the moment so oppressive. Suddenly Quöyeteva lifts the snake to his mouth. A few inches. A mad look in his eye. His face full of menace. And he takes the snake in his open mouth. Behind him, other dancers do the same and they all begin to dance. The first steps of this dance that is the most sacred of all.

Two by two. Side by side. One foot raised, then the other higher, swinging. And sometimes the movement slows, to start again in a long, bewitching spiral.

The sun.

It is through this dance that the rain must come.

The dancers go deep into the narrow streets. Noise everywhere, infernal. Young people shouting from the rooftops.

The sound of the clappers the men have tied around their thighs.

Drums.

Feet pounding, in an insistent call for rain. As if the rain should not fall, but rise up from inside an earth so dry it is as if it were possessed.

The men's knees, bent. Their backs too. All in movement.

One has to imagine.

To feel.

And hear.

The dance is taken like this throughout the village.

There are more than fifty dancers.

They form a single being. All of them. Intimately connected. At times the snake's face so close to their eyes.

The ritual is one of the most brutal, the most savage.

Quöyeteva can feel the weight of the snake around his neck. He can feel his own sweat. He dances. His blood is pulsing, throbbing violently. The streets are teeming, turbulent.

Where is Otto? He has not seen him for days. He looks for him.

He returns to the square. Until he is just outside the *kiva*. A few more yards. His jaws are like a vice around the cold body. He knows he must not yield any of the extreme pressure.

He clenches his teeth.

In a convulsion of anger, the snake twists. Quöyeteva feels the contact of the twisting body on his tongue, and the salt smell of fear mingles with his saliva. For an instant his eyes meet the burning gaze. Red flames. Messengers from the gods.

Quöyeteva smiles.

The rattlesnake is powerful. He will join the territory of the dead. He will unleash the lightning and the lightning will bring rain. In that moment the smile of the great priest shows he is certain of this.

A few more steps. Their union is intimate. This is how it has been ever since there have been snakes and the men who dance with them.

The end comes quickly. Brutally. Almost violently. The snakes are brandished one last time then released, with one gesture, and they flee, moving shadows among the white scree. The people all around, the crowds, already beginning to scatter.

Quöyeteva watches as his snake vanishes. He brings his hand up to his mouth. A faint smile, diffuse as a shadow, floats on his lips.

*

There is no one left in the *kiva*. Only the smell that the men and the snakes have left there.

Quöyeteva goes down the last rungs of the ladder. He sits down. It is dark and yet outside it was broad daylight. He stuffs his pipe with mountain grasses. Grasses that give vision.

He hears voices outside. So far away. The voices move off. Then come again. Like a slow buzzing.

A sudden heat. He feels for his mouth, his lips. There is no sensation. He has no more face. No more hands.

He thinks he is speaking.

His saliva has turned bitter. Black. He tries to spit it out. He is drooling.

On his lip is the blue mark. The place where he has been bitten.

Alice pulled her shawl tight around her shoulders. She was cold. They had probably stayed in the shade too long.

"Hopi dancers are not afraid of snakes. Quöyeteva was bitten because he knew he had committed a sin. And that knowledge made him vulnerable."

She left the bench where we had been sitting. We went into the conservatory.

"An Indian cannot be bitten unless he has offended the gods. Quöyeteva knew that. And that certainty was his antidote. It protected him. That's the way it is sometimes. If one believes death is impossible, one can elude it."

"Do you believe in such a thing?"

"In what?"

"In the punishment of the gods?"

Boxes laden with flowers had been set on a table. Some of the flowers had withered. Others were still mere buds. Sitting majestically in the middle of all the plants was an empty birdcage.

"I believe that the certainty that one has committed a sin does make one more vulnerable, and in some cases it can lead to death."

"Quöyeteva did not commit a sin."

"He was the keeper of the masks . . . And Otto was his son."

"His ritual son."

"The son he chose . . . These things matter."

Here and there, plastic basins were filling with water from the leaks in the roof.

"Breton was the one who told me about Quöyeteva's snake bite. Years later. When I saw him again in Paris."

A plant with red petals: I knew you were supposed to keep it thirsty to make it beautiful.

"We left very soon after that. My father had the mask, you see . . ."

"The blue mask . . ."

"The *Ang-ak-China* . . . I remember when we crossed the square. It was packed solid. The dancers still had the snakes in their mouths. They were returning to the entrance to the *kiva* . . . I saw Quöyeteva. It was impossible not to see him. I saw him as I see you, just before he spat the snake back out . . ."

She propped herself with both hands pressing on the edge of a trestle table.

"I think he had figured out that we were the ones who were going away with the mask."

She turned to face me. She held her hand out to my lips. Without touching them. And yet she was so close.

"I saw living snakes in the mouths of men. It made a great impression on me."

She turned away.

"Do you still believe in all that?" I said.

"That there are some thoughts which protect and others which kill? I cannot help but believe it."

It was hot. The air was heavy with humidity, hard to breathe. She sat down in one of the wicker armchairs. Her head back against the headrest.

I could not stop looking at her.

"When Otto was caught, we had already gone a long way down the road to Gallup."

She turned her head. Her eyes were shining. Her brief silence.

And then she said, in that voice that was so unusual: "That country bewitches you, you know."

She lifted her chin. Her hand. I sat down beside her.

She placed her hand on my arm. Her fingers were icy.

"What happened after that?" I asked.

"After what?"

"With Otto?"

"Nothing."

"You said he was caught. Did they notify the police?"

"That's not the way they do things, out there . . ."

"How do they do things?"

"It's an internal law . . . Otto became a pariah. Wherever he went, whatever he did . . . People would look away. Doors closed. He no longer even had the right to use the well water."

"I don't understand."

"And yet it's obvious . . . When no-one speaks to you anymore . . . Your friends become shadows. Your mother . . . The punishment of rejection, the worst of all. No-one can survive it."

"For a scrap of leather . . ."

"We belong to another civilization. We cannot understand. We can get closer, yes, but understand . . . No matter how close we get. Even with all the books and drawings and rituals, even if all that were given to us, we would still be outside."

"And yet they say they are a peaceful people, hostile to any form of violence . . ."

Alice swept my comment away with the back of her hand.

"You are white. A white man's view is limited to the world of the visible. The Hopis' view is much vaster."

"We also have our beliefs."

"Our beliefs have borders. Out there, there are no borders."

Purple shadows darkened her eyes. Her lips were dry. She ran her fingers over them. Several times.

"One morning Otto left the village. Some say he took a train and went to New York. Others say he walked until he obtained the gods' forgiveness, and then he went back to live among his own kind."

"But you – do you know the truth?"

"Which truth? There are so many possible truths."

A spot of white condensation had formed on the lenses of her spectacles. She took them off and wiped them with a corner of her shirt. She stood up and walked over to the door of the conservatory. Leaned her forehead against the glass. It had begun to rain.

She was looking out at the garden. Only the garden.

"He hanged himself."

That was all she would tell me.

For the rest, silence.

On my way home I wanted to buy a bouquet of flowers for Anna. Gladioli. Daisies would probably have suited her better but the shop assistant suggested gladioli. She said, women like these flowers as a rule.

The bouquet was too big for the vase.

Anna asked me if the flowers would shed that orange powder that so often stains tablecloths.

What could I say?

I looked out the window. It was evening. The beach was deserted. The sand, grey-brown. I thought about everything Alice had told me. Before leaving, I had asked to see the mask. She refused. Not today. Not this time. She told me she was tired. And she was, but that was another issue.

Anna put the flowers in the vase and set it on the table.

I went out onto the terrace. I lay down in the deckchair. She came to join me.

"Have you started smoking again?"

I handed her the cigarette. Before, we used to smoke like that. One cigarette for the two of us. Lying in the grass. I have memories of the two of us in the Luxembourg Gardens.

One would have to be able to return to the beginning.

Those few hours before the beginning.

Anna was standing next to me. Her legs. Her thighs naked. In her short skirt. Her panties. Anna's little cotton panties. I slid my hand between her thighs.

She smoked, looking at the sea.

Afterwards, the girls came out of their room. They came stampeding down the stairs. Like a great herd. When they saw us, they stopped short. Stuck. On the last step.

They stared at us. Anna's thighs, my hand. My hand lost up their mother's thighs. Beneath the fabric. They looked at each other and burst out laughing.

I removed my hand.

Anna went to prepare the meal.

The girls stayed there, sitting on the steps, playing, fingers touching, hand games they made up. Their own games. With words like nursery rhymes that they recited in a language known to them alone. I looked at them and wondered what sort of beauty would be theirs when they were grown-up.

Anna lit the lamp on the terrace and insects came to circle round it. Moths. Some of them burned their wings.

The night was balmy.

The air smelled of citronella. Echoing with the girls' laughter.

I had promised the girls I would take them by car to see the beaches at Trouville. I had promised them, too, that I would treat them to an ice cream in Deauville, but when they saw Trouville, they did not want to leave, so we ate our ice creams there. They went to play at the water's edge. Anna and I sat at an outdoor café. Facing the sea. We watched the girls. The boats. The girls, again. At one point Anna placed her hand on mine. She asked me if I wanted something to drink.

My hand.

The girls were waving to us. Behind them there were sailing boats where children were learning how to use the tiller.

Anna. Her skirt. Her legs in the sun.

I took out Alice's photograph. I slid it across the table to Anna. "That's her."

She looked at the photograph.

"What do you find so fascinating about all that?"

I tried to explain it to her.

The girls had made a sandcastle and they were building a dam to protect it from the sea. A rampart of sand.

The sun had moved around. We were in the shade now.

I put the photograph back in my pocket.

The sea continued to rise. It was eating away at the girls' dam.

The sailing boats were further and further away.

Anna wanted to move so that we would be back in the sun.

The sky was grey. The air was heavy.

Out to sea, in the distance, a tanker was heading for Boulogne or Calais, or even further still, Rotterdam, Amsterdam.

The girls lay down to make a dam with their bodies.

Anna said, it's late, and she called to the girls to dry off. The girls did not want to leave, because of the sandcastle.

I looked at Anna.

"Do you think I'm a coward?"

Anna did not answer.

The twins came over to us. Their cheeks were red. Sand in their hair.

We went back along the wooden walkway. The Savignac path as far as Roches Noires.

When we turned around we saw that the sea had destroyed the sandcastle.

The next day I went back to see Alice. It was just after five o'clock.

I found her in the conservatory. The bottom of her trousers rolled up. Both feet in a basin.

"Seawater baths, you're the one who told me about them."

She lifted one foot out of the water, up onto her thigh, and she began to dry it.

"A bit of water and some Guérande sea salt, that's practically the sea, don't you think?"

I stood there next to her.

"I'd like to see the mask."

"You've already seen it."

"I'd like to see it again."

She dried her other foot. She spread the towel over the back of the chair. She took the tub and went to empty it onto the gravel in the lane.

"What does Anna have to say about your coming here the way you do? She cannot just keep silent . . ."

She smiled. No doubt because I did not answer. And for her that was also an answer, in a way. A more obscure form of answer.

She went over to the door.

The weather was fine outside. Little blue butterflies were gathering pollen in the flowers in front of the house.

"Shall we go over to the bench?"

I followed her. The sun, over the garden. The water, evaporating. The plants with their flowers open wide, as if they were drinking in this new warmth.

The boxwood lane, dark green. Almost blue.

Alice pointed to a corner of the little slope that was sheltered from the wind by a row of bushes.

"Here, when it gets dark, you can see fireflies . . . All you have to do is sit and wait."

She walked on. A few steps.

"Did you know that the male firefly is only adult for two weeks? Two short weeks, that's all the time he has to find a mate and repro- duce . . . But why should you know that? You are from Paris. No-one knows these things in Paris."

"And what if the two weeks are not enough?"

"To reproduce?"

"To find a mate."

"Too bad for him, he will die."

She was digging through the grass.

"In any case, whether he reproduces or not, he will die all the same. A fate worthy of one's sympathy, don't you think?"

There were many creatures living in that garden. The daytime ones, and others that came out only at night.

Alice started towards the bench.

"There are fireflies that live in the ocean . . . They are a kind of lanternfish. Only the females grow. When they reach adulthood, the males choose a female and cling to her body. Then they degen- erate into a sort of pitiful sack of sperm. Quite peculiar, don't you think?"

"Yet they ensure the survival of their species all the same."

"Yes, of course . . . But nevertheless, the way they go about it is hardly poetic. Why are you looking at me like that?"

"Poetry bores me."

"It bores me, too, but from time to time it is useful. Are there any fireflies at *La Téméraire?*"

"No, I don't think so. In any case I've never seen any."

"Just because you haven't seen any doesn't mean . . ."

Alice paused, raising a finger, attentive.

"Do you hear? The sea . . . It's slack water."

I could not hear a thing.

She shrugged. She went over to the bench.

"This is where I would like to be buried. Beneath this tree. Near this old bench. In winter, when there is snow . . . The snow on this bench . . . That is why I never cross the Seine. They want me to go to Paris next winter but if I die there, they'll stick me in Père Lachaise or somewhere, they don't care where, they wouldn't hesitate."

She walked around the bench.

"And if they don't want to, if it's not possible, then they'll have to burn me. With ashes, naturally, there aren't the same difficulties . . ."

She leaned down to pick the bud of a poppy that was growing there against the foot of the bench. Green sepals. She plucked them and then unfolded them one after the other. Until she reached the inner flower.

She showed me. The wrinkled petals. Blood red. Like a dress made of crêpe paper. In the middle was the black, shining pistil. Its scent, slightly peppery.

"This is the most sexual flower there is," she said.

In the sky a few clouds passed over, driven by the wind. They were drawn inland, and would go to die further away, towards Offranville.

Alice sat down on the bench. She looked at the clouds.

"Where we see only clouds, others see the souls of their dead . . ."

Clouds, the dead . . . Was it possible to believe such a thing? I sat down next to her. Where the clouds went to die I saw only curtains of rain.

"Is your father buried here?" I asked.

"Buried? No . . . Ashes . . . Out to sea . . . We had to wait for a windy day. Go West! as he used to say."

She turned her head.

"Well, well, here's Voltaire . . ."

The cat came up to us. His tail upright. He rubbed against Alice's legs. Then mine. He went back and forth between us, leaving a few hairs to cling to our trouser legs.

Then he jumped up onto the bench and came to roll on her lap. Alice caressed him with *an attentive hand*, as she said that day.

"One must never caress Voltaire any other way."

His green, almost yellow eyes, a sort of luminescent powder, like stardust.

"An odd thing, really, cats, how they growl at night when they're on heat. The strange ballet of their lurking shadows. I watch out for them. The males in particular, so skinny they're frightening. They gather on the roof. And in spite of that, in spite of how thin they are, they still find the strength to howl their desire."

The cat was purring with delight.

"But this cat, if he were to disappear . . . If you could hear him at night . . . One should always howl one's desire. Yet one doesn't. One desires with restraint and then, you see, one day it is gone and one wonders why."

She was talking and looking at the cat. No longer stroking him. Only with her gaze.

"I would have liked to work with the insane. To live with them in one of those places where there are so many lives, and lives that are so unusual that our own, in comparison, seem quite insignificant."

"Are you fascinated by the insane?"

227

"Don't call them insane!"

"Well, you just did."

"Well, I can. But you cannot – that word, coming from you . . ."
She made a face.

"But let's not talk about that, if you don't mind. And anyway we shouldn't be talking about anything. It should be enough to enjoy the approach of evening, and wait for the night."

She pulled that old wool shawl closer around her neck; she never seemed to be without it. In any case it was never far away. As if it were always within reach.

"Are you always so silent? Your gestures . . . How do you manage, with women?"

I did not reply.

There was a wisteria plant running all along the wall. She told me that that wisteria had not bloomed in the spring, and now that all the other wisteria plants had stopped flowering, the flowers on this one were opening at last.

"This morning I saw a child on the beach. I think it was the child who goes to your garden. He came and sat down close to me. At one point I moved and he left. There aren't many children who behave like that; that's why I thought he was the one from your garden."

"He's an odd child."

"I don't know where he went."

"He's there and then he isn't there. No-one knows."

A butterfly alighted on the bench.

Alice held out her hand. To be closer. Her fingertips almost touching it. The cat was staring at the butterfly, too.

"I would like to see the mask again. That's why I came back."

Alice said that she knew. She could tell that that was all I was thinking about. And that I would see it. Later.

"You're so impatient . . ."

She let her gaze wander over the garden. As if she were indifferent. The border of perennials. The daisies. The place where she wanted her ashes to be scattered.

"Do you often think about your own death?" I asked.

"Everyone thinks about their death. It is part of life, the idea of death. And when you get old, all the more reason . . ."

The butterfly was still on the bench. For a split second its proboscis was right up against Alice's fingertips.

"I wonder what would happen if I died?" I said.

"Nothing would happen."

"Nothing . . ."

"The girls would cry. Anna . . ."

Alice turned her gaze to me. The cat held out a paw and the butterfly flew away.

"What are you thinking about?"

"Anna's face this morning. Her eyes. She'd been crying. I didn't hear her."

"What would you have done if you had heard her?"

"I don't know."

"You see . . . And what did she do?"

"She went into the bathroom. She put cold water compresses on her eyes. She asked me to make some coffee. She drank it, without sugar, just like that, standing by the window."

"And then?"

"And then nothing. She went to join the girls who were playing on the swing in the garden. She didn't want the girls to play on the swing because they were wearing clean dresses. She didn't want to take the swing away, either. She explained to them that they had to be capable of looking at the swing without wanting to climb on it. The girls gave some sort of answer and Anna slapped them. That's the first time I've ever seen her slap the girls. She turned around to see if I had noticed."

"And then?"

"During the night Anna woke up. She got up, took her pillow and spent the rest of the night on the sofa. In the morning when I saw her again she was standing by the window. She was looking outside. Lovely weather, she said. Without turning around. And as I did not answer, she said again, Lovely weather, isn't it? Her voice somewhat forced. Her reflection in the window. Her face. She had left some coffee in the pot. Switched on all night long. I poured myself a cup. It was lukewarm. Bitter. Outside it was raining."

Three days later. It was morning. The cat in the garden. No-one in the conservatory. Alice had been unwell during the night, and the doctor had come; he was supposed to call again during the day.

"Well, aren't you coming in!"

That is what she said when she saw me.

She was pale. Her features drawn.

She let me look at her, something that was unbearable to her as a rule, and then she waved her hand towards the window.

"The sun . . . It's coming out, do you see it?"

"I see it."

"Is it already high?"

"It's ten o'clock . . ."

"One day it won't rise anymore. I'll be dead."

"It will rise for other people."

"It won't rise anymore."

"Because you'll be dead?"

"That's right. Because I'll be dead."

She showed me her hands. Open. As if all the proof of what she had just said could be found there. And all her anger, too.

Her impotence.

"And what do you see through the other window?"

There was nothing.

"There must be something. Take a better look."

"There's nothing there, I tell you."

"The sea?"

"Far in the distance. You can't see it."

"And there's no-one?"

"No-one."

"Not even the cat?"

"Not even the cat."

"And the child?"

"He's not there."

"Look again. Over by the gate."

"He's not there."

"Then let go of the curtain and come and sit down. You can look again in a moment . . . You didn't answer my question."

"Which question?"

"The one I asked yesterday. You are so slow . . . How do you manage with women?"

"That wasn't yesterday."

She gave an ironic laugh.

"You are quibbling . . . but you always answer in the end."

We heard a sound in the passage. It was Clémence. She was bringing medication and a glass of water. She left the tray on the table. Before going out she looked at me and at the tablets.

Alice took a sip of water, then put the glass down.

"You'll answer that one as well."

She glanced at the pink and white pills that were in a saucer. And one plastic capsule.

"I have always known that one day someone would come. I might have preferred someone else. But it was you, don't you see . . ."

She turned her head. The wind was blowing. The branches of the wisteria were rubbing against the window.

"Sometimes you're there and I don't even see you."

"Your tablets," I said.

"What about my tablets?"

"You have almost no water left."

"So?"

"You have to take them, Alice . . ."

"Have to! You're a fine one to tell me that!"

"I want to look after you."

"Who asked you to? We don't know each other. We are strangers, don't ever forget that. Just because we spent a few hours together . . ."

She removed her spectacles. Put them down on the table.

"I'm tired of you."

I stood up.

"What are you doing?"

"I'm leaving."

"You always leave . . . And then you come back. It doesn't surprise me anymore."

She turned her head to one side.

"Even Anna, you don't dare leave her."

She gave a short, bitter laugh.

"Of course, you have your daughters . . . But children are noisy when they are little. All the things they say. And when they are big they become insolent. Am I shocking you? I can tell when you are shocked. You are wrong."

She was looking at her glass. It was transparent. You could see the liquid inside it, so clear. The way it caught the light.

"When one has no children, one cannot know what one has avoided. Both good and bad. You never stop wondering . . ."

"What did the doctor say?"

"What do you want him to say? That my blood pressure is low. That my heart is getting tired. Nothing that I don't already know."

Her hand, closed. Curled into a fist, held tight against her throat.

"Never mind what he said, he's an idiot, he doesn't understand a thing."

She leaned forward, opened the dresser drawer. She took out a packet of cigarettes. She could no longer roll them, because her hands had begun to tremble. The ashtray was on the hearthstone. She asked me to hand it to her.

She turned the striker wheel on the lighter several times.

Her face, sallow. The tablets in the saucer.

"Alice, what happened out there?"

Her eyes, just then.

"How dare you."

She made a face.

"Leave me alone."

"There are things you say, and then others . . ."

Her gaze. Her voice. Everything about her suddenly seemed to erect a barrier. I went over to the door. I could hear her breathing.

"Where are you going?"

"To fetch the mask."

"I forbid you!"

"Then I'm leaving."

I pressed the latch. I opened the door.

"Leave, then, if that's what you want."

I was in the passage. The door had not quite closed.

"But when you come back, think to bring some brioches. Because you are going to come back, aren't you? The brioche you brought the other day was good but you can find far better at Monsieur Paul's *boulangerie*. With little crystals of sugar, and praline at the centre. Would you do that for me? You're not answering . . ."

I went out.

Clémence was in the garden, trimming the withered blooms on

a rose bush that climbed high against the façade. She was using a long handle with two blades attached to the end. Some of the roses she cut fell to the ground. Some got caught on the other roses. There was a particular atmosphere in that garden, always the same, peaceful, as if time passed without lingering. Merely grazing the surface of things.

I went back up the lane, to the gate. And then I turned around. I saw the curtain move behind the window, just where I knew Alice had her armchair.

I smiled. Alice was wrong. We were not strangers anymore.

I went back to the conservatory. I sat down in one of the armchairs and waited. Clouds. I gazed at them through the glass roof. The clouds of the dead.

I imagined myself dead.

I imagined myself as a cloud.

I closed my eyes. I thought about Otto. The mask he stole, for his dream of New York. And his death, just a body dangling from a rope.

Now the mask was here, in this house, at the back of a cupboard. Hidden from our eyes. From memory. The blue mask. Hidden, as if there were something shameful about it. And yet for a brief time it was a messenger of the gods.

For a brief time, men had worn it to become spirits themselves.

That very mask.

Had the mask taken its revenge?

My thoughts were confused. For some time now I had been unable to sleep.

I simply could not.

I wondered if I could go on living with Anna much longer.

I closed my eyes.

When I opened them again there was a bowl on the table next to me. Fruit cut into small chunks. Three raspberries.

A little piece of paper was rolled up inside a thread. I opened it.
I read:

*. . . with both arms he held up the monstrous stone; but the moment it
was about to reach the summit, a sudden force caused the stone to fall
again, and it rolled all the way down.*

Homer, The Odyssey, *XI,* 594

Sisyphus.

I ate the fruit, one bite after another, until it was all gone.

Alice was behind me, in the doorway. I could not see her but I
sensed her presence.

She came up to me. She took the paper and read it in turn.

"Of course . . ."

That was all she said. She let the paper fall on the table.

"When you have finished, follow me."

I followed her. Along the corridor.

The stairway.

"The electrician has been here. He checked the wiring. He said
the rats had gnawed at the insulation of the wires, somewhere in
the eaves. That all we need to do is change the wiring and we'll have
electricity again."

She switched on the torch.

"I am not sure I want to have electricity again."

She sat down at the desk.

"Here, light this candle, and then you can light all the others."

She pulled one of the candlesticks towards her and used it to light her cigarette. Just like that. Straight from the flame.

She inhaled deeply, kept the smoke in for a long time.

"It makes us eternal, don't you think? The fact that there is no light . . . But you are still too young to want eternity."

Her dry lips. Around the filter. The smoke coming from her. And that haunting voice. Even when she did not speak. The walls resonated with her voice. The way one remembers the caresses of a lost love. Murmured words. An echo.

She pulled her shawl tighter around her shoulders. Her hands beneath the wool.

I went over to the wood stove.

I took some sheets of old newspaper. Little logs that were there in a pile. I tossed in the match. The wood was dry.

Alice said nothing about my lighting the fire. Or not. We were there. We had time.

We had all night.

I saw the flames bite into the wood behind the thick glass window. Light. All around us night had almost come. There were only the other flames, from the candles.

Alice got up.

She walked over and held her hands out to the fire.

"And there is this, as well, the need to understand why we are together . . . Why you are here, that I can understand, at a push, but why I let you come here, that I cannot understand . . ."

She placed her hand on my shoulder.

"You aren't going home?"

And then she grazed my neck lightly with her fingers.

"You ought to. Anna will be worried . . ."

A painting hung on the wall. Very close by. It was illuminated by the flames.

"That is Mary," she said. "Mary was strong, so much stronger than Christ. She never humbled herself. Even in the face of the things He asked of her. The things He imposed on her. She accepted it all. Women are so terribly strong, are they not?"

She was there, almost touching me.

"One day in Paris a woman came up and stopped me in the street. My name is Atalanta, she said, and then she went on her way. It was a long time ago but I still remember it. How extraordinary to have such a name and to want so immodestly to make others hear it. Atalanta . . . Really, doesn't that surprise you? Gracious, nothing surprises you, does it?"

I put more wood on the fire. The heat was spreading. A gentle heat. The scent of burning wood.

"Have you ever been unfaithful to Anna? You aren't answering . . . So the question does bother you, in fact."

"It doesn't bother me."

"What, then? . . . You've never been unfaithful to Anna. I know you haven't. It's obvious. You would have to be a different person from who you are."

I turned around. For a brief moment we faced each other. My gaze. Against hers.

She stepped back. A few steps, to the desk.

238

"I never told you it would be easy. With me. Being here, that is. I never hid it from you. Remember, that first day, you were the one who came. You helped me carry that basket full of pears. I hadn't asked you for anything. It was you and you alone."

She picked up a pen from the desk. She rolled it in her fingers. First one direction then the other.

"In any case, nothing is ever easy."

She crushed out her cigarette. Lit another one immediately.

"Do you know that your presence is driving me mad? It makes me torment myself. You do know that, don't you?"

Her expression.

"What will you do with me once I've gone mad? And anyway, I'm already mad. Hasn't Clémence told you?"

She could shout. Scream. Pour out her resentment. I had time. I told her so. The rest of the day and all night. I did not want to go home.

She shrugged. I heard her sigh.

"Sometimes your silence . . ."

"What do you mean, my silence?"

"Let me finish!"

She put the pen back down on the desk.

"If you constantly interrupt me, we'll never get anywhere."

She picked up the packet of cigarettes and tossed it to me.

"And then there's the fact that you don't smoke, when you're dying to. This creates tension between us, you've no idea . . ."

Her voice was trembling with anger.

"I feel like killing you when you're like this."

Her smile.

"I am quite capable of killing, you know . . ."

"You could kill me?"

She burst out laughing.

"You are very arrogant to believe that," she said.

"You didn't answer my question."

"I suppose it would suit you, if I were to kill you. Your death would put an end to all your questioning."

"It would empty your house of my presence."

Alice went and sat down again. Behind the desk. I could hardly see her.

"But if I wanted to empty my house of you, all I would need to do is to open the door. That's all. A simple gesture with my hand and you would leave."

"I would not leave."

"But of course you would leave."

"Are you going to ask me to?"

"I don't know. I probably will. Sooner or later we all do. It becomes necessary to make others leave, don't you think?"

"I don't know."

"You don't know! That is what is so exasperating about you. No matter what one asks you. You don't even struggle . . . And anyway, it hardly matters. I already said as much, that's just the way you are . . . Would you stop making that noise!"

"What noise?"

"You are clicking your fingernails. Ever since you got here. It's irritating. You do things and you don't even realize."

I had picked up the packet of cigarettes. I was flicking it over and over. I eventually opened it.

"If you struggle, you sink more quickly," I said.

"And if you don't struggle you sink anyway."

"I prefer to sink gradually."

"You have no idea what you're talking about . . . You ought to be thinking about how to add some substance to your life."

"I'll do that."

"That's right, you do that."

I took a cigarette from the packet.

Alice was staring at the wood stove, the little window through which you could see the flames.

"Have you noticed how tense it is getting between us? . . . No matter what one does, tension between people is unavoidable."

She opened a desk drawer in the desk.

"This is a *paho*."

She handed it to me. The prayer stick was wrapped in a cloth.

"Otto sold it to my father. He probably sold a great many other things, that summer . . ."

Three feathers. Coloured fibres.

Alice stood up.

"He also gave me a necklace."

She went to the cupboard. She opened one of the doors. I heard the necklace sliding against the wood.

"It is a ceremonial necklace. Otto told me that no-one must know he had given it to me."

A rustic-looking cord held the stones together. Stones of all different sizes. Turquoises, roughly carved. Without a clasp. The necklace was heavy.

"I've never worn it. I couldn't have."

She went back to the desk. She opened another drawer. She took out a large envelope.

She handed it to me.

In the silence that followed I thought I could hear her heart beating.

I opened the envelope.

Inside was a photograph. It was the same photograph as the one I had found in the studio. Except that this one had been enlarged. It was sharper, too. I held it up to the light. Alice's eyes. Her thick cotton dress. In the darkest corner you could just make out the black rungs of a ladder.

I took the photograph out of my pocket. The two pictures.

Side by side. And in Alice's hand, at the end of her arm, which seemed so heavy it might sink into the ground, was the turquoise necklace.

"That was the day it happened," she said. "The day of this last photograph."

Her words. As if the world had suddenly shrunk. High walls. Walls of silence.

I sat down on the floor, my back to the stove.

I waited.

"It happened in that room – the only way out was through the roof. You see the ladder there, in the picture . . . The entire village was built like that. That village and all the others as well. All the villages on the plateaux. Wobbly ladders to go from one roof to the next, flat roofs, like half-terraces, and there were other ladders leading down to the street . . . I was in that room. With my father. It was the day of the Snake Dance."

She was speaking in a low voice, her words interrupted by silence. She did not see me. She was no longer speaking to me. She was using me. To have someone to go there with her. Through my scarcely breathing presence.

A strange monologue.

"The door that gave on to the roof was open. The light came in. A long beam, vibrating with dust. My father was sitting against the wall. I think I had fallen asleep. Otto arrived. I heard his voice in my sleep. And my father's. I didn't want to wake up. My father picked up his satchel.

"I opened my eyes. I saw him. He was climbing the ladder. Otto was at the top. I remember, he was swaying from one foot to the other. I asked my father where he was going. He told me to stay there in that room, to wait for him, that he wouldn't be long."

Silence again. Growing deeper all around us. The moment Alice stopped talking.

was behind him. I followed them with my gaze for as long as I could and then they disappeared."

Alice crushed out her cigarette. She lit another one. Immediately. Even though the first one, that she had just crushed, was not even finished.

"I sat with my back to the wall."

I looked at her. Her eyes, pools of silence. And the silence could bear it no longer.

It was oozing.

A wretched smell.

I recoiled. It was the smell. It made you recoil, if you guessed it was there. An instinctive movement, of survival.

Alice smiled.

She guessed what I was feeling.

"I heard someone walking overhead. On the roof."

She fell silent again. That memory. She had kept it at a distance. She seemed to want to keep it there still. The visible depths of her wrinkles. And then other depths. Internal fissures.

"I heard talking, and laughter. I called out. I thought someone could hear me and that they would put the ladder back and help me to get out. I called out again."

She smiled and her smile faded. Vanished.

"There were three of them. They weren't Hopi, they were boys who had come from the town, judging from their clothing, you could tell, from Flagstaff or somewhere. One of them pushed open the door. He leaned in. When he saw me he whistled to the others. I couldn't see their faces very well because the light was behind them. I asked them to put the ladder back. They began to laugh. I didn't like the way they laughed. They spoke among themselves, I couldn't understand what they were saying, and then one of them began making obscene gestures with his fingers. He put his hand on his sex. Stroking himself. I looked at him. I was there. In that hole, like a pit. On the other side, in the street, life went on. My father was going to come back. I told them so. They didn't believe me. The one who was making the gestures put the ladder back. He came down. Just him. The others stayed up on the roof to keep watch."

Alice ran her hands over her face, then her hands one over the other. Several times. Silence again.

And after that silence, what she still had to say.

"Outside, the dances began. The long procession, with the snakes. Through the entire village. The infernal sound of drums. People shouting from the rooftops. I tried to call out again but he slapped his hand over my throat. He was strong. His body stank of sweat. I thought he was going to kill me."

She took a last cigarette and lit it.

"When he lay on top of me, I could feel his mouth. The stink of alcohol. I turned my head to one side and threw up."

In the silence that followed I could hear the terrible pounding of my heart. Her words.

I was watching her. A shiver in my neck. Burning. And the burn spreading like a wave through me.

I was silent. Waiting for something else. More words.

"My father came back . . . He was holding a package under his arm. He put the package in his bag. 'You're angry, is that it?' he said. Because of my silence. My pallor, perhaps. He came over to me. He looked at me and said, 'So pale, against this adobe wall . . .'

"He took out his camera. He asked me to take a few steps back, he wanted my face in the light. In my hand I was still holding the necklace Otto gave me. It's strange, isn't it . . . That turquoise necklace. I had not let go of it.

"My father took the picture. That photograph . . .

"After that, he told me we were leaving. That we had to get our things together. I didn't want to go out. I couldn't. There were too

245

many people outside. I was afraid. My father thought I was angry because the dances had started and I hadn't seen them. He told me that in any case we had seen the dances at Mishongnovi. And that we would see the end of this dance as we crossed the square. He had to drag me, by force. The dancers were on the square. The high priest. For a moment I was directly opposite him. His gaze. A horrifying vision. And the snake he held in his mouth. Breton saw us and he leaned over to say something to Elisa.

"We went back to the car. My father drove fast. For a long time. Hours. Six, maybe eight, as far as Gallup. I was in the back seat. Wrapped in a blanket. I could see the back of his neck. His eyes in the rear-view mirror.

"'Are you still angry?' he asked.

"The satchel was on the seat next to me. The mask was inside."

Alice moved one of the candlesticks that was on the desk. She moved it without lifting it. Slid it over. The light from the flames.

The mask had been there on the table all along, while she was speaking. It had been there, in the shadow, and now it was in the light.

"It's always the same, whenever you see it . . . You look at it. You don't dare touch it."

She took the mask in her hands and held it as close as she could to the light.

"For a long time it frightened me. For a long time, too, I couldn't look at it."

She handed it to me.

I took it. The way she had. With the same gesture. The blue mask.

Its slit-like eyes. A beard of black horsehair. Rough. Three small cords were mingled with the horsehair and at the end of each of those cords was a feather. In the lower half of the face there was a bandeau made of coloured squares, yellow, red, ochre, grey . . . Eight squares in all.

The dancer's gaze seemed to vibrate in the deep black of the space for the eyes. As if all the sculptor's faith were emanating from that mask. Coming to light, still, a century later.

I turned the mask over. On the back, impregnated in the leather, were the traces of the sweat of the men who had worn it.

I do not know how long I stood there looking at it. A long while, I suppose.

"That's enough for today, you have to get back to Anna."

I looked at Alice. I suppose I did not understand.

"Anna. Anna and the girls. You have to go back to them now. They must be waiting for you."

I put the mask back down.

"I'll come again tomorrow."

"Not tomorrow. Let a few days go by . . ."

She went with me to the door and took my hand. A hand I had not held out to her. She pressed it gently against her cheek.

"A few days for you without me, that shouldn't be impossible."

I was back in the car, my hands on the wheel. I could do nothing but sit there.

I could do nothing at all.

I could not listen to Alice.

Or see Anna.

The taste of saliva in my mouth: I left the car and threw up, and when I went back to the car I realized I had been sweating and that my sweat had taken on the taste of that brackish water I had just spat out. My skin was drenched. My shirt. I was cold. I went back to the pub in Dieppe where I had been with her. I began to drink. At the bar. With my face in the mirror across from me, I was staring at two empty holes and at one point I realized that those two empty holes were my eyes.

The eyes of the mask. Those two carved slits.

I thought back on everything Alice had told me. The unexpected confession that I almost failed to receive.

Why had she not told her father? How did she manage not to scream?

And how did he, her father, fail to understand? She was seventeen. I thought about my daughters. About the silence that gags women.

The waiter asked me if I was there on holiday. Just to say something. I suppose he could see I was not well. I did not answer.

I stank, my shirt, my hair sticking to my forehead. I drank another whisky. When I went out night had fallen. I told myself I could not go back to Anna and that I would have to find somewhere else to spend the night.

Which is what I did.

I did not go home.

Why did I not go home?

If I had gone home, I would have been with Anna again. Anna and the girls.

"We said a few days . . ."

And it was only the next morning.

I put the brioches on the table.

She looked at the bag.

"You didn't buy them at Monsieur Paul's boulangerie."

"It was closed."

"What kind did you get?"

"Round, with sugar on top."

"The sugar is never as good as the praline. It will never be as good."

She opened the bag.

"There's one for Clémence," I said.

She took a brioche from the bag.

"I'll eat this one and keep the other one for tomorrow."

The cat was on a chair. His nose between his paws. When he heard us he opened his eyes.

"Why did you come back?"

"Because of what you said."

"And what did I say?"

"That Mary was strong. Much stronger than a man. Much stronger than He was."

She shrugged.

"That's obvious. Mary Magdalene was strong, too. All women

are strong. But you didn't come back because of Mary."

I shook my head.

I would have liked to touch her. It seemed impossible. I reached out and placed my hand next to hers. Very close. On the table.

"A graze . . ." she said, looking at my hand, and I wondered if this word that I had never heard really could be used in that way, or whether she had just made it up.

A graze. An ineffable moment.

Soon I would not see her anymore. I knew that. Because I was going to leave. And she was going to die.

"That was something I liked about you, your astonishing simplicity."

"You say it in the past tense . . ."

Yes, that was true, I had spoken about her in the past. I was talking about her, with her voice.

A blackbird came to perch on the windowsill.

"One day you asked me what I would say about you when you were dead," I said.

"And you replied that you would say nothing."

She smiled.

"I like the fact that you speak about me in the past. That you dare to do so. As if I were already dead. Perhaps you like the idea as well?"

"The idea of you being dead?"

"Yes."

"I don't know. I don't think so."

"Go on talking about me as if I were dead."

I tried to imagine it, the garden, the house.

She was eating her brioche, little pieces she broke off with her fingers. The blackbird was still there.

"There are two ways in which we die. The first, actual death, and then the second, when no-one speaks about you anymore. That one must be the most unbearable."

Two little crystals of sugar fell onto her trouser leg. She took them in her fingers and then lifted them to her mouth.

She said, "For a grocery brioche, it will do."

"It's not a grocery brioche."

"Anything you buy that is not from Monsieur Paul's is grocery produce, you must know that."

"Is that an *idée fixe* with you?"

"No, it's obvious."

I looked at her.

"You are stubborn, Alice."

She made a face, moved her lips, suddenly sullen.

"You see, there it is again, that tension between us. We cannot help it. Perhaps we are already an old couple . . ."

She tossed what was left of the brioche out the window and the blackbird flew away.

"Perhaps we should stop seeing each other, too."

Her hands on the cloth of her trousers, brushing away the last crumbs. And then her hands one against the other.

"You should work on your muscles," she said, standing up. "And put on a bit of weight, but I've already told you that."

Her gaze, her indiscreet attention.

"It's strange that you're so thin, actually . . . Don't they feed you in Paris? And why did you choose Paris? Paris is an impossible city, everything is so terribly complicated there. You don't answer? Here we go again, your silence . . . We'll never get around it . . ."

She closed the window.

The blackbird came back.

"Where did you sleep last night? Because you didn't go home, did you? Not after what I told you. That would be impossible. You could no longer bear being with me, nor could you bear seeing Anna again . . ."

"A hotel in Dieppe."

"I got up. I saw Otto's face and I understood he was there because of the mask. The mask he wanted to sell. I began to climb the ladder. My father was already at the top. I had heard that terrible things happened to those who sold masks. I didn't want anything to happen to Otto. I said so, to my father. I remember telling him that. Saying that people would die. My father got annoyed. He told me that if he didn't buy the mask, then Breton would."

Alice had spoken carefully. As if she were determined to include everything. Good and Evil. Slowly.

And the memory of that day, rising to the surface.

"I remembered the necklace Otto gave me. I wanted to give it back to him. I don't know why . . . I thought it was important for me to do that. The necklace was in my bag. I had to go back down the ladder. Everything happened so quickly . . . I bent over to search through my bag and when I turned around my father was removing the ladder. I can still see it, the ladder being lifted up. The shadow of my father above me. Don't worry, that's all he said.

"Don't worry . . .

"And he left."

Alice lit a cigarette. She began smoking, fitfully. Abrupt gestures, like the words she had wrenched from within. And which she now seemed to be spitting out. Snatches darkening her memory.

I listened to her. That memory, suddenly gaping. Like a wound.

That memory, where she was searching.

"There were no windows. Only two tiny openings. Like slits carved directly in the wall. I dragged myself up with both hands on the edge. And I could see outside. There were a lot of people. It was early afternoon. The dances had not begun yet. I could see people going by with drums. Children playing hide-and-seek. I tried to call to them. There was too much noise. They didn't hear me . . . Breton and Elisa were there, on the square.

"I saw Otto when he made his way through the crowd. My father

"A hotel? I hope the sheets were clean, at least?"

"Yes, I think so . . ."

"You must find out. And if you have the slightest doubt you must ask for them to be changed. The bathroom?"

"A shower."

"A shower, that's alright. Better in any case than a bath. But you must be careful never to touch the tiles, they're often dirty, not cleaned properly. Zones of contact in those places, if you see what I mean . . . You are wrong to smile, one can never take too many precautions. Will you think about what I said, about your body?"

"I will think about it."

"Now leave me, I am tired. And besides, the doctor said he would come. If he finds you here . . ."

She called me back when I was at the door. She was holding a book. She handed it to me.

"Inside you will find the journal André Breton wrote when he was out there."

I took the book.

The journal was short.

I read it in the car, before going home.

## ANDRÉ BRETON'S RETURN TO PARIS

What words does Breton murmur in Elisa's ear when he sees Alice's father leaving?

In a few days he too will be leaving the high plateaux.

Has he already begun to sense that it will be impossible to go back there? He takes with him the vision of hordes of tourists clinging to the red cliffs to approach, to violate the most secret rites.

These Indians are great artists, he is sure of that. They did not create Beauty. They created objects that were in the image of their beliefs, and it was only later, through other means, through the gaze that other men brought to them, that those objects were seen as something beautiful.

Only later.

Through the gaze of others.

Breton is one of those who know how to see. He has been the instrument, the hand, the voice. He has contributed to the metamorphosis.

And thus the sacred thing has become a work of art.

*

A few weeks later, not yet the rue Fontaine, still New York. The *kachinas* are in boxes – Eagle *Kachina*, Fly *Kachina*, Hoho Mana, Little Fire God and Miss Butterfly. A precious booty.

Breton removes them from their boxes and sets them side by side on the narrow doorledge.

Jewellery, children's drawings, newspaper cuttings.

The mature man has rediscovered the child he once was.

*Here, I find another reality, a new coherence to the world, closer to my early childhood.*

*

The war is over, Breton leaves New York. With him are Elisa and his daughter Aube. On 25 May, 1946, after a long crossing, they arrive at last in Le Havre.

And from there, Paris.

Pigalle. Place Blanche. And, only a few steps from the Moulin Rouge, the rue Fontaine. A steep street. Number 42. Behind the door is a passage leading to another door.

*As far as I'm concerned, I shall continue to live in my glass house, where at any time of day one can see who has come to visit.*

The inner courtyard. The familiar smell.

Breton is again in his studio after five years of absence. In all likelihood he is no longer the same man. In all likelihood his ideas have changed. Have been transformed.

In all likelihood Paris has changed, too.

What does he know about this new Paris?

His boxes have arrived. They have been set down. Piled up. To make his way through the flat he has to skirt round them. Clear a path.

It is the month of May. Paris, the cafés, tables on the pavement.

Girls in flamboyant skirts. Breton is still in pre-war Paris and this new Paris astonishes him. He rediscovers Montmartre, the narrow streets leading up to the Sacré Coeur. The banks of the Seine. The *quais*. There are meetings again at the Deux Magots. A joyful post-war ferment.

He has come back to Paris but he is still filled with out there. When the journalist Jean Bedel comes to interview him, immediately after his return, when he has hardly had time to settle in, he will say: *I am going to write about a people who are gifted with a fabulous sense of art. You will see, you will see . . .*

His fiery spirit is intact.

In the flat, the *kachinas* hang from the wall. The Snake *Kachina*, the Sayastasha, the Koyala, the Mana Hopi, the Palhik Mana . . .

And then the leather Hopi mask he bought in New York, and the other mask, the Salimboya. The Salimboya has been placed on a shelf, the leather mask has been fixed to the wall.

Presences. Here. The studio is charged with a new energy.

Breton sits down at his desk. Contemplating.

Beauty, prevailing.

*

Breton renews his ties with the Parisian intellectual movement. He thinks that everyone will gather round him. That they will adhere to this new philosophy. This new current of thought that he has brought to them.

*I am the instrument.*

He wants to see them gather round, as if round a great bonfire.

At the same time Max Ernst, who stayed in Arizona, is building his house.

The town where he has settled is called Sedona.

*

Primitive peoples hold their dreams to be a far greater reality than real life itself.

*

In Paris Breton sets objects that should never have been together side by side. An Inuit mask, a necklace from Nepal, a statue from Easter Island or the Marquesas, a mask from New Guinea.

And all of it, all these objects, brought here from so many different places, seem to find a harmonious refuge between his walls.

Only Breton would dare to create such a juxtaposition of unlikely companions. The studio has turned into a sort of baroque cathedral, a fantastic arborescence where objects from every culture have come together. Every available nook has been invaded, submerged by this uncommon idea.

Breton has guests. He shows them.

He provokes them, too. He likes to quote this sentence from Baudelaire: *What is intoxicating about bad taste is always the aristocratic pleasure of displeasing others.*

Does he need to return to Hopi country to feel he is *out there?*

*

Those who have the good fortune to visit his studio say they leave again overcome by emotion.

An emotion enhanced by the host's presence.

*The object is particularly moving to me, insofar as I know neither its origin nor its purpose.*

Thus, the masks that surpass the limits of our world.

Breton will spend the rest of his life at the rue Fontaine. From the moment he gets up in the morning, and all night. During his insomnia. He wanders, in his dressing gown, which he sometimes wears even when he has guests. The little boy from Pantin, this man, has become the king of his realm.

Wherever his gaze happens to wander. In the shambles of his studio.

At night, the silent dialogues.

Breton will never see the desert again. In a drawer he keeps a handful of sandy earth.

The red sand.

Time goes by.

His features grow heavy. Between his eyes, two deep wrinkles. Two wrinkles also define his mouth. His life becomes a solitary conversation with the sacred.

Is Breton afraid of death?

He has fallen out with his treasured friends – Éluard, Dalí, Picabia, Aragon, Tzara. He has also fallen out with Giacometti. And Victor Berthier.

His time is precious. He knows that.

All around him, the objects are the strata of his life. Certainly one might think that his journey to the Hopi Indians had marked him deeply.

But this man who always sought to understand, to reach, had to live with the devastating certainty that he had remained outside.

*

André Breton dies on 28 September, 1966.

He is buried in the Batignolles cemetery.

On the announcement of his death is written: *A. Breton 1896–1966.*

And this sentence, a few chosen words:

*I am seeking the gold of time.*

The same words will be carved on his tombstone.

\*

Elisa stays on in the studio for a few years. And then the doors close.

Inside are the *kachinas*.

The masks.

The studio has become a sanctuary.

Then there is Elisa's death.

And that black day when the doors of the studio are opened. The constant traffic up and down the wooden staircase of those who come to see. To buy.

The objects are picked up, handled, greedy hands. Everything is wrapped up.

Lots, hundreds of them. And included in those lots, the *kachinas*.

\*

The sale is held at the Hôtel Drouot. Between the 1st and the 17th of April, 2003. The pavement is packed with people before it even opens. Many intellectuals condemn what they term a senseless waste. A petition is launched. To no avail. The sale begins. For two whole weeks. The auctioneer describes the lots, sells them to the highest bidder. One minute per lot. A sorry spectacle. Sordid. Some people leave the room. Fake banknotes with Breton's effigy are passed around. On each note, these words: *Your money stinks of the corpse of the poet you did not dare to become.*

The notes fall to the floor. Some people pick them up. Stuff them in their pockets.

The *kachinas* belong to lot 6138, *Objects in sculpted wood, called Hopi Indian dolls.*

In that lot are the Snake *Kachina* and the black leather mask.

The Salimboya.

It is a madhouse.

Everyone grabs what they can.

Which means that Breton's studio is scattered, according to the whims of the auction. Some *kachinas* are bought by museums, others by private collectors. Still others are bought to be sold again, such as the touching Mother Crow.

"I went to Breton's place. A few months before his death. In 1966. I remember the studio . . . You cannot forget a place like that. I had called him. I needed money. I had sold a few of my father's photographs. I wanted to sell my *kachinas* as well. TRINITÉ 28 33. That's it, I remember, TRI 28 33. Strange, isn't it, when I have forgotten so many things . . . A woman answered. She told me that Breton was busy and to ring again in an hour. She said Breton, not André. I rang an hour later. And he answered. He told me to come the next day. I arrived rather early. I waited out on the pavement. He lived on the second floor, no. 1/2, a building at the back of a courtyard. I climbed the steps. Slowly. His name was written on the wall next to the buzzer. There were two doors. I went through the first one, which led to the study. The two rooms were joined by a few steps. It was dark. There were books everywhere. The shutters were closed. And the curtains. It was a very unusual place. It was like being in an old museum. Breton was at his desk. I hadn't seen him since Arizona. He had aged. He said, who are you, exactly? I told him. He didn't remember me. My father, yes, vaguely. But not me. He hunted through one of his albums and found a photograph where the four of us were together in the streets of Oraibi.

"His *kachinas* were on the wall. There were skulls on a shelf . . . A ball hanging from a thread, and when I went to touch it, he said, don't, without telling me why, and I later found out that it was a work by Giacometti. He wanted me to talk to him about Varengeville. He didn't remember the house or the garden, but he remembered the *manoir d'Ango*. I took the *kachinas* out of my bag. I put them down on the desk. He looked at them, one after the other. He took his time. I told him that these *kachinas* were all from *out there* and he said that he knew that. He bought three of them. For the others, he gave me the address of an art dealer on the rue de Seine. After that I showed him the mask. I remember his face. His emotion when he saw it. He took it in his hands. He said, this is the *Ang-ak-China*. And he looked at it. For a long time. Then he put it down but even when it was on the desk he continued to look at it.

"'I had never seen it,' he said. 'But I know it. I know the story behind it.'

"And he told me how Otto died."

Alice lit a cigarette. The same cigarette that she had just lit. And that she had stubbed out almost immediately.

"It was a few months after the dances. Otto had no house anymore. No shelter. He lived out of doors, in the cliffs. His mother left a little food for him on her doorstep. He would come and get it at night, while the village slept. Winter passed. Spring. One day Otto went into a bar in Navajo territory. He made a deal with an Indian. He gave him his horse and everything he had on him and set off on foot down the road. He walked for an hour. Perhaps two. Along the railway line. It was hot. The Indian followed him and killed him. Then he hanged him from the branch of a tree so that his tribespeople would find him. A tree by the side of the railway tracks. He died watching the trains go by."

She looked up at me.

"Suicide is forbidden by the Hopis, so sometimes this is the way things are done when one wants to die . . ."

A bouquet of roses stood on the table between us. Roses with wrinkled petals. Almost white. The flowers were not particularly pretty, in any case, they were not the way you expect roses to be, and there were prettier ones in the garden.

Alice picked up one of the petals that had fallen on the table.

"Breton told me about Otto's death and he wrapped up the mask again in its paper. 'Don't sell it . . .' That's all he could think of to say.

"After that, he had to leave because he had an appointment in a café on the Place Blanche and he was already late. He asked me if I wanted to go with him. I didn't.

"We said goodbye in the street. He walked away. It was winter. He was wearing a long grey overcoat. My eyes followed him until he reached the end of the street. When he got there he stopped. He turned and waved to me. And then he disappeared to the right, towards the Boulevard de Clichy. I never saw him again.

"A few months later, in the newspaper, I read about his death."

Alice got up. She walked over to the window. The weather was stormy. The air stifling.

"What is the matter with all the swallows today? Why are they all so excited? It's as if they had gone mad. Do you see how they're flying?"

"It's the storm, out at sea."

"But why are they flying like that? They look as if they are about to crash into the windowpanes."

She opened the window. A sudden powerful draught swept into the room.

"You're right, it's the storm ... Can you hear that shutter banging? It is going to rain."

I was looking at her. The reflection of her face in the window.

She closed the window.

She came back over to the table.

I was thinking about Otto.

These interwoven destinies. Acts of violence, hidden by indifference, shattering the tranquillity of a person's life. All the dreams one has. Dreams that carry us and sometimes destroy us. And if they do not destroy us, they diminish us. In the form of untold disappointments. Unfulfilled love.

So in the end, yes, of course, one looks for a solution. Otto could have boarded a train. And gone away. Did someone really have to die for that mask? I refused to believe it.

Alice touched my arm as if to call me back to her. To the reality that we shared.

"That child who comes into the garden . . . I don't think he exists. He's a mirage."

"I saw him on the beach. He was sitting next to me."

"What did he smell like?"

"I don't know."

"Every child has a smell. That one doesn't. He doesn't exist."

She gave me a strange look. We had been together for hours. We were tired.

"Are you thirsty?"

She went to fetch some wine.

"Women begin to die long before they are dead. The moment they begin to get old. And are no longer desired. That is the first death."

She snuggled up to me. To my back.

"You must love Anna."

The sky had turned black.

"The storm . . . Do you hear all that noise on the roof? There will be mud in the garden."

The hour did not matter to me. Or time.

I was with her. Beyond tiredness. And I knew it was not over. She had told me, there is still more for you to hear.

We drank the wine. A wine with a taste of the earth.

We went on talking.

The rain. The sky, uniformly grey. It might have been morning. We no longer knew.

"Where is Clémence?"

"Somewhere . . ."

We should have turned on the lights.

Alice was looking at me.

"Do you believe that somewhere in the world there are two other people like us? Two other people who, although they are not who we are, are experiencing what we are experiencing?"

"What are we experiencing?"

"We are together . . ."

She smiled and said, "If two people like us exist, and those two people are experiencing what we are experiencing, then I would like them to die."

"When an elephant senses his death is near he leaves the herd. He goes to a secret place, a tree or a source of water. The others watch as he leaves, and then they go their own way."

"Where do they go?"

"I don't know . . . They keep going. And sometimes, along the way, they find the bones of elephants. And then a strange thing happens. The entire herd stops and they pass the bones from trump to trump. It's like a dance. Sometimes they take some of the bones with them. People who have seen this say it is unforgettable. That it is burnt into their memory for life . . ."

"Why are you telling me this?"

"I don't know. It must be the wine. Listen, someone is ringing at the door."

"Let them."

"They're still ringing."

"Clémence can open. She's the one who takes care of it as a rule."

"Clémence isn't here. And they're still ringing. That's the third time."

"I know. Do you think I'm deaf? You can do what you like but I warn you, it is raining."

I went to have a look. There was no-one at the gate. Nor was there anyone on the path.

"It must have been some children . . . I told you, children have to be the worst thing there is."

Night fell. We were still together.

"Perhaps we ought to get some sleep. Or some food. Do something."

Alice turned to me.

"Perhaps we are doomed to stay here . . ."

It had stopped raining. The first stars were in the sky.

"You can sleep here if you like."

There was a guest room right at the end of the house. With its own entrance. I rang Anna. She asked me why I was not coming back and I told her that I needed to be alone.

She said, you're not alone, since you are there.

I lay down. On the bed. Fully clothed. Flowered wallpaper. I went from one flower to the next.

Otto died because he did not know how to leave. Sometimes that is the way it is, Alice had said as much, a person's destiny is made up of the people we meet, of strange turns of fate.

I got up.

I took the car.

*La Téméraire*, in the night. Without me. Just Anna and the girls. A light in Anna's room.

The little light, too, just above the front door.

A traveller's light, or for a late-night passer-by. A lover's light.

An unfaithful husband's light.

I went along the garden and down to the beach.

Some young people had lit a fire. They were playing the guitar.

I asked them if they had anything to smoke. I hunted through my pockets. I came up with 50 euros, a pack of chewing gum, a box of matches.

They wanted my running shoes, a pair of Reeboks.

I gave them everything.

They shared the chewing gum. The euros. The boy who rolled the joint kept my Reeboks.

I smoked all on my own. Off to one side. Looking at the light in Anna's room.

Afterwards I went back up to *La Téméraire*. Anna had left the little side door open. I went in. I spent the night on the sofa.

I woke up with a terrible headache. I took two aspirins. Two more immediately afterwards.

Anna must have heard me because she got up. When she saw my face she poured some powder into a glass. She added water and mixed it with the back of a spoon the way she did when the girls were sick. It was viscous. I swallowed it.

My headache went away.

The taste remained.

I went out onto the terrace. It was morning. The sun was shining. The light. I raised my hand to shield my eyes. The girls were at the window. I could hear them. I could not see them. They were making fun of me. Anna sent them to play on the beach.

A ferry crossing, in the distance. I lay down on the deckchair.

I closed my eyes.

When I opened them again, the girls were no longer on the beach. Or behind the rocks, or on the path that led up through the trees.

There was a note from Anna on the kitchen table: *Gone shopping.*

"My nephews are coming. Will you stay? Just long enough to meet them. After that, you can leave . . . Or not. You can do as you like. In the meantime let's play a game of solitaire. I'll sit by the window, that way all I have to do is pull the curtain if they ring at the door."

She began to play.

"That's them I hear, no?"

I pulled the curtain.

"Not yet."

"What time is it?"

"Two o'clock. What did they say on the telephone?"

"That they were coming at two. They should be here. Take a better look."

I went to the front door.

"Do they have a long way to come?" I asked.

Alice sighed.

"Perhaps we should have bought something to eat. Or at least some refreshments."

"Don't you have anything?"

"We have wine."

"Only wine?"

"Yes."

She tapped her finger on the edge of the table.

"I hear a car door, is that them?"

"No."

"Who is it?"

"I don't know. Neighbours."

"We don't have any neighbours. We are suffocating in this house. Did you check that the telephone is properly connected?"

"Yes."

"Check again, one never knows."

I went to the telephone. I picked up the receiver.

"It's working," I said.

Alice tilted her head to one side, as if she were trying to remember something.

"Perhaps I got the days mixed up. It does happen . . . Perhaps they're not coming. Or they'll only get here tomorrow."

I went up the stairs. I opened the door and called out to Anna. She was not there. It was cold in the room. I had forgotten to close the shutters and the rain had got in.

I went back down to the kitchen.

The mirror in the corridor. My face. My beard had grown.

I took a beer from the vegetable crisper. It was the last one. I went to drink it in front of the television.

The thought occurred to me that Anna would be coming and there would be no beer left for her. I went out onto the terrace, thinking she might be down on the beach.

A shutter banged in the girls' bedroom. I went to close it. I continued to wait.

I was beginning to feel hungry. I thought she would be coming back and we would be able to call and have some pizzas delivered, and we could eat them in front of the television. With a beer. And then I remembered there was no more beer.

I thought of going back out but then I reasoned that if she came home while I was out, she would not see me and she would leave again.

I waited some more.

Night fell.

It was too late to go out. I broke two eggs into a frying pan. I did not let the oil get hot enough. The eggs stuck. It was soft and damp, the egg white was like mucus. I stabbed it with my fork and the yolk ran into the white. Inedible.

Some young people arrived on the beach.

I asked them where they had got their beers and they told me there was a petrol station open on the main road to Dieppe.

I took the car.

When I came back, Anna's scarf was on the kitchen table.

I called her.

I thought she was in the shower. I went to see. She had taken her suitcase, the big one, and all her clothes.

She had eaten the last apple. The peel was on the edge of the sink, with the core and the knife.

There were the marks of Anna's teeth on the core.

I slept. An hour. Maybe two.

It was the telephone that woke me. It was Anna. She told me that everything was fine, that she was with friends in Les Andelys. She would bring the girls back in two days, and then we would see. Would that be alright?

There was a football match on the television.

I did not know Anna had friends in Les Andelys.

At half-time I looked for something to eat. I opened the cupboards. I found some *biscottes*. As there was some butter left, I took the *biscottes* and carried everything through to the television.

I spread the butter with Anna's knife, the one she had used to peel her apple.

On the edge of the sink the apple peel had begun to turn brown.

I took the car. I went to Dieppe.

Dieppe, at night.

I looked for a café. The centre of town was deserted, I headed down the back streets. I eventually found a bar for prostitutes. With a pathetic live orchestra. Girls. You could drink, dance, fuck. I began by drinking. And then I danced, too. I fucked. A black woman. Something I had been wanting to do for a long time.

In the morning, I found myself outside. It must have been six a.m. The sun was rising. I could not remember where I had parked the car.

I stank. Sweat. Smoke. The girl's perfume. Her sheets. I had a thirst, for water. I thought, the sea's not far, I'll go for a swim.

The morning swim.

The narrow streets were gloomy. Bin bags everywhere. My headache was coming back. A sharp pain behind my eyes.

It took me a while to find the car.

I thought of going back to *La Téméraire*. To sleep and wait for Anna.

I also thought of going to Les Andelys. I remember thinking, I'll sleep for an hour or two and then I'll go and get Anna.

It was very early in the morning when I arrived at Alice's place. The gate was still locked. I climbed over the wooden fence.

There was no noise. No light. For a moment I thought of going back to Varengeville. Or heading out on the national highway. To drink a coffee in a transport café, there was one not far from there.

A pink light was beginning to glow faintly in the sky. The grass was wet. A cricket. A few beetles.

I went over to the bench. That place where Alice had told me she would like to be buried. Or failing that, to have her ashes buried. The scent of pollen lingered here and there. The smell of leaves. I thought about out there. The images that had grown stronger through the long night. Too long. A night of fatigue. Otto's face. Even with my eyes closed. Alice's face. Wherever I looked.

I sat down on the bench.

Anna had left. We would have to sell *La Téméraire*. And what about the flat in Montreuil?

I took my head in my hands. And there, in a patch of grass so deep in shade that it was still night, I saw two small lights. Almost blue. I stood up. The lights vanished so I sat back down on the bench and then I saw them again. I did this several times. And each time I wanted to go closer, the lights disappeared. They were fireflies. I was sure of it, even though I had never seen any before. A light that is said to be so bright, some people say, as bright as the glow of a fire in the desert.

I looked at them. For a long time.

I looked at them until it was impossible for me to see them. Their firefly light was gradually absorbed by the brighter light of the day. I looked even when it was impossible to see them. Because I knew they were there. Tenacious little lights.

Fragile.

I turned my head.

Something had moved in the grass. Right next to the spot where I had seen the fireflies. There, between the feet of the bench and the first roots of the magnolia. It was a frog. One of those little green frogs known as tree frogs which you can hold in the palm of your hand. I knew that the cat hunted for them. And killed them. He did not eat them. Alice found their dead bodies on the doormat. This frog must have come from the pond nearby, in the next field. I bent down. Now captive between my two palms. I could feel him. The accelerated rhythm of his heartbeat. The terrified pulsing.

I opened my hands. I saw the frog. And the light. The light from inside. Through the transparency.

In the very belly of the frog.

It came from inside, passing through the fine membrane of his skin. I took a closer look. The tree frog in the hollow of my hand. It did not move. At first I did not understand. Only afterwards. The light was from the firefly larvae the frog had just swallowed. Larvae, not yet dead but in that in-between state.

And which continued to shine.

Alice was standing there. Silent. She did not ask me anything, as if it were perfectly normal for me to be there so early in the morning in her garden.

"That star shining just before the morning light. Do you see it? It's the last star, the Morning Star."

She pointed to a spot in the sky.

"The name of that star is Talàwsohu. The summer moon is called Talà'mùyaw. And there are other names for the other moons, too. Otto taught me . . ."

She turned towards me. Her shoulders wrapped in her woollen shawl.

"Let's go in, shall we? The coffee should be ready."

In the kitchen there was a smell of toast. Jam.

We sat down, facing each other. The bowl Clémence had used at the end of the table. A few crumbs around a knife.

Alice took the toast from the grill. She had heated croissants in the oven.

"There's something else . . ."

"Something else?"

"Your face . . ."

As if that were an answer. My face. I wiped my hand over it. My eyes, my lips.

"Anna has left," I said.

276

She nodded.

She poured the coffee. Her mug. Then mine. She pushed the box of sugar over to me.

"These things happen, it's not that serious . . ."

The coffee was scorching. Very strong.

Alice took a sip.

"What else?"

"Nothing."

"What did you do in the garden?"

"I sat down. I saw fireflies shining in the belly of a tree frog."

She smiled.

She said, "One day I saw the larvae shining in the fireflies' eggs. Through the shell. I also saw a female devouring the male."

She put her mug down.

She took a slice of bread and buttered it.

"You could have opened the frog's belly . . ."

"To save the fireflies?"

"Of course."

She spread jam on the butter, a mixture of apricot and bitter orange.

"One day we shall go and sit next to the pond and watch the toads, there's an entire colony. Would you like that? . . . You're not answering . . ."

"I told you, Anna has left."

"So?"

"So you aren't listening to what I said. You think of no-one but yourself! Only yourself!"

"And you think all you have to do is be silent to find a solution?"

For a moment, her eyes meeting mine. She did not look away. On the contrary. It was as if she were stubbornly holding my gaze.

She pushed her mug into the middle of the table. Without

finishing the coffee still in it. I suppose it had gone cold. Or was still lukewarm but hardly worth drinking.

Her mug, almost touching mine.

"I don't even know your name . . ."

She lifted her hand towards my mouth. As if to order me to remain silent.

"Don't tell me. It's too late now."

She stood up.

The mug. Her chair behind it, slightly to one side.

She turned to me.

"Let's remain strangers, that's it . . . Two strangers."

She smiled at me.

Her hands pressing against the edge of the table. Then she went over to the door.

"Where are you going?"

She did not answer.

It was her fault that I had left Anna.

I stood up. I caught up with her. I told her. It's your fault that I left Anna.

She turned her head. Ever so slightly. I suppose she knew she did not have to show me her face any more than that. That her words would suffice. Her words alone.

"You didn't leave Anna, she's the one who went away."

She turned from me.

"But I agree to take responsibility for that."

"Don't go imagining things. I tried to tell other people this story. I found no-one. Only you . . ."

She closed the door. We were in the room with the fir tree. Near the table.

She walked around the table. Slowly.

"It was Christmas . . . the first Christmas after the war."

With her hand she stroked the chair backs.

"My mother must have been sitting here, and there, that was Clémence's place . . ."

She continued. Naming each of the guests in turn. The guests of absence.

"This was my father's place."

Her gaze wandering over the table. As if she were indifferent.

"It was snowing that day."

She made a dismissive gesture. Then regained her composure. She began to tell her story.

"If it hadn't snowed . . . but it was snowing and my father was a photographer. There was snow in Étretat. He said he'd just go and come right back. He would be back by late afternoon. Clémence decided to go with him. I wanted to go, too. We had an argument in the car about it. When we arrived at Étretat, Clémence didn't want to get out of the car. We left her there. We set off on foot along the base of the cliffs. It was low tide. An equinoctial tide. I

279

remember that everything was white because of the cold weather, the snow . . . The tide was coming in. We had to be quick. My father took a few pictures. There was light against the cliffs. A very unusual light. At one point, I looked away. Clémence had got out of the car. She was heading up a path along the cliff. The sea had already covered the coastal path we had taken to come. My father said it didn't matter, that we could climb up by the iron stairs set into the cliff. We had already done so on several occasions . . . It began snowing again, thick flakes. It was very beautiful. The colours. The seaweed on the rocks. And then the sky darkened, all of a sudden.

"The tide kept coming. Strong waves. Driven by the wind. I remember, the snow was coming down on us in gusts. I went to shelter in the hollow of the cliff. I wasn't afraid. It wasn't the first time we'd been caught out by the tide. My father was walking along the water's edge. It was cold. I was sorry I'd come. I had a rope ladder in my bag. I began to take it out. At that point my father shouted and waved to me. I went over to look. The cliff was red. With the snow in front of it. The falling snow. The wind, whirling. And behind us, in contrast, the sea had turned black. That was the moment he wanted. The light at that exact moment.

"He began to take his pictures.

"When his feet were in the water he was obliged to come back. But he was still taking pictures. After that he had to run. With his back against the cliff, he placed his hands to give me a leg up. The water was coming in. We had to hurry. I stepped on his hands, first one foot, then both feet on his shoulders. I felt his hands as they gripped my ankles like a vice, then he hoisted me up. Almost at arm's length. Two iron handles were set in the rock higher up. I couldn't see them. I groped for them. I remember how they felt when I found them, that cold contact beneath my hands. I grabbed them and hoisted myself with all my strength up to the platform.

"I gashed my lip on the way up. I had blood in my mouth. My lip was swelling. I could feel it. Pain numbing an entire side of my face. I swallowed the blood. The water was already filling the back of the cave. Splashing against the walls. My father told me to throw him the rope ladder. The deafening roar. I stood up straight. I saw the water. I remember . . . The slow inexorable rising, heavy waves. Equinoctial waves . . . And the taste of blood in my mouth, the strength of the waves, my father's voice . . . The waves . . . Sometimes at night in my dreams I still hear them. I couldn't move. My father was shouting. The light grew brighter. Like on that day in Oraibi, the light, against the adobe wall . . . The same white light. The day my father left me to go with Otto, and then he came back but when he came back it was too late. He showed me the mask. I didn't haggle over it, you know . . . That's what he said, I didn't haggle . . .

"It had been over a year earlier. And it all came back. There. So brutally.

"I fell down on my knees on the rock. I was looking at my father. I was weeping, swallowing everything, blood and tears mixed all together. I was back there . . . The two moments had melted together. The two places. I began scratching at the rock with my nails like an animal. Earth in my mouth. That taste of rusty iron. I was chewing but I could not swallow, it stayed in my mouth. I can still feel how it crunched. The rope in my hands, burning. And I rubbed the rope into the burn. Right into my skin, tearing it open. The way I had been torn open, back there. When that Indian threw himself on me . . . The same burning . . . I thought I'd be able to forget. I thought that if I didn't speak about it I would be safe. I remember biting into the rope. My teeth, too, in the Indian's shoulder. No matter what you think, you don't forget . . . My father was in water up to his waist. He was clinging to the cliff. It was like chalk. It crumbled beneath his fingers. At one point, he tried to let the water carry him. The waves were too strong. They sent him crashing against the wall. A first time, then again. So he tried to get out of the cave. I suppose he thought he could swim to the port. He was holding his camera up out of the water. You cannot win against an equinoctial tide. He knew that. He tried. At one point he turned onto his back. He floated. A wave submerged him. Then another. And one last time I saw his hand . . . The same hand that had removed the ladder. That hand . . . The camera. Right up to the end he wanted to save his pictures . . . I didn't see when he disappeared. But I felt it, on me. In me. I leaned over. There was water everywhere. A seagull cried out somewhere above me, in that too-white sky.

"I looked up. Clémence was right at the top. At the edge of the cliff. Her hands over her mouth. Her hands like two fists.

"I threw the ladder into the water and I waited, sitting in the cold, for someone to come and get me. And they came and took us away, Clémence and me. They asked us who we were and what had happened.

"Clémence didn't say a thing.

"I was the one who told them. I said my father had drowned.

"The Coast Guard found his body a week later. It had washed up on the shore. He had managed to tie his camera around his neck. It was his last film. My mother tried to develop it . . . The newspapers said my father had died because he was trapped by the tide. An unfortunate accident. Everyone said that . . . Even I could have told you that . . ."

"Do you still love me?"

That was the last thing Anna asked me. She had already asked me a thousand times. Do you still love me?

But this time . . .

What was I supposed to say . . . That is why she left. Because I was no longer able to answer.

We can go and live somewhere else, I said, a house in Provence. We can have a meadow, with a donkey. The girls have always wanted to have a donkey, and you know how much they love the sun.

She said no.

She said, it's too late.

Before leaving she said, you look after the girls. Three days. The time it takes for me to make a few arrangements. I'll come and fetch them on Thursday.

She explained everything to the girls.

She did not tell me what those arrangements were. In the morning, at breakfast, it was just like with Anna. Bread, butter, jam. Just the same, only Anna was not there.

I looked after the girls for three days.

When Anna came back to fetch them, I did not ask her what she had done.

I looked at her. I thought, Alice was right, women are strong.

There is everything we understand, everything we are capable of transcribing while trying to be as accurate as possible. And then there is all the rest. The world of appearances, of silences. The vastness of the unnameable.

This world cannot be transcribed. It obeys a different logic. There are even times when it has no logic.

One has to decode it.

The imperceptible shift. I suppose that is what is meant by André Breton's beloved step to one side. Just how far one must step to change one's vision.

One step can be enough.

And how many have fallen trying to take that step? Fallen because they failed to measure the danger of the one step too far, as they tried to go beyond who they were?

And that is probably what brought all those men together, Talayesva, Quöyeteva, Otto and Breton, their need to see differently. Not to suffice unto themselves.

All in search of the same dream. Fleeing the same everyday life. For elsewhere.

The Hopi spiritual leaders have a knowledge that we do not have. They recognized the bombing of Hiroshima and Nagasaki as the fulfilment of their ancient prophecies.

*The first world was destroyed by a devastating fire that came from the sky and the earth.*

*Second prophecy: The second world ended when the earthly globe veered off its axis and everything was covered with ice.*

*Third prophecy: The third world was destroyed by a universal flood.*

For them, the present-day world is the fourth world.

I thought about all of that in the train taking me back to Paris. The train was a local one and stopped everywhere. At every station. Sometimes out in the middle of the countryside too, and it was impossible to know why. Passengers boarded, others got off. The outskirts of Paris. Allotments. I thought about Breton. About Pantin.

I went to the flat.

Anna had taken all her belongings. The girls' as well, except for a few dresses and winter jumpers.

I knew this. She had told me, wait a few days, a week if you can. After that you can come back.

I went to wander around the Île de la Cité. The weather was fine. The leaves on the trees were turning yellow.

The *bouquinistes*, along the riverbanks. A café, a table on the pavement next to Notre-Dame. I had finished reading *Sun Chief*. For a bookmark I had been using a sheet of paper where I had copied out a poem by Simon J. Ortiz.

The bookmark was gone. It must have fallen. Slipped out in the train.

I looked for it.

I had read that poem so many times, when I was at Alice's. And I had lost it. I tried to retrieve it from memory, a first word and then another, and I am the sort who never remembers anything, but I realized that I was able to recite that poem to myself. It was inside me. I had carried it with me. Learned it.

> *I wonder if I have ever come close*
> *to seeing the first seed, the origin,*
> *and where?*
>
> *I've thought about it, says Coyote.*
>
> *Once I thought I saw it in the glint*
> *of a mica stratum a hairwidth deep.*
> *I was a child then,*
> *cradled in my mother's arms.*
> *we were digging for the grey clay*
> *to make pottery with.*
>
> *That was south of Acoma years back;*
> *that was the closest I've gotten yet.*
>
> *I've thought about it, says Coyote.*

And that thing which I had read and remembered, not wanting to learn it, that thing had overwhelmed me.

I let a few days go by. Until the last days of September. And then I took the *métro*. To the Blanche station. Right in Pigalle.

42 rue Fontaine. I opened the door. The passage, the inner courtyard. The tree in the middle of the courtyard. I could hear Alice's voice telling me, you have to go upstairs.

I went further. A woman at the window on the ground floor. She showed me a door.

Wooden steps, with very high windows overlooking the courtyard. It was old. The electric wires hanging out of their insulation.

I climbed all the way to the top, to the second floor, flat 1/2. Almost under the roof. Two doors, now two separate flats. In Breton's time, it was one flat.

I could have rung the bell.

Asked to have a look.

I sat down on the steps. I smoked a cigarette.

When I went back down, the woman was still at the window. She said, one day they came and took everything away.

She said it had been quite a business, all the coming and going, an entire day of it. Cratefuls at a time.

I went for a walk. And then came back. I asked her if there were any flats to let. There, with a window on the courtyard. I wrote my name on a scrap of paper, my telephone number. She promised to ask the concierge.

I wandered around the *quartier*. Boulevard de Clichy. I looked for the old café where Breton used to go for his coffee in the morning. An old man told me the café had been called Le Paradis, but it no longer existed.

Breton's studio was just above. Right at the top, under the eaves, the glass roof. I walked around. I do not know how long I waited.

Nor what I was waiting for.

I was there.

Then I went up the Boulevard de Clichy as far as the *métro* station. Sacré Coeur.

It was noon. I was not hungry. I drank a beer on the square.

A few solitary artists were painting the streets of Montmartre.

It must have been close to four o'clock when I took the *métro*. The Batignolles cemetery. The station exit only a few steps from the *boulevard périphérique*. The guard asked me if I were looking for someone in particular and I said, André Breton. He showed me on the map. A photocopy that he gave to me. It was right at the back. At the far end of the cemetery. He told me I would find Benjamin Péret's grave quite close.

Along with Blaise Cendrars, Édouard Vuillard, and Paul Verlaine.

He informed me that the cemetery closed at five o'clock, because it was already four, and it would take some time to go all the way there and back.

I took the central path. The air was warm. A faint breeze scattered the first leaves from the branches of the chestnut trees. They fell onto the path. Onto the graves. Some got caught on other branches. In the arms of statues. There were a few clouds in the sky that the sun managed to pierce.

I walked. Slowly. As if I were on my way to meet someone.

The ground on the path was red. Sandy. There were chestnuts underfoot. Some of them were crushed. Their skin, burst and shining.

The guard had said, right to the end, 31st division, 12th row, 18th plot. I went to the brick wall that surrounded the cemetery. I did not find it right away. I had to search. Retrace my steps.

And then I saw it. A simple stone stele. Practically abutting the *périphérique*.

Breton's name. And a second name, more recent, Elisa's.

The wind had deposited a few brown leaves at the front of the grave. A few chestnuts out of their burrs.

The light was pale the way it often is in Paris come September at the end of the afternoon.

I took out my mobile. I rang Alice. Heard it ringing. Four, five times.

And then she picked up.

"Is that you?" she said. And immediately afterwards, "So you are . . ."

"I'm there."

"What do you see?"

I placed my hand on the stone.

"The letters of his name."

"What sounds?"

I turned the phone to face the wind, the *périphérique*, the dense traffic at this time of day.

I could hear Alice's breathing.

"Do as we said."

I slipped my hand into my pocket.

The girls' walkman.

The cassette was inside. I placed the headphones over my ears.

The tape began to play. For a moment, nothing. As if silence had been recorded. Then the first words, incomprehensible. A man's voice. The first chants in the Hopi language.

Silence again, after the chants. The wind. The wind from over there. Silence again. And that sound, just barely audible, which she had made me listen to there in her sitting room the first time, and I had not recognized a thing.

291

I turned up the volume.

I heard the wind, or what I thought must be the wind, the air hardly stirring, that was all there was, that sound of burning air, and then behind it came another sound.

The recording ended.

Alice said, "Go back. You'll understand . . . It is impossible for you not to understand."

I went back. As far as the chants. I listened again. It was like raindrops but it was not rain. I listened again and I eventually grasped it. That was the sound of the first drops before they even reached the ground. Evaporating raindrops. Her father had been able to capture that moment. And that phenomenon, both rare and magical, was something she had given to me to hear.

"Well?"

I smiled. And I sensed Alice's smile on the end of the line. Her smile answering my own.

"I knew you would be able to hear it."

I imagined her back there in her house. So far away.

"Where are you? Which room are you in?"

"In the conservatory. The wicker armchair."

"And Voltaire?"

"He is here next to me."

I could hear her breathing. As if she were here. Or I were there by her.

"What are you wearing?" I asked.

She did not reply.

I took the *paho* out of my bag. I placed it on the grave.

A little longer then Alice hung up.

The story of the Hopi people was her story. She had passed it on to me. And her story had become mine. I understood. Her silences. Her stubbornness. I understood what she had wanted to grant me before confronting it herself, not the idea of her own death, since she had been carrying it within for a very long time already, but death itself.

The onset of difficult days.

I promised myself I would go to see Anna again. To explain it to her. To try and show her. To learn with her.

A chestnut fell on André Breton's grave. It was a chestnut just like all the others. Brown skin. Almost red. I picked it up. I kept it in my hand for a moment and then slipped it into my pocket.

I felt my fingers close around a piece of paper. I thought it was Simon J. Ortiz's poem. I took it out. It was a sheet of paper from a notebook, folded in four.

Inside, large, steady handwriting, with a felt-tip. Alice's hand-writing:

*I hope that from time to time you will go closer to the tenuous light of the fireflies.*

I put the paper back in my pocket. With the chestnut. And headed for the way out.

# BIBLIOGRAPHY

André Breton 42, rue Fontaine – 17 April 2003 – *Arts primitifs*, Camels-Cohen, Paris. (Catalogue, sale of primitive art from André Breton's collection.)

*La Danse des kachina: Poupées hopi et zuni des collections surréalistes et alentour*, Exhibition, Paris, Pavillon des arts, 22 July–25 October 1998, Paris Musées, 1998.

*Esprit kachina, Poupées, mythes et cérémonies chez les Indiens hopi et zuni*, Galerie Flak, Paris, 2003.

Julien Gracq, Gilles Ehrmann, *42 rue Fontaine, L'Atelier d'André Breton*, text by Julien Gracq, photographs by Gilles Ehrmann (Éditions Adam Biro, 2003).

Marie-Elisabeth Laniel-le-François, José Pierre, Jorge Camacho, *Kachina des Indiens hopi* (Saint-Vit: Danièle Amez, 1993).

Don C. Talayesva, *Soleil hopi* (Paris: Plon, 1959, 1990).

Aby M. Warburg, *Le Rituel du Serpent, Récit d'un voyage en pays pueblo*, translated from the German (Paris: Macula, 2003).

Frank Waters, *Le Livre du Hopi, Histoire, mythe et rites des Indiens hopis*, translated from English (Paris: Payot, 1978).

\*

I would like to extend special thanks to Professor Éric Mickeler for his valuable information.

CLAUDIE GALLAY was born in a Bourgoin and now lives in Provence where she works as a writer and part-time teacher. Her novel *The Breakers* was a huge commercial and critical success in France, winning a number of prizes and selling more than half a million copies.

ALISON ANDERSON's translations include Muriel Barbery's best-selling novel *The Elegance of the Hedgehog* and *The Breakers* by Claudie Gallay.